SHOCK
WAVE

SHOCK WAVE

ANDREW VACHSS

Pantheon Books · New York

All rights reserved. Published in the United States by Pantheon Books, a division of Random House LLC, New York, and in Canada by Random House of Canada Limited, Toronto, Penguin Random House companies.

Pantheon Books and colophon are registered trademarks of Random House LLC.

Library of Congress Cataloging-in-Publication Data
Vachss, Andrew H.
Shockwave : an Aftershock novel / Andrew Vachss.
pages   cm
ISBN 978-0-307-90885-8 (hardcover)
ISBN 978-0-307-90886-5 (e-book)
1. Psychopaths—Fiction. 2. Murder—Investigation—Fiction.
I. Title.
PS3572.A33S56 2014   813'.54—dc23   2013040808

www.pantheonbooks.com

Jacket design by Pablo Delcán

Printed in the United States of America
First Edition

9   8   7   6   5   4   3   2   1

I didn't want to be doing this.

Not ever again, not any part of it. It was all wrong. Every interlocking piece of it, wrong.

The worst part was that, once I started, it didn't *feel* wrong. Not once I found that place inside me that didn't feel anything. Inside that world of ice-pure emptiness, there is only this: *la mission est sacrée.* As a child, I had been directed to that world as another might have been to a boarding school—to learn how to conduct myself in a place already reserved for me.

I left for one world; the man who told me where I must go left for another. I was forbidden to follow him, and there was no question as to my obedience. How could I not obey the only person who had ever loved me?

I was certain I'd forever left that place I'd been sent to, but later I found that I could return at will. And I wouldn't need a map. That place wasn't a geographic location—it was an implant.

Until Dolly, the training I got there may have kept me alive, but I felt no gratitude for that. Instead, I often blamed it for my always empty life.

Before Dolly, no matter what path I walked, the road would seem to fork at every juncture. But those were nothing but illusions—there never had been more than one path for me to walk . . . not if I wanted to *keep* walking. The destination never mattered, only the departure.

But those who had abandoned me, used me, even paid me—

their implant never reached my core. Deep inside myself, I waited. Should I ever come across a chance—a *real* chance—at another life, I'd take it.

If anyone tried to stop me, I'd take theirs.

It wouldn't matter whether I had to hack my way through vegetation, or flesh and bone. If I ever saw such a chance, I knew it would be a tiny candle, burning in a black cellar. A flickering candle, with very little remaining light.

Whatever that cost—I'd pay. Or I'd make others pay.

The only way I knew to leave the place that trained me was to use that training.

By whatever miracle, I'd managed to do that. The opening appeared. The instant it did, I leaped blind. And landed at the one place I'd always been seeking.

In my world, secrets were weapons, and you never abandoned your weapons. Surrender wasn't an option—not when you were fighting those who didn't trade prisoners, and being paid to fight by those who had no prisoners to trade.

Whatever had compelled me to leap so blindly had been true. I thought I'd paid in full, but it turned out that all I'd paid was the price of admission. If I wanted to stay, I'd have to return to what I once was.

And, that time, it *was* my choice.

It took a lot. A lot of lives.

Once I'd done all that, I couldn't just throw a switch and put things back to the way they'd been before.

The life Dolly and I had worked so long and hard to make for ourselves was gone forever.

But all it had taken was a single backward glance to push us both over to the other side of the line. Back to using what had cost us so much to learn, and so much more to leave behind.

But even the cost of stepping back across that line hadn't separated us. We were still one.

I knew that if I ever slipped, if I ever dropped back into Hell, Dolly would follow me. And bring me back, too. She'd done it before.

When our paths first crossed, I was a professional soldier.

If you prefer, a hired gun; an assassin. Or a freedom fighter; a liberator. What I was called depended on who was saying the words.

Dolly was the other side of the coin I was paid in. I was paid to take lives; her mission was to save lives . . . and she wasn't paid at all. I, a mercenary. She, a nurse with Médecins Sans Frontières, switching between French and English as smoothly as if both were her native tongues.

That first time Dolly came into my life, she healed my wounds. She asked no questions—my skin color alone would have told her that I didn't belong where I'd been found. There weren't any tourists in that zone—even the missionaries gave it a wide berth. That didn't leave much . . . and my camo outfit would narrow any guesses down to one.

Regardless, Dolly wouldn't have asked my motives. Her team's only way to continue its mission was to maintain its role of pure impartiality. It must be always apolitical, never judgmental. To Médecins Sans Frontières, a gunshot wound was a gunshot wound, a machete slash was a machete slash— they were there to heal the wounds, not aid the cause of the wounded.

But even the mosquitoes knew the difference. In Africa, everybody gets malaria sooner or later, but the native-born have a much better chance of coming out the other side of that hideous ague. Coming out alive. Darwin ruled that world in all ways. Only survivors can breed—some genetic resistance to malaria became the native heritage.

The extraction of that chunk of metal from my leg in the field hospital had left me woozy, disoriented.

So I don't remember much about the evac to Switzerland itself, but the message that I couldn't *stay* came through clearly. As soon as my wounds were healed enough for me to move under my own power, I was expected to move on.

By that time, Dolly was long gone.

I asked about her, but all I got in return was blank stares. Another clear message: Whatever we know is ours, not yours . . . and a man such as you could never be one of us. Could never *become* one of us. Blood washes off a healer's hands. But it forever remains on those of a professional life-taker.

As the years passed, I began to believe that Dolly was an apparition I had fever-dreamed.

It was easier that way. Even if she *had* been real, I knew the chances of our paths ever crossing again were too remote to imagine.

But even the longest odds aren't the same as absolute zero—otherwise, all the world's roulette wheels would have stopped spinning long ago.

When I saw Dolly walking out of a hospital in San Francisco, I had to shake my head violently and refocus, just to be sure my eyes weren't playing some cruel joke.

But this was no mirage in the desert of my life—it was Dolly, and she could not have been more real. I don't know why she'd been inside that hospital. But I knew what had brought me there. And it was no mystical, magnetic pull—I was coming into that hospital to do something to a patient. Actually, *for* a patient, but I knew the law wouldn't see it that way.

I called her name—"Dolly" was all I knew—and she turned to face me.

And she remembered—I could see her eyes flash a decision.

We didn't have much time then, but Dolly answered my questions as if she knew why I was so desperate for the answers. She even told me her secret. She was finished with the unrelenting parade of hurt, crippled, and wounded people. Not just soldiers. Gang-raped women. Children missing both their forearms, left alive only to send a witch doctor's message— the trademark of the Lord's Resistance Army was to force a child to hack limbs off his own sister. The child knew if he refused he would die . . . and his sister would follow, raped to death.

The child who did not refuse was maintained on a steady diet of hallucinogens until the witch doctor's words became the only truth in his life. Once he had surrendered to that evil magic, he would become what those who had infused his life with horror had been. And carry it on.

Dolly stopped because she couldn't make *it* stop. Nobody could. It was as much a part of the jungle as the ever-renewing undergrowth. A kill-zone inhabited by targets, all tracked by human predators. And those who hunted those predators.

The cycle never changed—a river of blood, limbs, and organs, all flowing into the same delta. When that delta filled, it would disgorge itself, forcibly reversing the current with an even stronger backflow.

And then it would all begin again. Names might change, allegiances shift, new weaponry be introduced . . . but killing, rape, torture, they never stopped. In that part of the world, only the seasons change, never the climate.

I'd never heard of "post-traumatic stress disorder," but I'd *seen* it. Seen men paralyzed by something that went way deeper than any fear could. Seen men never stop shaking inside. Seen men grab their rifles and start shooting at empty darkness, certain "they" were out there.

And I didn't find out what *secondary* PTSD was until much, much later. Had I known, I would have understood why the relentless inevitability of the broken, bleeding, suffering, and dying had made Dolly flee for the same reason I had, so long ago: to save herself. Not her life, her *self*. I couldn't think of another way to put it.

The French—not the men I served with, but the privileged elite who spent their lives in cafés, smoking their cigarettes, sipping their espressos, analyzing a world they would never enter—never stopped talking. None of them ever listened; their empty-room lectures always ended the same way. They would shrug off the pain of others, devoutly proclaiming their anthem, *"Chacun fait ce qu'il peut."*

"One does what one can." For such people, "can" was always limited to talk. Endlessly, they would discuss, argue, debate. Circles within circles. That was their self-assigned role. That men such as me had our roles assigned by others, even forced upon us, that was not their concern.

And certainly not their *fault*. So there was nothing to stop them from judging us. And they have not stopped to this day.

Maybe it was different for those who wore their own country's uniforms into battle.

The frontline medics who patched up the wounded and

sent them back into combat, maybe they believed that a war was made noble by its necessity. To protect democracy from dictatorship, that was worth whatever it might cost.

Still, it was sometimes all down to them. That ultimate decision: would the soldier they had just repaired go back to the fighting, or would he be sent home?

And who better to make such judgments? They were un-armed warriors, always under fire. Whether a man truly de-served the medals others pinned to his chest—that was a political game. The true test was black-and-white clear: had he placed himself in harm's way? From the dawn of combat between men, there were always those who could avoid this. But no medics did—the only time *they* went home would be in body bags.

Dolly's people didn't have even *that* luxury. Their cloak of neutrality had no room for pinned-on medals. They were always in harm's way, but when they returned, not even grati-tude awaited them.

Soldiers obey orders. Soldiers can be conscripted, but Médecins Sans Frontières personnel were all volunteers. And they had to know that some of those they saved would soon be creating new patients for them, or even be returning to take *their* lives.

The truth of their mission mattered not at all to those whose only mission was to kill . . . sometimes in combat, sometimes at their leisure. Why else would the Médecins Sans Frontières nurses have "rape bombs" strapped to their belts?

What Dolly wanted more than anything was to live the rest of her life in peace. Not some "paradise," just a place where the climate wasn't a permanent rainy season, an unending down-pour of violence and death. She'd even found a place where she believed she could do that.

From the moment I was entrusted with that secret, my

mission—the only one I had ever truly volunteered for—was to give Dolly that life she wanted. I never lied to myself, never pretended unselfishness. Every step I took toward finding that place of peace Dolly wanted came with my prayer for a chance to share that life with her.

Against insane odds, I got that done.

And once my prayer was answered, I thought I was done, too. Not dead, but finished forever with doing the only work I knew how to do.

For a long while, it seemed as if the dream would hold. Dolly had a place in that little community, and I had . . . Well, I had Dolly. All I wanted.

But then I was forced to start a fire that drove the rats from their hiding places. That was no accident, and I didn't act alone. Dolly had been the one who handed me the matches.

To live in peace, we'd both had to leave our lives behind.

Not just the work, all the ID, too. We had to be different people.

Dolly had to give up being an R.N. She still had all the skills, and she was always finding ways to use them—healing isn't always about the wounds you can see or stitch.

I still had my skills, too. But no real use for them. Not anymore. Yes, even after we came here, I had done some things I would never tell Dolly about. But once I was satisfied that our perimeter was secure, I was done working.

Dolly never stopped nursing. Teenage girls flocked to her as if she were the only flower they could feed from.

Dolly cared for them all. She didn't make judgments, but she always had rules. You do what's right, or you do it somewhere else.

But even though Dolly was able to go back to her own mission—the one she created for herself—I couldn't tell if she was feeling what I was.

I didn't think so. A soldier and a battlefield healer would share the awareness of some things, but not all—same jungle, but very different reasons to be there. Ever since we put those heads up on stakes surrounding our village, my soldier's sense could feel a dirt-gray haze hovering overhead.

Part of the climate now. Not the climate people in this part of the country are always bragging about. Maybe they don't look close enough to see it—or they deliberately look away. For most of them, even if they did see it, they wouldn't know what they were looking at.

Rats always return. Survival is their sole genetic heritage—they breed constantly, and they'll kill each other as quick as they'll kill anything else. Food is food. Put up all the barriers you want, spray all the poisons you like, some of them will still get through.

Rats only tackle what they can handle alone—they don't work in packs. They only tolerate the presence of others of their kind up to the point where the food supply is threatened. Then they use death to achieve maximum volumetric efficiency. Put a thousand rats inside a cage that any two of them could tear open if they worked together, come back a few weeks later, and the cage will be intact. With only one rat left.

The only difference between rats and human vermin is that rats don't have food preferences. But once human vermin taste something that fires every synapse inside them, that's *all* they want. Such humans are always hungry, and they stick to their chosen diet as closely as they can.

No rat ever dies from obesity. Except lab rats, force-fed by humans experimenting on them.

When you work a jungle for the first time, you find yourself under a canopy of leaves and vines so thick it blocks out the sun.

Until you learn better, that canopy creates an illusion of safety. You can hear the planes overhead—supply ships carrying food, death dealers packing missiles. But you don't worry about sounds: you can't see them, so how could they see you?

If you live long enough, you learn that the only thing that jungle canopy protects is its own undergrowth. It won't stop a bomb, or turn a missile off-target. That kind of delivered death has its own vision.

And the shade-shielded undergrowth is perfect for constructing camouflaged deadfalls, with poison-tipped punji sticks awaiting anyone who takes a wrong step.

If you walk a wrong path, every step is a wrong one.

Those deadfalls were the handcrafted weapons of the primitives. The more sophisticated enemies used land mines. "Sophisticated" doesn't mean non-native; it means subsidized.

No paid invader is half as dangerous as those born in the jungle. The professional isn't defending his home, he's just . . . killing. And soon enough, those he's been paid to hunt become the ones hunting him.

Sometimes, there's more than one paymaster pulling the strings. If the strings they use to pull the pins are long enough, they can detonate their grenades at a safe distance.

In the jungle, there's no such thing as property rights. No deeds, no titles, no mortgages. Those who hire invaders don't want the land—they want what's under it. "Extractable resources" is their term. In the jungle there's only one law of property—if you can't defend it, you don't own it.

And if it's valuable enough—diamonds that can be mined, oil that can be sucked out—some land is worth much more than any human life. Those inert riches tempt the wealthy more than life itself . . . as long as the lives are not their own. Not just diamonds and oil; some of the land covers gold, even radioactive yellowcake. All prized because the supply is finite—diamonds can't breed more diamonds. But there's never a shortage of humans who have to be moved off the land that covers those riches—so there will always be work for a man like the one I'd once been.

The equation has only one common denominator: human life. That's what it costs to take what the "investors" want, and that's what it costs to keep their pipelines open.

Everybody walking that jungle is part of the same death chain. Labels don't matter. The government soldiers hunt "rebels." That turns the hunted into "guerrillas" who hunt the government soldiers. If the guerrillas prevail, they become the rulers.

This will never change. Just recently, not far from where Dolly had first come into my life—that place had a lot of names, but to us, it was just "the Congo"—native soldiers who took the city of Goma were "deserters" who had formed themselves into what they called M23. They said the rulers had deserted *them,* paying them next to nothing, keeping none of their promises. The world, as always, withheld judgment. Waiting on "reliable data" before making a commitment, they would say.

But profiteers know they can't afford to wait—they know others of their kind are in a permanent state of readiness. When there's enough of a prize at stake, you can't wait your turn—if another force gets in first, you won't *get* a turn.

They can always find "rebels" to subsidize. Profiteers can

range from individuals to a collective of private investors . . . even to entire countries. If those other countries are open enough about it, any non-native who signs on to defend the existing regime becomes one of those universally hated "mercenaries." Those non-natives sent to aid the rebels are "private contractors."

Such labels are as twisted as the centuries-old vines that are powerful enough to hold even a dead tree upright. Subsidized "rebels" can hire their own soldiers. Countries with an interest in the outcome can send "advisors."

What is written on labels depends on who does the writing.

In all such wars, the winners become the government. And "winner" soon becomes a synonym for "legitimate."

In openly declared warfare between countries, ships and planes carry markings. But most wars are never declared. On *that* ground, there are no uniforms—no insignia is worn on camouflage. There are no battle lines. There is no "front." No rules of engagement. No Geneva Convention.

No POWs.

There's only one rule both sides agree to, and actually obey. Never, under any circumstances, can there be truth. Some journalists are sent in already armed with the "reports" they are expected to send back. Sometimes, it's the reporters themselves who are sent back. In plastic-lined canvas coffins. When the coffins stack up too high, the journalists are called home. The ones that can be located, anyway—a fax message can't be sent to a tree; a shattered sat-phone can't take a call.

When you watch from a distance, like on your television screen, you see only what is shown to you. Mercenaries only "change sides" in movies. Who would trust a hired gun, anyway? When you soldier for money, it is understood that your loyalty is *to* that money.

The people who lived on land before value was discovered under it never try to fight off the invaders. They can always find more land. Invaders come in all colors, but there's one sure way you can tell who the true natives are—they're the ones running for their lives.

In such places, there are endless ways to die. *How* doesn't matter. *Why* doesn't matter. The jungle undergrowth doesn't care who feeds it—all blood is red, and the earth it enriches is always black.

This is what you learn: Only the jungle itself is permanent. Self-renewing. Not like you—what *you* are is replaceable.

La Légion taught us that we could always count on our comrades. Weren't we the finest fighting force in history? The best-trained, most sharply honed soldiers on the planet? And were we not bound by an *esprit de corps* that made us all one?

Only the officers asked that last rhetorical question. All the soldiers knew the true answer. And none would ever speak it aloud.

I left as soon as I could.

The five years I served granted me French citizenship, under the name I had picked. For most of us, that was the reason we enlisted—that new name; that chance to create our own pasts.

The name I picked wasn't really a new one—I had never known my true name, only what I was called. Maybe there was a birth certificate somewhere, perhaps inside the "clinic" I had run away from when I was still a child. But, somehow, I thought not.

I was taught to survive by an old man who had survived the invaders, and the Gestapo they left behind. I don't mean he was a collaborator—he had been a valued member of the Resistance. But when the Nazis were driven out, his usefulness was over.

And when he knew his own time was up, he sent me to the one place he knew would ask no questions.

Prior service as a *légionnaire* was enough of a credential for any merc outfit.

And once I went freelance, even that transparent *esprit-de-corps* curtain was lifted. We might be called "teams," or "units," but each of us knew every man was there for his own reasons. Some more complicated than others, but each one personal. Reasons rarely shared, and, when they were, never believed.

The only thing we were good at doing wasn't anything a civilized society would allow us to do. Not openly, anyway.

"Civilized"—that's another word for countries that have laws, or rulers who *are* the law. When we were paid to attack such rulers, we were "rebels." If we were successful, we instantly became "freedom fighters." But we were never invited to stay and share that freedom. We were respected for our skills, but never trusted; who would trust a man whose loyalty was to his paymaster?

"Citizenship," that we had—what we never became was citizens. We might be welcomed, even invited to march in triumphant parades.

And then be told to leave.

No matter—there was always another job waiting.

The deepest areas of any jungle will always be free-fire zones.

For a mercenary, "jungle" is just a word. It doesn't have to be tropical. It could be a desert, or a mountain range. Any place that has value—under its ground or off its shores—qualifies.

But even the most arid ground could be valued purely for its strategic location. Portugal didn't give a damn about those who called the territory they occupied "Biafra" when it broke from Nigeria. But it backed the new country anyway.

Of course, not for the humanitarian reason it so piously proclaimed. Portugal couldn't launch its jets from Lisbon all the way to Angola to strafe and return without refueling, so a much closer air base would have been a prize. Thus, the tiny island of São Tomé—a Portuguese slave colony just off the coast of Nigeria—became the staging area for planes carrying "relief supplies" to the breakaway country.

But when Biafra disappeared under the tribal-religious slaughter that was never called "genocide" by world leaders, Portugal lost the last of its colonies.

Before that, after that, always . . . every new area teaches the same lesson. Don't trust. Know when to look closer, when to look away, and when it's time to go.

You never sign on when part of the inducement is an opportunity to loot. Even if the paymaster isn't lying about that, nobody mourns a dead merc. Looting isn't a safe thing to do, not even when the enemy has abandoned the area. If the temptation is strong enough, your backup can become your murderer in less time than it takes the thought to occur.

Some signed on to market the only skills they'd ever learned. Some wanted a lawless place to practice their perversions.

Some left their homeland to forget a betrayal that could never be avenged. Others left because they had already taken that vengeance—some so excessively that they could never return.

I could understand most of the reasons, but the addicts always puzzled me. They followed wars like fans followed their favorite soccer team. Hard-core fans, the kind that attend all the games in person, even when they have to travel some serious distance. They never miss a match. And they don't know what to do with themselves when the season ends. All they can do is wait for it to come around again.

It always has. It always will.

A mercenary is a paid soldier.

He doesn't wear a uniform; he never gets exchanged for a prisoner taken by the other side. International law says a mercenary is anyone "fighting under a foreign flag." But international law doesn't matter in places where no flags fly.

Mercenaries are paid, but that pay isn't what drives them all. I served with men who already had more money than they could spend. Family money that had withstood everything from currency fluctuations to global conflicts. I don't mean the long-distance men, the ones who could launch an assault with a sat-phone conversation. I mean the men who had to be on the killing ground to feel—I don't know—just whatever it was that they felt once the fighting started.

I was done with that. All that. I had never chosen that life— it had been the only "choice" my life had offered. A boy who is freezing to death will enter the first door that opens. Even if the devil is standing behind that door, at least it's warm in there.

The only man who had ever called me "son" had promised that, if I could be strong enough to walk past that devil's door, the time would come when another would open. And *that* door would be the passage to the only thing I had ever truly wanted. If I survived five years in that furnace, I could be a person. *Become* a person.

"La Légion Étrangère is the only way for you, my son. Listen very carefully, now. You know where their recruiting office is, that place I showed you. I don't know how old you are, and they won't, either. You are a good size, you shave, you tell them you are eighteen, they will not argue.

"But they will ask questions, and you must know the answers. So! Why do you want to enlist? Because you want to be a professional soldier. *'Parlez-vous français?'* You answer *en anglais:* 'Only a little bit.' Where are your parents? You are an orphan. And you didn't want to stay with the caravan. They will understand from this that you are at least part *gitan,* a Gypsy. Probably a runaway, but that will not concern them.

"Then they will test you. How far can you run before you collapse? Will you get up and run some more if they order it? Physical pain will be your daily diet.

"But the hardest test will be the strength of your mind. That, they will test again and again. You will go without sleep for days at a time. For them, 'adaptability' is all. When they see how easily you can accomplish this, they will not ask where you learned, or who taught you—a stolen knife cuts as sharply as any you buy in a store.

"Whatever name you give them cannot be the truth. For you, this is natural—you don't know your real name. But this you must never admit. So, to the recruiter, your name is Luca Adrian. It is the only version of my name that I can give to you—mine might still call in the hounds."

Like everything else Luc had told me, that had proved true. But it was only part of the truth. What he never told me was that being a person doesn't lead you to a place where you belong. What can a man who knows nothing but war do with the rest of his life once he leaves the battleground?

I didn't blame Luc. How could he tell me? Luc had abandoned the search for that answer long before he found me.

From the moment I stepped past that first door, I never allowed my thoughts to wander beyond the next step. That's how your mind works when you're paid to walk trails to find those you've been paid to kill. They know you're coming, so your *next* step is all that matters. Congratulating yourself for slipping past a land mine can occupy your attention long enough to make you walk into a no-escape ambush.

When Luc first found me, I was afraid all the time. But from the moment he sent me away, I never knew fear.

I don't mean I was brave. Or even reckless. But fear doesn't take the high ground when you know the worst thing you might encounter would be better than what you had already escaped. When you already know how the story ends, there's no suspense. I always knew there was only one way a life like mine could end—the only mystery was its timing. The skills we were trained in were useful only for delaying that ending.

For some of us, those skills were vastly overvalued.

That was my life, never to fear death, and never to be unwilling to kill.

But I had seen too many become addicted to that life, and I was terrified of becoming like them. So, when I put together enough money to last me the rest of my bare-bones life, I stopped.

What goals did I have? Companionship? Who would want me? I carried so much weight that I couldn't add another's to mine and still keep walking. Friendship? I'd had friends. I'd watched Luc walk away. I'd carried the shredded body of Patrice back to base. Not back to his home—that was a journey he'd never make.

A mercenary might have comrades. But friends? Never. For me, that was never *again*—I knew that the loss of a true friend would be another slice off my ever-diminishing heart. And expecting every man in my unit to come back would be insane.

One reason I had so much money was that I had nothing to

spend it on. Nothing I'd ever wanted cost more than an hour of a whore's time. But even if I'd saved every penny I'd ever earned, I would not possess the ridiculous wealth I had accumulated. That money had come from simply following the instructions of a man I'd never met.

He may have found me when I took a job that came over the wire. How he found out that my "team" was only myself, I don't know.

I don't know what drove such a man—I'd never met him—but it wasn't any force I knew about. He was the one who told me when to put all my paper money into gold, when to change the gold back into cash. Time and time again. He was never wrong.

I liked to think he had been a comrade of Luc's in the Resistance—he would be a very old man by now, but he wouldn't need youthful strength to do what he did. The only thing I knew for sure was that I would never know his identity.

What I did know was that he could ghost past coding barriers the way I could a sleeping sentry—he'd proved that often enough. All I knew was how to access the encrypted line. Whoever was at the other end could waft through info-banks at will. A soundless breeze, too gentle to flutter a single leaf, never touching ground long enough to leave tracks. He'd helped me before. I wasn't sure why, and never asked.

I guessed he *could* have been connected to Luc, somehow—I *wanted* that to be true. And I reasoned that this was logical—perhaps the cyber-invader's father had passed his skills to his son as Luc had passed his to me.

I often told myself I had no need of either money or friends. But when that ghost asked me to do one last job—the one in that hospital—there was no way to refuse.

The job had been paid for in advance, by people who couldn't bring themselves to do what their dear friend wanted them to do so terribly.

Their dear friend, dying. Kept alive because experimenting on humans wasn't allowed in America, and nobody had yet decoded HIV.

That's when I found Dolly, but finding her didn't push either of us off our paths, not right away. She left for some place where they were treating advanced cancer patients with black-market stem cells. I stayed to finish my job.

I could have told her a bunch of lies. But considering what I'd been doing when we met, that would have been stupid. Not stupid because she would have seen through them, but stupid because I didn't want her to think I would lie to her. Ever.

Just because I couldn't explain any of that to myself didn't mean it wasn't true. I somehow knew I needed her to trust me if there was ever to be a chance for . . . for things I couldn't allow myself to think about.

A few months passed.

She never called the number I'd left with her, and I tried to make myself stop wishing she would.

Even though I now knew that Dolly was real, I had been trained never to wallow in hope—such feelings would only drip acid on my heart. *Je ne regrette rien.*

But I *did* hope. Not despite my will, but because of it. And every time that acid rained, I welcomed its burn. If my heart would only be strong enough, maybe that acid would etch in an image I might never again see with my eyes.

It was as if trying so hard not to wish for something *made* it happen. When she called, I didn't waste the chance. I asked her if she would sit with me long enough for me to say what I wanted to say. She didn't bother with a bunch of questions, not even "Why?" She just told me where she was.

I didn't tell her a story. I told her the truth. Not just about what I'd been, but what I wanted to be.

We had plenty of time then. Almost a week. Mostly, I listened. I found out that Dolly had seen too much war—too much pain, suffering, death. The worst had been right in Switzerland, in a place where they treated torture victims. She told me she'd had to get out before she became like one of them. I didn't understand what she meant, not then.

Dolly's dream was to live somewhere on the Oregon coast. She loved the idea of being so near the ocean. One day, she was going to buy a little cottage there. She had scouted around for a long time before coming to that decision. But now she was sure—all she wanted was to be in a place where she could live in peace.

Only the last part of what she said I felt inside myself, as well. True North. That had always been my dream, too.

I'd had only one reason to live—it was second nature to me to avoid death. But, afterward, I had two more: to make Dolly's dream come true, and to be part of it.

I found the place Dolly wanted—it *had* to be, I told myself; it was just as she'd described it.

I asked her to come and see it. Just *look* at it for herself—see if I hadn't truly been listening.

And to look at me—look at the man I *could* be. She had to know what I'd been doing in that jungle. So much blood had leached into that ground that even the most beautiful blossoms were poisonous. But I told her the whole truth of my life anyway, pushing all my chips into the middle of the table. Everything I had. Even the heart I thought had finally died with my last friend, Patrice.

I had to start from the beginning. The beginning as I knew it—the first years of my life were gone forever. That "clinic" in Belgium told me—in English, not in French—that I had "retrograde amnesia," as if that explained everything. But they wouldn't tell me anything else. Not even who put me there, or who was paying the bills.

All I knew for sure was that English—American English—was my mother tongue. That was as close to "mother" as I was ever to get.

No visitor ever came for me. I wasn't envious—nobody in that antiseptically clean, soulless place ever got a visitor.

I think I was somewhere around nine or ten years old when I escaped. It was so easy, as if moving in the dark had always been part of whoever I was.

I got as far as the gutters of Paris. Always hungry, always afraid, always cold—until Luc took me home with him.

When Luc neared his end, he knew. That's when he pointed me toward that only door open to me: La Légion Étrangère. I never looked back—that last memory of the old man standing on his own feet, that was the picture I needed to keep in my heart forever. My last chance to show him my love and respect.

For years, that memory was a pacemaker, the only thing keeping my heart alive. Before its batteries ran out, Patrice had come into my life, and they recharged. But my heart never grew powerful enough to pump on its own.

That's when fear left me forever, I thought. I hadn't watched Luc go—the old man would never have wanted that. Years later, I'd carried the bullet-shredded body of Patrice all the way back to base. When I dropped him to the ground, the officers praised me for bringing him back.

Our orders: we were never to abandon our dead, our wounded, or our weapons. But the officers were wise enough to understand that even the dullest of our despised band would never actually obey any such order if it meant even the slightest reduction in their own chance to survive.

I knew I still had a heart only because blood continued to pump through me. But after Luc, after Patrice, I didn't have any other use for that heart.

Not until Dolly.

Once Dolly accepted whatever was left of my heart, I was forever finished working at the only thing I knew.

Cutting my ties to my past was easy—I didn't have a past. Dolly never told me why she'd been no less willing to sever whatever ties she'd had, and I never asked.

But just to stop working at my deadly trade wasn't enough. Dolly told me I had to find a way to atone. This wasn't any religious thing—nobody who'd seen what Dolly had seen could ever believe there was any "God." Not on this planet, anyway.

If there was a Hereafter, we'd find out together. Whoever went first would wait for the other. I prayed that would be me, because nothing in Heaven or Hell would stop me from staying wherever I landed, so Dolly could find me when she arrived.

Regardless, Dolly said I had to atone for war because it was the only way I'd ever be at peace. I don't know how she knew this, but I trusted anything she said. So when she told me there was no reason to search—the opportunity would come to me—I trusted that as well.

Dolly was right.

A man who had access to the same network I once used reached out to offer me a job. The job—a job I would have refused, as I'd refused so many in the past years—was to bring his daughter to him. *To* him, not *back* to him. He'd never been her father; she was just some carelessly spilled seed.

Unwanted children are unprotected, and the unprotected are always the most clearly marked, the easiest of prey. So this man knew he was responsible for his daughter's willingness to go with a flesh trader. I knew that was the truth—her "choice" was the same I'd once made.

Finding the target was easy. There was nothing special about him—all I did was use the photos the father had supplied me with. Then follow the girl when oncoming morning drove all the night-birds "home."

He was a young prettyboy with nothing but some fraud-flash—zircons, fake fur, and a tired Cadillac. A galaxy's distance from a place he could never reach. Just a nasty little punk with no training, limited to running one girl at a time. Without the trappings to compete with professionals, he couldn't enter the same clubs frequented by serious pimps without being laughed out the door.

He didn't even try to pull a girl already in The Life—no working girl would go near a nothing like him. He did his recruiting on Facebook.

His product lasted only until a better offer—or a degenerate with a knife—came along and took it away from him. All he could do then was restock his empty cupboard.

He would have kept that up until . . . Well, an amateur like him never thought more than a few hours ahead.

I atoned for the killing I'd done for money by killing for free. I disposed of him quickly, and left his body to rot under a couch—an eventual message to anyone experienced enough to read it.

The girl never saw it happen. I told her some lies to get her to come with me. Once the car was moving, I told her that her father wanted her. More than anything in the world. She didn't believe me, but she came along without a struggle or even a protest. As she would have with anyone who took her, for any reason.

I told the man that the vermin who had taken his daughter would never call out to her again. And if he made the story I'd told the girl into the truth, none of his kind ever would.

His atonement was to be a father. He had a lot of ground to make up, but his commitment was strong enough so he could go the distance.

When I refused his money, the man was puzzled. When I wouldn't take a higher offer, he was mystified. Then he told me, if I ever needed anything, I had only to call, but I shook my head. The only way to make sure he accepted his own burden was to put what I'd promised into his hands, and leave with nothing in my own.

Maybe I could have explained that leaving without payment was my only path to what no amount of money could buy. But I didn't even try to explain. My debt was to others, not to him.

That man did become a father. The baby girl he never wanted became the most precious thing in his life. I never told Dolly how I'd made that happen—in truth, only given it a *chance* to happen. I told her I had found a way to atone for lives I'd taken. And I had done that. She accepted what I said, and never mentioned the subject again.

No invader can claim he killed with justification—only to protect himself, as if he'd had no other option. But I could claim—*now* I could claim—that I had killed to create an option. An option for a life. For *two* new lives.

A couple of years ago, a girl who'd been the high school's most prized athlete—"Mighty Mary" in the sports pages throughout the state—gunned down a popular boy, killing him with a pistol she'd stolen from her drunken father.

Dolly knew this was wrong. Not the killing itself, but the way everyone was looking at it. Even though it seemed a day couldn't go by without the national news reporting another "school shooting," Dolly knew this wasn't any such thing.

When I say I know something, Dolly never questions it. I never question her, either. Not because of trust—that is a permanency between us—but because we know where the other's knowledge came from. And what we learned was embedded so deeply that it has become part of who we are.

Love came to us much later, arcing like an electric current over the chasm between life-taker and life-saver. Since then, whatever we are now, that's how we'll always be.

I guess I could have passed. Maybe if I had, I never would have learned what a foul human sewer ran beneath this pretty little town. It wasn't that Dolly asked me to try—it was her absolute faith that I *could* do something that drove me back to where she'd first found me.

Not to that life itself, but to what that life had taught me.

Not all jungles have canopies. But they can still have land mines, and they all have enemy patrols. There's only one thing you can always be sure of: they're all ruled by the same laws.

After it was all over, a whole bunch of folks around here finally realized what they had to do.

They came to understand that theirs was no different from any other village: unless they surrounded it with the image of a ring of human skulls planted on stakes, they were inviting predators to a party.

I thought it was all done then.

I was wrong. So now I was an invisible part of the underbrush on a little hill that sloped down to Lovers' Lane. Waiting for a little red dot to pop into life. A little red dot that would tell me he was back to work.

I didn't know his name, or where he lived—although he thought I did. I didn't know what demons drove him to film the action down below. Still, I knew *him*. I'd just have to turn the right key to unlock the rest of what I needed to know.

That first time, I'd snapped him into a choke and held him tightly in the one embrace no man seeks.

When I gently ran the serrated edge of my black-bladed Tanto across his Adam's apple, he'd almost collapsed in terror.

This time, he responded as though I was a guest he'd been expecting. An unwelcome guest, to be sure. But an inevitable one.

"It's time for us to work together again," I whispered. "You know you can trust me, don't you? You know if I wanted to use this blade, you'd be gone, yes?"

"Yes," he said. Or maybe I could just feel him say it.

"You don't always have to wear the same outfit," I said. "Here, you wear it to blend with the night. But, sometimes, you have to blend in other places. To film what you need, yes?"

That time, I was sure he didn't speak. But I could feel the "yes" again.

"That body, the one the ocean spit out on the beach . . ."

I felt him quiver, but he stayed silent.

"It was marked with all kinds of Nazi tattoos. The head was shaved, but the whole back of the skull was caved in. No shark could do that. Not even those razor rocks just a few yards past the shoreline. But there's still a dozen different ways that body could have gotten into that ocean to begin with."

He stiffened.

"You took that picture," I said. Not an accusation, a statement of fact. Indisputable fact. "The one that was on the front page of the paper."

"How could you—?"

"The quality," I said, slipping a thread of admiration into my voice. "That was no cell-phone snap—it was the work of a top professional. The papers around here are too small to have their own staff photographers. The reporters take what whoever their story's about gives them—like a picture of some politician. Anyone can take a picture, but that body on the beach, *that* was a work of art."

He longed for just that kind of praise, but he couldn't risk the blame . . . which is why he'd sent the photo to the papers. So he took another feeble stab at throwing me off his scent. "There's more than one photographer in—"

"Studio men." I dismissed them all under the same blanket of disdain. "They're not photojournalists. And they aren't night workers, either. You got a first-light photo. So you had to have been right there when it happened. When the body first washed up."

It was a safe guess. This wretched little man I was talking to would know all the spots where he might capture what he hunted. Images. Images of people doing what he . . . I stopped myself from speculating. It didn't matter why he did what he did, only that he'd never stop. I didn't judge him. All that mattered to me about his sickness was that it ensured I could always put my hands on him if I needed to.

"I wasn't doing anything wrong."

"Did I say you were? I found you once before, didn't I? And I know where you live, too. But I never said a word, not to anybody. I said we were going to be friends then, didn't I? Aren't we still friends?"

"I . . . guess."

"If we were enemies, I could hurt you a hundred different

ways," I said softly. "I could hurt you right now. Very badly. Much worse than death, if I wanted. Two quick little pokes with this"—tapping the point of the Tanto lightly on his cheek—"and you'd never use your eyes again. But I'd never hurt a friend. I'd never *let* anyone hurt a friend, either."

He wasn't my friend, but I wasn't lying to him. Torture is stupid. All it achieves is pain and terror. If you want someone to talk, you have to put more incentive in front of him than just making the pain stop. The thought of a hidden protector somewhere out in the darkness he prowled was stronger than any fear I could have induced.

He went silent again, but I could feel the calmness settle over his spirit.

"Just tell me about that photo. All I want to know is what was happening just *before* you took it. You were there, so you know. You tell me and I'm gone. Just like last time. I kept that promise, didn't I? And remember what I told you then: someday, you may be thankful you have a friend like me."

The body had washed up way north of where we live. Not far from where a huge chunk of concrete pier torn loose by a monstrous tsunami in Japan had floated all the way across the Pacific.

For a while, that pier had been a tourist attraction. Some just wanted to see it, so they could e-mail the sight to their friends, or post it on Facebook if they didn't have any actual friends. Some brought metal detectors, "prospecting" for whatever valuables might also have made the journey. "Salvaging," that's how they'd describe their hobby. As if they were deep-sea divers taking risks, not scavengers looting a corpse.

Finally, the government managed to chop the whole thing up and turn it into concrete granules that could be used for road fill. "Recycling"—that's a magic word around here. I knew more about recycling than any of them ever would, but it wasn't knowledge I'd share.

Oregon doesn't have private beaches. You can pay millions of dollars for oceanfront property to sit out on your deck and watch the beautiful sunsets with nothing blocking your view, night after night. If you stayed there until after dark, you could listen to the sounds of eardrum-destroying "music" . . . and the accompaniment those lying on the sand a long way below you create when the meth kicks in. The next morning, you walk down your "private" staircase and self-righteously clean up the mess those disgusting people always leave behind. After all, you didn't pay a fortune for a landscape of garbage.

All along the beach, skull-and-crossbones signs were posted, warnings of what people call "sneaker waves." You can't see them coming—they reach out like the tentacles of a giant octopus and pull you under. You just vanish, as if you'd never really been there at all.

That didn't stop some drugged-out fools from sleeping under those signs. Or stop perfectly sober people from letting their dogs "run free." Or not watching their kids close enough.

Every time one of those waves took a child, the sand would be dotted with heartfelt "memorials," artistically arrayed by anguished locals. It wouldn't do to plant a row of tombstones blaming the grieving parents—the self-proclaimed liberals who populate the coast would tolerate just about any lifestyle, but "anti-tourist" conduct was strictly prohibited.

Those same sneaker-wave tentacles are as capricious as they are deadly—they don't just whip out and drag people under, they sometimes fling things back up on the beach, too.

Like that body.

As soon as I saw that photo, I knew the strange man I always thought of as a video ninja had been there, doing his work. The original ninjas were trained as spies, working in darkness centuries before artificial light existed. And that was him—part of the night—incessantly spying in service to the overlord who lived inside him.

So I knew that the ninja had already been in place for hours when the ocean disgorged the body of that man, patiently waiting for any new players to step into his frame.

But why send that photo? Maybe he couldn't resist the opportunity to see his work displayed on paper—not just on whatever back-channel Internet site he'd set up to show his videos. Maybe he needed to tell himself he really was the photojournalist I'd called him. An artistic documenter, not some degenerate, compulsively seeking more captives for his master's dungeon.

It didn't matter. I wasn't there to analyze him, even if I could. What I needed was what he could tell me.

What I knew he *would* tell me.

"**W**hat time was it?"

The video ninja knew what I was asking, and didn't hesitate—the digital photo he'd sent was date/time-stamped, and that couldn't have been some accident on his part.

"Four-oh-nine a.m."

"That angle in the photo . . . ?"

"I was . . . I was between some rock formations. There's a little place under there that—"

"Only you know about," I finished for him, twisting my disgust into what would sound like a respectful acknowledgment of his skills.

"Yes."

"Did anyone else see it? The body? When it first hit the shore, I mean?"

"No."

"You just snapped the shot and took off?"

"Yes."

"And you e-mailed it to the papers from a proxy address?"

"Yes."

"What about that *Undercurrents* thing? The online . . . blog, or whatever you call it?"

"No. I knew the regular papers would call the police, but I didn't think they . . . the people who run the blog . . . I didn't think they'd cooperate with the police—they're more like watchdogs than reporters."

"Did you do a little work on it first? Artistic work, I mean."

"No!" he snapped out vehemently, probably surprising himself more than me. "I don't need that stuff," he explained, instantly reverting to timidity. "That's not photography, it's just playing with a computer program."

"I understand. And we're still friends, right?"

"Yes."

"So I don't have to put you to sleep this time? You'll just keep looking straight ahead, not look behind you as I leave?"

"Yes."

"Have you ever heard the sound a silenced pistol makes?"

"Only in—"

"Movies. Okay. I have much better equipment than that. You'd never hear it. Neither would anyone else."

"But I'm not going to—"

"I believe you. But we're friends, so I have an obligation. Friends always warn friends about risks they might not see for themselves. I have to explain what would happen if you *did* turn around, do you understand?"

"Yes."

By then, his fear-stench was overpowering, and we were upwind from what he'd been there to film. So I vanished from his life. Again.

It had started with Dolly, a few nights before.

"That damn ocean. I love it, but I'm afraid of it, too. It's so beautiful, so calming. That must be where 'Pacific' came from. But now it's like something . . . malignant, Dell. I know it sounds crazy, but it's almost as if someone lobbed a grenade into our lives."

"It's only a picture."

"On the front page of the paper."

"It's still a picture, no matter where it's put."

"But that . . . body. That's what they do. Over there. You know."

Yeah, I knew. Coming across the mutilated body of a soldier from your outfit was supposed to make you fear going any deeper into the jungle. Maybe it did, for some. For those trained as we were, it only served as confirmation that we were where we wanted to be—close to the enemy we'd been hunting.

"Dolly, honey, it came out of the ocean. If a gigantic chunk of concrete could float here all the way from Japan, that body could have been dumped into that same ocean anywhere between Canada and California."

"It was a fresh kill, Dell."

I didn't question how Dolly knew that—anything the local hospital found would be shared with her as soon as one of her nurse pals came on shift. "So—less time to float, sure. But 'fresh' doesn't mean all that much, especially in salt water."

"But it still feels like an . . . invasion."

"A dead body isn't an invasion. It could be a warning to anyone *thinking* about invading, sure. But who invades the ocean?"

"I know. I know it's logical, what you're saying. But you know I don't spook at shadows, baby. And I have to trust my . . ."

I couldn't put a name to what I knew my woman had always

trusted. "Instincts," "intuition," whatever it was, I knew she'd had it—inside her, I mean—before she ever entered that kill-zone where we'd first met. Maybe it was what *sent* her there.

But all that really mattered was that it hadn't kept her from trusting me.

It was another ten days before any public info started to emerge.

I read the press release that passes for "news" here to Dolly. The dead man had been ID'ed by his prints: Welter Thom Jordan, born August 21, 1980—so age thirty-three at time of death. White, male, five feet ten inches; two hundred and twelve pounds, hazel eyes. No facial hair, head shaved. Two prior prison terms, both for assault, with the last one flagged as a "hate crime." The local papers didn't have much more, other than his "racist tattoos."

"What kind of name is 'Welter'?" I asked.

"Probably supposed to be 'Walter,'" my wife said. "You'd be amazed at how many times a birth mother misspells a baby's name, especially if she's alone and frantic. Or the hospital itself might have screwed it up."

For a slice of a second, I wondered what my own birth certificate might have on it. The thought passed almost before I was conscious of it. An instant reflex, the kind you work hard to develop, always narrowing the gap between "see" and "shoot."

"Hate crime?" I asked my wife.

"Probably the assault was against anyone that fits one of the categories: different skin color, gay, a mixed-race couple. . . ."

"If he did a good jolt on that last one, he'd have been a young man when he was locked up for it. But that kind of crime would carry status with certain people—he wouldn't have been alone in prison. And that height-weight ratio sounds like he spent a lot of time pushing iron, even if it was only the bars on his cell."

"All they have so far is what was on file when he was arrested. That was quite a while ago, so the autopsy would be a lot more accurate—he could be anything from muscled up to a flab bucket when he was killed. I haven't seen the autopsy photos, but I could if you—"

"Dolly . . ."

"What, baby?"

"What's this—*any* of this—got to do with us?"

"His watch. Wristwatch. The police found it on a homeless guy, and they're holding him for the murder."

"So?"

"So Mack says there's no way the guy they arrested could have done it."

"Mack?"

"The man who works with . . . Well, he works outdoors, mostly, but he has to interface with the hospital, too," she said, as if repeating something I should have already known.

"It's still 'So?,' Dolly. If it's not going to touch us, then—"

"It already has. There's already talk about some crazy homeless man, but it's just smoke, I think."

"Why not just let the cops work it out?"

She gave me one of those "Are you for real?" looks she must have picked up from the teenage girls that haunt this house. I've only got two places just for myself: that "den" Dolly fixed up for me on the first floor, and the basement. The kids know they can walk into the den if the door's open . . . and not even to knock if it isn't.

The basement door is always closed, always locked, and the only way to get to it is down a hall, after a sharp left turn.

Nobody ever follows Dolly down that hall. Rascal's usually pretty indifferent once Dolly lets anyone in the house, but trying to follow behind Dolly when she walks away will get you a warning growl . . . if it's your lucky day.

Like I said, rules.

"They may not be investigative geniuses, honey. But . . . I mean, who cares? A dead Nazi, some homeless guy, a nut job—who cares?"

"Dell, I already told you. Mack says—"

"People are probably *saying* everything."

"You never met him. Mack, I mean."

"I don't need to meet him."

"Dell . . ."

I sat back in my chair and closed my eyes. I knew that tone.

"I know Laura. The guidance counselor at the high school. She worked on the rez before that."

I didn't say anything.

"Don't you give me one of your looks, Dell. When I say 'counselor,' I'm not talking about some New Age healer—around here, those people, they're like . . . everywhere you turn. 'Counseling' means what it sounds like. Not aroma therapy or toxin-releasing massage."

"Okay," I said, but that didn't slow her down.

"And I don't mean one of those 'I've been there' idiots who think having been a dope fiend makes you an expert on drug addiction. To work inside a school, you need a license. Which means going to school—*graduate* school—and passing exams afterward. So, if the school hired her, she was qualified for the job."

"If that was the rule, they'd have to fire some of the teachers."

"Will you *stop*? Aren't you the one always saying the tribe should spend some of their casino money on a program for gambling addicts?"

"I said that *once,* sure. But come on, Dolly. You really think that's what the tribe wants, *less* gambling? If it wasn't for those casinos, they'd all have to find jobs."

"Very funny. The fact is, those casinos were a smart political move. Even in this state, this *side* of the state, anyway—where most of the voters are concentrated—a lot of folks just plain resent them. The tribe, I mean. So—"

"How do you know that resentment's wrong? You can resent a person who's a different color than you for reasons *besides* their color."

"Like what?"

"Like all that phony 'Native American' worship, like the TV ads about respecting their 'culture,' like all the garbage about how they're always 'giving back.' It's all about money, period. Hell, they're even running their own payday loan rip-offs now. What's it matter whether the person bleeding you white is a genuine Native American?"

"Dell . . ."

"What? All you have to do is show you've got some percentage—I'm not sure how high, but it isn't much—of Indian blood, you get all kinds of job opportunities that others don't, never mind those 'allotments' you can collect. With so many people out of work . . ."

"It's not that way everywhere. Plenty of Indians live in the worst kind of poverty."

"Sure. In states that don't have casinos."

"Dell, you're the last person I'd expect to—"

"Why? Just because I can't tell a thing about myself from a blood sample, you think I'd resent other people just because they can? And they *do* swing a lot of weight with all the politicians, don't they?"

"Sure they do. But it's not like they're fighting each other, so they're not paying negative money."

"What's negative—"

"Like when those two tribes were fighting over who would get the 'casino rights' in Texas. That's what sent that king lobbyist to prison. Abramoff, I think his name was—he was taking money from *both* sides for payoffs to politicians. It happens all over—some 'tribe' with eight members claims a few acres, and, all of a sudden, they've got some real heavy hitters 'advocating' for them."

"And that *didn't* happen here?"

"No," she said, tartly, "it did not. The casino business here, it's not owned by one single tribe—they're a confederation. So it's not the percentage of any particular tribe you need, just a percentage of Indian blood."

They should have done that centuries ago in Africa, I thought to myself. *If they'd ever confederated . . . But those tribes never will. Why join forces to fight off non-native invaders? They know they'll eventually go back to wherever they came from. Then the different tribes can start killing each other again. Just like they were before strangers with a different skin color showed up.*

"Anyway. It wasn't counseling gamblers that got Laura in trouble on the rez—it was working with young girls."

"She changed her own job?"

"No. She added to it. Her forty-hour week was more like sixty. But she did break a lot of their rules. Like when an Indian woman—no matter how young—gives birth but she can't take care of the child. Or doesn't want to. Or even . . . Well, it doesn't matter. If the baby ends up a candidate for adoption, their rules are that only an Indian family can adopt.

"There was this one case: a newborn baby was put in 'foster care' with a Mexican family for nine years. But when that family wanted to adopt him, the tribe objected. They *objected* when the only family that baby had ever known wanted to adopt him! There's some federal law that lets them do that, and they won in court.

"But there *wasn't* any Indian family that wanted to adopt a child that age, so guess what? Back to foster care, only with a *different* family!"

"That's nuts," I said, my mind flicking back and forth between "the only family that baby had ever known" and "nine years"—the age I'd probably been when I escaped from that "clinic." It took more effort than usual to push all that back where it belonged, but I managed it. "Anyway, don't they have Mexican Indians? Like Aztecs and—"

"It's not the same thing. Not to them. And you're right, that *was* nuts. And Laura said so. In public."

"They fired her for that?"

"They said she wasn't fired, just 'laid off.' But nobody could miss the message. By then, she was seeing so many school-age kids that she had a . . . 'following,' I guess you'd call it. So, when that nasty old crone that used to be the guidance counselor at the high school retired, Laura got the job."

"'Nasty old crone'?"

"That's what the kids always called her," Dolly said, making it into an unchallengeable truth. "All of them. If any of them had a . . . secret of some kind, or even wanted to talk about how they were feeling, she was the *last* person they'd pick.

"Besides, nobody really wanted that job. It doesn't pay much, and the only other applicants were just college grads, without a counseling license.

"Laura didn't have any political backing, but you'd be surprised at how many people told the school board that they wanted the most qualified person for the job. Maybe it's all those school shootings—" She cut herself off, and I stepped in quick, so her last words wouldn't just hang in the air.

"I wouldn't be surprised," I told her. "Anyway, with that psycho who blew himself up building a pipe bomb a while back, and then that . . . horror show in Connecticut, folks would *want* the early-warning signals now."

"Uh-huh," Dolly said, not interested in going any further down that trail. "*Now* can we get back to why that homeless guy couldn't have been the killer?"

"What's that got to do with Laura?" Which got me another acidic look from the only person I loved still able to walk this earth.

"Laura is what they call a 'sit-down therapist.' This kind of thing, that's Mack's work. I told him I'd let him know. When he could come over, I mean."

My wife was telling me she'd given her word. That was enough. If your word doesn't mean much, neither do you. So you can't just warn anyone off—a threat is a promise. And my life was a simple equation: you hurt my Dolly, you hurt me. I was taught very early on—you let anyone do something bad to you, they'll come back and do something worse. Since then, it's been very simple: hurt me, you won't get another chance to do it again. Ever. But all I said was "It's your house, Dolly. I'm not—"

"Dell," she said, hands on hips to let me know she was really running out of patience, "it's you I want him to talk to. And you know damn well it is. So I'd have to make sure you weren't planning on being off somewhere when I tell him—"

"Tonight's fine," I cut her off, this time earning a dazzling smile and a sweet kiss I didn't deserve. All I wanted was to get whatever this was over with, and I knew the only way I could do that was to show Dolly it had nothing to do with us. Or her girls.

I'm not a hermit, but in a town this size, I'd already been way too visible for my taste.

Dolly, now, she was all over the place, all the time. That was fine with me. And it was no secret that we were married. When we'd walked away, it was understood between us that I was finished with what had once been my work. I'd never expected the same from Dolly. I knew healing was in her blood. And I needed to believe that killing wasn't in mine.

So I'd gotten used to the flocks of teenaged girls—and the boys who kind of followed them around—being in the house. And to Dolly going off to one of her endless meetings—I guess "fights" would be a better word, like when the town tried to close the animal shelter. But the last time I went back to my past, I'd reacted as if I'd been waiting for the chance. That state of readiness bothered me—I didn't want to go near that place again.

That last time, everyone knew "Mighty Mary." But how many knew that Cameron Taft—the man she gunned down in a high-school corridor—was the boss of a gang-rape "society"? One that only plucked the lowest-hanging fruit: girls who were underage, undesirable, and unwanted by anyone else. Those who *did* know never told anyone, not anymore. What would have been the point? When the earlier victims had told the Sexual Assault Nurse Examiner on duty in the ER exactly what had happened to them, when the SANE nurses immediately reported the rapes, complete with their own medical findings for confirmation, nothing happened. Nothing at all.

After a while, everyone believed the gang rapists who called themselves "Tiger Ko Khai" had some kind of special immunity.

I found out a lot of things then. In between the work I'd had to do and a jury finding MaryLou not guilty, a lot of . . . violence took place.

And even after that verdict, I'd killed another man. That was keeping my promise to MaryLou—the promise that had finally convinced her to help the lawyer we'd paid for and the experts Dolly had assembled to defend her.

Before that, she'd been a stone. *La mission est terminée. J'ai fini. Il n'y a rien d'autre à faire.* I'd seen that look before, when I soldiered for La Légion. Always the same: "The mission is over. There is nothing left to do." Nothing left of me, either.

That tree had been pulled out by its taproot. Chopped up into stakes just right for impaling. Those heads turned into skulls, now surrounding the village.

It wasn't my job to protect anything other than my own perimeter. If Dolly hadn't pulled MaryLou inside that perimeter, I wouldn't have done a thing.

So I'd listen to whatever this Mack guy wanted to say. And then the only work I'd have to do would be to keep Dolly from pulling him or whoever else he might be talking about inside our perimeter. If what he wanted was money to hire a lawyer, I knew a good one, right in town. And we had the money, too. But that was as far as I was prepared to go.

La Légion held all kinds of men, the full range of the human spectrum.

But we lived under the same rules, some official, some cultural.

To ignore orders when there were no officers around to enforce them was part of that culture. As was hero worship of men who had most flagrantly disobeyed *all* rules, those who *chose* a life of violence, despite knowing how all such lives must end.

That was why a famous criminal named Mesrine was admired by every *légionnaire*. First for his battlefield courage in North Africa, later for his international string of bank robberies, the beautiful women he always seemed to have with him, and his many escapes from custody.

It was assumed some of his exploits had been financed by the Organisation Armée Secrete—those former soldiers who still regarded de Gaulle as a traitor for abandoning the fight to keep Algeria a French colony.

But Mesrine's journey proved to be longer than the distance

between continents. He slid all the way from the fascist-loving Right to the overthrow-obsessed Left, moving like a superb tango-dancer, never missing a step. Or losing a single worshipper.

To a *légionnaire,* it was not whether Mesrine stood to the left or to the right—it was that he stood with *us.* Politics were for fat men who sat behind desks—fighting was for the soldiers they sent out like one-way carrier pigeons. We existed solely to deliver death messages. Whether we returned or not was of no great interest to them. So Mesrine's motivations meant nothing to us—what mattered was that he represented everything we respected.

I remember a passage from a pamphlet one of the men in my unit showed me:

La prison, cest un puit nausabond de haine, de peur et de désespoir. La bourgeoisie bien-pensante veut nous faire croire que sa fonction est de nous "transformer." Après tout, quel esprit sain aurait envie de retourner dans cet enfer? Mais comme le bourgeois na aucune idée de ce qu'est vraiment le désespoir, il ne peut pas comprendre ses effets.

He glanced up to see if I was still looking over his shoulder; then his eyes returned to the page, stopping only when he reached the point where his own life was a tribute to his hero.

Je fais le vœu de porter le titre de HORS-LA-LOI jusqu'à ma mort. Et je fais le vœu de mourir dans la lutte sans merci qui m'oppose aux ennemis de tous ceux qui ont un vrai respect pour la justice.

I could have translated the gist of it easily enough. But, as Patrice had cautioned me many times, I never spoke more than a few words of French aloud—only those words the officers required us all to know. So I just glanced at the passage and shook my head in frustration. That didn't matter. The man who held the pamphlet was very passionate about it—he couldn't wait to recite it for me in English, with a few embellishments of his own. He was an Aussie, maybe as much as twice my age. All I knew about him was that he called himself "Mal."

"Listen to this, mate. Here speaks a man who knows the truth of things." He translated: "Prison is a foul pit of hatred, fear, and despair. The pious bourgeoisie claim that living in pain will 'rehabilitate' us. After all, what sane man would want to return to such a palace of horrors? But they do not understand: the pain they inflict produces only total desperation. True, none of us wish to be thrown back into Hell. And perhaps such a prospect frightens the weak and the cowardly. But for the warrior, there are only the choices of the jungle: kill, or be killed. Prison itself is an instrument of evil, designed not to 'change' convicts, but only to protect the wealthy from the poor. I reject their bourgeois 'values' as I reject them all. I vow to proudly wear the brand of OUTLAW until I die. And I vow to die in battle, in mortal combat against the enemy of all who truly revere justice."

Mal knew I was much younger than him, but not so young that I might not have already tasted prison wine and found it too sour to ever drink again. I didn't know if those words he quoted had actually come from Mesrine himself, or if the Aussie was reading some leftist French "analysis." In France, the Left specializes in explaining things to those too uneducated to understand them. They are certain that no one is too ignorant to understand the messages of the Right.

I knew that the Aussie had no plans to earn a living by unskilled labor. And I guessed that "Mal" wasn't short for "Malcolm," just his way of proclaiming that he would be a bad person to have as an enemy. He didn't mind fighting—he was a courageous man, and adept as well—but the only work he'd ever do would end in his death. Or, worse, capture by the enemy. Either way, OUTLAW boldly tattooed on the outside of his thick right forearm would be with him always, even if only in a shallow grave.

If it hadn't been for Dolly, I might have followed him. Not to any political ideology. La Légion had shown me that those are all the same—excuses to take power, or to keep it. No, I would have followed Mal to the only two depots where the trains for men like us ever stopped: prison or death. And for those willing to risk death to escape prison, even those two were really only one.

It was as the Aussie had said—those with the power to make the laws can brand "outlaw" on whoever they choose.

And even if those with that power took it by force, so what? No real power is ever acquired legitimately, because the conqueror is always the final authority.

I will never forget two men I'd served with. Hard men from America. They didn't look alike, but they had the same look.

One was a Cherokee, I think. I knew he was from one of those tribes that fought to the death rather than be captured and enslaved, and I knew that this was no political position—it was something inside him. The other one was black—not an African, like Idrissa, a Senegalese who preferred to fight with his sword—but an African born in America. His English was the same as mine, but he never talked to me. And I never started a conversation in all the time I was a *légionnaire*—more advice from Patrice.

I thought that maybe the Indian blood in Dolly's friend Laura had risen to the surface—better to fight than surrender, tribe trumping race, as it always does—but I never said anything.

Why would I? She had a really good way with those girls who were always around. And I knew she had Dolly's trust. Otherwise, she would never have allowed Laura to take one of the girls into our bedroom—the only place in the house that was unmonitored.

Rascal—a mutt Dolly had rescued from the shelter—made a noise deep in his chest. Not a threat, just an alert. People usually didn't come near the house after dark. If I wasn't around, he'd guard Dolly. When Dolly left the house, Rascal would go along. I guess he figured I could take care of myself. Or he didn't give a damn.

I understood that. All of it. Rascal had his job, and he'd do it—that was all that counted, no matter what it might cost.

I'd already seen a car pull in. The camera we had set up in the driveway didn't throw a monitor image sharp enough for me to see exactly what kind of car it was, but I could tell it was a good twenty years old . . . and it hadn't been an easy twenty years.

I heard a car door close—sounded more like a screen door than a bank vault. Watched an unfamiliar figure walk around to the back entrance. Soon as Rascal got the man's scent, he relaxed.

"This is Mack," Dolly said. "Laura knows him, too."

No more "Maksim" for you, huh? flashed in my mind. I know a Russian when I see one, and this guy was right off a recruiting poster: close-cropped blond hair, flat blue eyes, heavy cheekbones, and that squared-up stance they always took—relying on strength, not flexibility.

We shook hands. He didn't go for a bone crusher, like some do when they first meet me, but he let me feel he had more in the tank if he needed it.

Dolly moved her head and he sat down. No surprise to me. Dolly never played hostess—if anyone wanted something, they knew where the refrigerator was. And the coffee urn, where you could mix your own brew.

"I work two jobs," Mack said. Speaking to me, no preamble—I guessed that Dolly already knew whatever he was telling me. "Actually, three. But they all overlap. I deal with two of the permanent homeless populations, and I'm on call if the jail gets a prisoner who could be losing it."

"I never heard of a shrink that worked with homeless people."

"You mean, worked with them outdoors, right?"

"I guess so. I never really thought about it."

"I'm not a medical doctor. I'm a social worker."

"A guy's on suicide watch in the jail, they call in a social worker?"

"Mack is an L.C.S.W.," Dolly said, "a licensed clinical social worker." She wasn't being defensive with me. She wasn't really talking to me at all. Mack wasn't going to play the credentials game, fine—but she'd be damned if he allowed modesty to get in the way of information.

I just nodded, as if I understood what she meant—I knew Dolly would explain it to me later.

"One homeless population has really advanced coping skills," Mack said. "For them, being homeless is a lifestyle, not something they were forced into. Maybe they were travelers, once"—he paused just for a second, maybe he could see the *gitan* in my blood as easily as I saw Russian in his—"like they jumped off a freight just to see what they could scrounge, and found they liked it here. The weather is good year-round—that could have played into their choice, too.

"The other group is completely different—mentally ill or addicted to something. Or both."

"Drunks?"

"Alcoholism, sure. Around here, meth is more common.

But anything you can drink, snort, shoot, or . . . It's a long list. Still, just about any way you play that, getting locked up somewhere along the way is part of their deal."

"Wouldn't some of those 'advanced coping skills' get you locked up, too?"

"That's the truth," he said, smiling thinly. "But there's a difference between the merchants who don't want homeless camps blotting the scenery during tourist season and locals who are scared of people walking around who smell bad, look worse, and talk to themselves."

"I've seen those. Both of those, I guess. But I've never seen you before."

"You never saw my face," he said. "And I don't wear a suit and tie to work."

I nodded. No reason for this guy to know I could pick a visitor out of a crowd just by his stance. It was as easy for me as picking up a red dot on a black screen. Or putting one on an enemy's chest.

"The cops usually don't bother them. Any of them. The MICAs—Mentally Ill, Chemically Addicted—they could be carrying everything they own with them, or else they've got some kind of 'residence' . . . you know, a place to sleep, or even get help. The ones who *chose* the outside life, they don't want anything to do with the government. No 'programs' for them. If they've got a check coming—maybe from the VA—they'll have some local address, give the owner a piece to hold the checks. Just go down to the library any morning right before it opens, you'll always see a few of them. Waiting to check on their e-mail."

"Their e-mail?"

"Yep," Mack said, showing that thin smile again. "The library has free Internet access. It's a lot cheaper than a PO box. So many of them use it that there's a sign-up sheet."

"And this guy they grabbed—?"

"Homer. He's an ambulatory schizophrenic. Stays outside as much as possible, because the voices can't get to him as easily if he's not indoors. But he only really feels safe after dark."

"So how did he get that guy's watch?"

"God gave it to him," Mack said, not the faintest touch of sarcasm in his voice. "He was walking along the beach. Just before the sun comes up, you can see the sky start to lighten. The voices are really strong in the daytime. But Homer knows you can't rely on the sun—it can get so foggy near the ocean that you can hardly see it at all at sea level. That's why God gave him the watch—so he could keep track of time."

"He took it off the body?"

"That's my guess. It's not like they matched a serial number or anything. But who else besides a White Power guy would have an '88' with a pair of lightning bolts through it engraved on the back of his watch?"

"If the . . . crazy guy, okay? . . . if he was wearing that watch, how would the cops have seen the *back* of the case?"

"Homer took it off and showed it to them. He wanted them to know he'd have better control over the voices now."

"They weren't even looking—?"

"For suspects? Probably were. Not thinking any homeless guy actually did the killing, but they know those folks—the permanent ones, I'm saying—they don't miss much that goes on around here, so . . ."

"But wouldn't those people, the ones who are homeless by choice, wouldn't they keep lunatics out of their camps?"

"Well, see, there's more than one homeless-by-choice crew. The older ones—the ones with e-mail addresses and camping gear—they stay to themselves. But there's also the kids. The ones we call 'emancipated by abandonment.' Not runaways, throwaways. They won't have ID, won't have prints on file, and their parents—their biological parents—wouldn't file Missing Persons on them."

"There's another group of kids you haven't even mentioned," Dolly cut her way into the conversation, the edge of her voice razor-ready. "Some of my girls are 'homeless,' too. Their parents may not have a place to live, but they're *trying,* not giving up. You can be the best father in the world and still lose your job. You can be the best mother and get so sick—diabetes, cancer, it doesn't matter—that your medical bills drive the whole family into bankruptcy. That's the address some of my girls have: 'homeless.' And you know *where* that address appears? On their school records! And if you think *their* parents don't go over their homework with them, or that any of *my* girls treat them any differently, you'd be dead wrong."

You'd be dead to Dolly, I thought to myself. *You bring some weed over here, Dolly gives you a second chance. But you look down on other girls because your parents have money and theirs don't, you're not welcome in Dolly's house. Ever.*

Mack set his jaw, bowed his head very slightly, said, "I know," to Dolly. "*Everybody* knows."

Dolly flashed him a smile, unclenched her fists, and just barely stopped short of giving him a kiss on the cheek. Mack's posture changed, too—not as dramatically, but you couldn't miss how relieved he was. Alienating Dolly wasn't something a man who did his kind of work would ever want to do.

"I was talking about those kids who don't have anyone but themselves. Some were in custody. Abused kids in 'group homes,' JDs from 'community corrections,' all the same once they take off. They all hang together. And they don't ask questions. The only rule they have is that you don't get aggressive with them."

"You're saying it was *those* kids who let Homer hang around?"

"Yep. The permanents, they're scared of crazy people. Even the circuit riders, the ones who drop off for a while but never stay, they've got enough sense to keep their distance from them.

But the kids, they seem to actually like them. Damaged adults, I mean."

"As long as they're not violent," Dolly added.

"Yeah," Mack agreed. "Whatever's going on in their heads doesn't matter, so long as it's not telling them to get physical."

"And there's no way this Homer could possibly have killed that guy they found on the beach?"

"Possible? Sure." Mack shrugged. "*Anything* is, right? But that doesn't make any more sense than Homer does when he tries to 'explain' something. He's never . . . physical. Not with anyone.

"Plus, he's scared of adults. He knows they don't like him— that's the way he puts it—and he knows, from the state hospitals he's been in and out of all his life, that what he calls 'big people' will hurt you."

"Orderlies, you're saying?"

"I'm not saying anything; I'm repeating what Homer told me," he said, his voice going just a little softer. From the way Dolly put her hand on his forearm, I guessed his voice got softer when his temper got closer to the surface.

I just held his eyes, waiting for some information I could actually use.

"Homer's about five foot two, and he's damn near emaciated. On top of that, he's almost sixty."

None of that meant much to me. I once watched a little Filipino guy who was probably older than this Homer cut a man's throat so fast I barely saw his hand move. The other guy was a big merc with a bigger mouth. But nothing would have happened if he hadn't decided it would be funny to snatch the Filipino's beer off the counter and pour it over his head.

The merc should have known better—it was the kind of place where part of the help's job was to drag unconscious men out by their ankles and dump them in the alley, then throw some fresh sawdust over the floor. The merc didn't size up the bar, and he'd walked in alone. Maybe he spotted me and thought I'd back him up. Maybe he was already drunk. That wouldn't have made a difference—he was a stupid bully even when he was sober.

"He ever get beat up?"

"Homer?"

"Yeah."

"I told you—"

"Not in some hospital. Or criminally insane wing of a prison. I mean on the street."

"Not that I ever heard of. Why'd you ask?"

"To see if he was good at protecting himself."

"Yeah, all right. No, not a chance. Screaming's the only weapon he's got. And that's never helped him much."

"Then what's the big deal?"

I could feel Mack stiffen. Watched his eyes try to look through my skull to the wall behind me. When he took a breath, it was through his nose. The little whistling sound told me that whoever had tried to fix the break hadn't done a great job of it. Probably had a deviated septum by now. And health insurance. But he'd never gotten it fixed.

He was a young man, not a kid. But I'd seen harder stares, from harder men, before I was half his age.

About five seconds passed before he understood that he was wasting his time. Still, he said, "What's the big deal?" with more hostility than he probably realized.

"Yeah, that's what I said. This guy's got a guaranteed insanity defense, no matter what he might have done, right up to murder. So they put him back in some crazy-house, how does that hurt him, really? You said yourself, he comes and he goes. At his age, the way he lives, who knows how long his next visit would have lasted, no matter what the reason for it."

"Homer's terrified of being locked up."

"Don't they have drugs for—?"

"Homer doesn't need to be locked up to be on medication. He's got his disability check, and it's sent to us. We bank it, and we only give him so much a day—*after* someone watches him take his meds. That way, he knows he always has a place to go. And we're always sure he's taking his meds. The *right* meds, not something that'd turn him into a zombie."

"There's more, Dell," my wife said. "If Homer didn't kill that guy—and even the cops don't really think he did, but they had to take him when he showed them that watch—somebody else did."

"Dolly, I'm not trying to act cold-blooded, but . . . so what? Guy like that—the tattoos, his record—probably a lot of people could have a reason to kill him. That's a job for the cops."

"Which cops?" Dolly shot back. "The locals? The Sheriff's Office? The State Police? Knowing where a body was found doesn't tell you where a murder happened. Or even if it *was* a murder."

"Okay," I said.

"Okay?" Dolly and Mack, speaking as one.

"I'm not sure what you want me to say."

That made it Dolly's turn. "Dell, couldn't you . . . kind of find out something? Maybe it didn't happen around here—and you're probably right, that body was just another kind of driftwood—but if it did, there could be something really dangerous still out there. Something close. We have to make sure."

"We." Once Dolly said it that way, she was making it mine, too. And telling me it was time to take my turn.

Maybe I tried only because I didn't want Dolly to lose face—who knows what she might have told this guy about my . . . capabilities.

Or maybe because I couldn't resist that trusting look in my love's eyes.

That video ninja had been my one hope. And I hadn't banked on it. Sure, I knew it had to be him who took that picture. But I also knew he wouldn't have had his videocam trained on the ocean, so he wouldn't have tape of the body being thrown up on shore. He'd have nothing that would clear this Homer guy.

Plus, I'd never get that video man near a witness stand. His image capturing was another version of the movie those psycho mass-killers watch in their heads as they randomly mow down targets. For people like that, suicide is always their exit strategy.

So some *other* need had driven him to send that photo to the papers. That was the only hand I had to play, but winning such a small-ante pot hadn't amounted to much. Sure, I'd confirmed that the video ninja *had* been there when the ocean threw up that body, but I knew he would have been long gone before Homer arrived—he wasn't the kind of man who'd hold up under questioning, and he was smart enough to know it.

And, from what Mack said, if the beach *hadn't* been deserted, Homer never would have gone anywhere near the body.

No point in asking Homer what time that wristwatch was showing when he took it, or even if he actually took it off the dead man's wrist. I didn't speak whatever language a schizophrenic does, but maybe Mack could get some answers from him.

My best guess was that one of the local papers got the e-mails—no message, just the attached photo—before the cops knew anything about a body on the beach. But even if the first paper to check its e-mail that morning thought the picture was some kind of hoax—the composition was so intricate that it could be a Photoshop-aided prank—they'd still call it in.

Playing it safe. If the photo turned out to be real, they could run the story later. And the last thing they'd want to do was get on the wrong side of the local police—they were a great source of press releases.

The cops would have moved quick on this one: dead bodies on the beach weren't part of the town's image. The photo was anonymous, so the papers couldn't say they were protecting a source. Not that they'd ever hold anything back, not around here. Every elected official, every government office, every funded "program" . . . they all worship the same three idols: Cooperation, Collaboration, and Consensus. None of that requires any of them to actually *do* anything, but it's great for making it look as if they're all devoted to serving the public. And it's not like some "investigative reporter" is going to find out otherwise.

There was no way to know if the body was still wet by the time Homer took the watch, but that didn't matter. The video ninja said he'd seen the body thrown up by the ocean. And he had the total reliability of any sex spy—as long as he didn't feel judged for what he was, he'd tell the truth.

So what could Homer add? He hadn't actually seen anything happen, or he never would have shown the cops the watch.

Or would he? There's all kinds of crazy. Some people are really sick in their heads past the point of any cure. But Mack said Homer was on some kind of medication. . . .

I let it go for now. It was daylight, and I was a legitimate person—Adelbert Jackson, with plenty of paper to prove it. I was even a local, although I doubt anyone in town would recognize me. Except maybe those kids Dolly always had around, and they wouldn't likely be prowling that section of beach at this early hour.

So I put Dolly's ancient Subaru into gear and went to take a look for myself.

Damn!

I'd been hoping for a long stretch of sand, but it was actually kind of an inlet, with high promontories of rock on both sides.

I shrugged off that hope—easy enough, what with all the practice I'd had. So I climbed out of the car, dressed like a walker. Walking, that's a big thing around here—one of those "retirement hobbies" that some people really get into. There's special gear for it and everything.

And if that wasn't enough, I had a digital camera hanging from a strap around my neck. Taking pictures of the ocean, that's another thing people do—dentists especially, for some reason I couldn't even guess at. And tourists for sure—who knows, they might actually get a shot of a whale.

I picked the highest of the promontories. Noticed there was already a well-worn path going up. Not that it was paved, or even cut-through brush—just a path it would have taken a lot of years to make by walking up a hill of solid rock.

I wasn't worried about cops staking out the place to see if the person who'd created the crime scene would show up to view it. Finding good spots wouldn't be easy in daylight, and it wasn't as if they had a surplus of manpower, anyway.

Even if a cop was watching through a telescope, so what? Plenty of people must have passed this same way since the body had been removed, and the camera was all the camouflage I'd need.

The climb wasn't that steep, but I kept to a slow pace. When I got to the top, I could see it wasn't uniformly jagged—it flattened out to a mesa big enough to park a few cars on. More than enough for a couple of guys to kill a man and toss his body into the ocean, provided they knew what they were doing, and how to work together.

The camera's zoom lens helped me scan the area. I made

sure to snap off some shots while I was looking around, in case I needed to show why I was there to anyone who asked. Although it looked tall from sea level, I guessed the flat-topped peak was, at the most, maybe three hundred meters high.

I'd already taken some pictures from the ground, so I could be a lot more exact later, when I pulled them off the card and onto a computer screen. There's a program that will tell you the distance between any two points on a digital photo—all you have to do is input the focal length of the lens. And I'd already paced off distances on my way to the rocks and during the climb, so I was confident I'd be close even without the computer's help.

What I didn't know was the depth of the ocean just beneath where I was standing. But I knew that would vary with the tide, and I could find those tables easy enough.

That was as far as I could go without asking questions. I knew a lawyer who'd give me a letter saying I was working for him as an investigator. A lawyer who'd been nothing before I'd hired him to defend MaryLou McCoy. Now he was the heavy hitter for the whole county—a criminal-defense specialist who'd won an impossible case. But without a case, why would there even be a lawyer?

So I'd have to talk to Mack again.

Damn.

"**W**hat would I have to do?"

"Just be yourself."

"There's no such thing. I'm not asking you what to be; I'm asking you what I'll have to be to get them to talk to me."

"I already told you."

"So as long as I'm with you . . . ?"

"Yeah. You already look like you've got more than enough mileage on you, and I don't guess you walk around in a suit and tie."

"So I'd be your—what?—assistant, maybe?"

"My friend," Mack said. "That's the only kind of person I'd ever bring along. They all know that."

"You ever do it before?" I asked him.

"Not with a man."

"You took Dolly along?"

"More than once. Living the way they do, they get cut. And sick sometimes, too. But none of them would go near the hospital."

"But . . . Okay, maybe I don't get it. Even kids, some of them, they're crazy, right?"

"Sure."

"And crazy people, they can be dangerous."

"Uh-huh."

"So if one of them thought Dolly was . . . I don't know, maybe a witch or something, he could . . . You know what I mean."

"Some people you don't even have to guess about. Not the crazy part, the dangerous one."

"So you think Dolly can protect herself?"

"What are you really asking me?"

"Dangerous people who aren't crazy, if you've got something they want, if you get in their way, if you even—"

"I get it. So does Dolly. The good thing about people who aren't crazy is that they calculate. Compute the odds."

"So Dolly's safe with you, is what you're saying."

"That's true. But it's not what I'm saying. What I'm saying is that you'd have to be howling-at-the-moon insane to think you could get past Minnie."

"Minnie?"

"My dog. She goes everywhere with me when I work outside. Everywhere. I know Dolly brings her own dog other places, but when she goes with me, it's better if I bring mine."

"She told me you had a pit bull. Adopted from the shelter."

"Yep. That's Minnie. She's a sweetheart. Just finds a spot, lies down, and watches. You don't move, she won't move. You do, she will."

"Doesn't that make some of your . . . whatever you call them, clients or patients or—"

"I call them by their names."

"Okay," I said, thinking, *This one probably doesn't know all the signals he gives off.* "Doesn't that make some of them nervous?"

"I don't know. If they're there for the right reasons, they get over it real quick once they start talking about why they came."

"You don't have any dog with you now."

"No."

"And I'm a stranger to them, right? So the dog will be coming along?"

"No."

"You're saying . . . ? Never mind. You carry a gun?"

"No."

"I'm no expert on homeless camps, but I've been in some. Ridden some freights, too. Hitched rides. They've always got something to protect themselves with. Usually a knife, but there's other stuff. . . ."

"You *do* carry a gun, right?"

"Yes."

"If you don't flash it, they won't pick it up by scent or anything."

"I never do that."

"Meaning . . . ?"

"If I bring it out, it's going to get used."

"You don't look like you spook at shadows."

"I don't shoot at them, either."

"Tomorrow morning, then. I'll pick you up. Around seven, okay?"

"I knew you could do something, baby."

"Dolly, I haven't done anything. I'm just having Mack take me around so I can get some answers . . . provided there's any answers to get, and I wouldn't bet too heavy on that."

"Well . . . Anyway, I got those depth charts. Even when the tide's on full ebb, there's still a good eight, ten feet of offshore water before you hit those razor rocks. But that's tricky. Some of the underwater rocks rise much higher than others, like stalagmites in caves."

"So it could be even deeper—the water, I mean—at night?"

"Sure. Why does it matter?"

"If that body was thrown off the top of the rocks, depending on the time that was done, it could just stay underwater until the tide rolled it in."

"Do you think that's what happened?"

"I'm not there yet, honey. First, I have to look at what *couldn't* happen, see?"

"I think so. But that may not be so important. Let's see what comes back on the . . . dead man. If he was on parole, or even if he was a registered sex offender, there'd be an address for him—although it doesn't seem like they check those out. But if he really lived, say, fifty miles away, his body could have just drifted down. Or up—I'm not sure which way the current runs; I'm pretty sure it depends on the season."

"Fifty miles, that's an hour's drive."

"Meaning . . . ?"

"Meaning that even if he was one of those guys on some list, and even if he actually lived where he told the law he did, he could make the trip to where his body was found pretty quick."

"But there was no abandoned car—"

"Why would there be? It'd take at least two men to throw him over, so one of them could just drive his car away."

"Oh."

"Dolly, can you get a copy of the autopsy? The photos, too?"

"A look—a good, long look—that I can get, no problem. And I've got a good memory. But an actual copy . . . that's another thing."

"There's a way. You visit one of the nurses you're pals with, okay? She just happens to have it all on her desk. You signal her—she has to use the restroom or something. But even if there's a copy machine in her office, there's no guarantee someone wouldn't know. The way these hospitals run, they probably have all the machines connected to the billing department, so they'd know if copies had been made. Not *what* was copied, but that the machine was used."

"That's about right. Now even the morphine pumps are connected to the billing department. The patient—his insurance, I mean—they pay per hit, like the pump was a slot machine. But I could probably Skype a pretty decent shot with my—"

"No. Those things show too flat a perspective. There wouldn't be enough detail. And you'd trigger whatever wireless connection the hospital was using.

"There's a better way. I've got a cell phone you can use. Open it up, push the 'on' button, then use the volume button like it was a camera lens—zoom to macro. You'll be able to fit an entire image on the screen, or just a tiny piece, if that's what you want to highlight. When you've got everything, push the 'off' button. That'll store everything. This one's got a hundred-shot chip—should be more than enough, right?"

"Dell, where do you get these . . . ? Ah, never mind. I just thought I knew all the different stuff you had."

"You did, girl. This gadget, it's new."

"When did you get it?"

"Right after you told me about the body."

"Oh."

"It's kind of an experiment. But I tested it—it'll work."

That wasn't a lie, I thought to myself. I would never be the master jeweler–turned–bombmaker that Luc had been, but he'd taught me as much as possible before he had to go. Passing knowledge from father to son, the way it must have been done for eons. My inheritance.

I know Luc would have been proud of my perimeter-protector strike. It was preemptive, but not by much: a dangerous pervert had already worked himself inside, one of the boys who were always hanging around Dolly's flock. He'd already demonstrated his love of torture and worship of fire. I knew how that would play out, but I didn't know which of the boys was the afflicted one.

Planting the signal senders inside the staples of a magazine I'd carelessly left in my den had been Luc's craftsmanship, as had the explosive charge deliberately disguised as amateurism. "Very simplistic," their expert had declared. "You can get instructions on how to build one on the Internet."

An unfortunate accident. Jerrald had been a "deeply disturbed" teenager who'd filled his blog with the "creative fiction" that his therapist had deemed an "outlet" for his rape-torture-kill fantasies.

His therapist hadn't seen the crow-raven hybrid Dolly had named "Alfred Hitchcock," because he had such a dignified way of carrying himself. I found him in the woods behind our house—one leg had been wired around a heavy rock before the gasoline had been poured over him and ignited. It had probably taken him a long time to die.

When he stopped coming around, Dolly figured he'd gone off to find a mate.

When I came across his body, I recognized it immediately for what it was—that wasn't Luc's training, any mercenary would have seen that kind of thing many times. So I left the scene untouched, and went hunting. I wasn't seeking "justice" for Alfred Hitchcock. I wasn't after revenge. I was responding to a cancerous tumor that had already grown too close to my Dolly. I couldn't kill the tumor, but I could kill its carrier.

"And it *looks* like a cell phone?" Dolly asked me.

"Like *your* cell phone," I said, taking the duplicate from my pocket and holding it out to her.

"**T**his was no send-a-message beating," I told her a few days later, pointing at the computer's big HD screen. "This was a killing. A planned-out killing."

"How—?"

"See how his skull was punctured right down into the brain, and then a triangular wedge pulled out? That's a move you have to practice to be any good at."

"It looks like it was something like your . . . What do you call it?"

"A Vietnam tomahawk," I told her. I'd been carrying one when the people from her team had picked me up. It had worked so perfectly the first time I'd been forced to use it that I'd vowed never to be without one again. It's an ax on one side, with a long spike on the other.

If the Nazi the ocean had dumped on that beach had been hit from behind by a man who knew how to use such a weapon, the killer wouldn't have pulled back after the first strike, he would have pulled *up*.

"If people like him—the dead man—if people like him were thinking about setting up shop here, couldn't he have ended up being one of those heads on stakes?" Dolly said, unable to keep the hopefulness from her voice.

"If that's what whoever killed him wanted, they would have

left the body where it fell, not tossed it over into the water. For all they knew, it might have stayed in the ocean forever. And they were in a hurry to get out of there."

"How do you know that?"

"Those gashes on the body," I said, moving the cursor over the screen to blow up each of them as I spoke, "they're from the razor rocks. Not deep enough to keep internal gas buildup from pushing him to the surface. The killers would have known that—they'd have opened him up if they'd had the time.

"If there was a river or a lake to dump the body in, they could have *taken* the time. But who knows when some early riser is going to come strolling down the beach? And the ocean— they couldn't have known how deep it was, or where the body might float to. It might never come up at all. Orcas hunt out there, too, right?"

"What are you saying, Dell? I thought you and Mack were going to—"

"We still are. But that's only to see if Homer said anything to anybody. And even if he did, so what? A crazy man talking to some runaway kids, that's no kind of evidence."

"But Homer's still in jail."

"I don't think he'll be there long."

"Even on a murder charge?"

"Come on, Dolly. How many times have you heard your friends say that this weasel of a DA we got here isn't going to even *think* about putting someone on trial unless he's got a case that can't be lost? 'Soft as warm custard,' that's what they say about him. And that was *before* the whole town turned on him after his office managed to lose a murder case where they had security-camera tape of the whole thing."

"It wasn't that he lost the case, Dell. It was that he shouldn't even have brought it to trial. If he'd known about that Tiger Ko Khai bunch, it—what MaryLou did, I mean—it wouldn't have happened at all. But he didn't know. Or didn't care. I mean, the cops knew, but even *they'd* stopped arresting the leader—they knew he'd never go on trial."

"Okay. You're right. But it doesn't change anything. This Homer guy, no way he killed a man, especially one that size. The dead guy sure didn't turn into any 'flab bucket,' did he? That autopsy said he weighed in at two twelve. Probably still hitting the weights. And he was off a prison-food diet, too.

"So how are they saying he got killed? A crazy man half his size and double his age leaped straight into the air, hit him from behind, and wrenched out a piece of his skull on the way down, like in one of those flying kung-fu movies? And that *same* man couldn't wait to show the cops the dead guy's watch?"

"Still . . ."

"I know. Crazy people don't need a reason for anything they do. But where's the weapon? The cops must've already searched Homer's room at that 'residency' place."

"Sure. I know, Dell. But you're—?"

"Still going out with Mack? Jesus, Dolly. How many times are you going to get me to say it?"

"**Y**ou carrying a gun?"

"Yes," I told Mack.

"I couldn't tell by looking at you."

"They won't, either, right?"

"Yeah, I get it. Let's go."

Mack's car must have been fueled with miracle juice.

The rust bucket was way past "old." Both sides had been keyed a hundred times, the right quarter panel looked like a saber-toothed tiger had tried to chew it off, one of the back windows was duct-taped plastic instead of glass, and the engine sounded like a prolonged death rattle. But it ran okay. And we didn't have far to go.

Mack pulled in under a bridge. If the average person looked through the windshield from where I was sitting, he wouldn't see anything but tangles of brush, a couple of dead trees, and various machine parts that looked as if a wrecker had just tossed them out randomly.

I saw the flickering movements right away. I figured whoever was back there must have seen the car . . . and then I realized why Mack had never gotten it fixed. Or junked it. I don't know much about the kind of people he said he worked with, but I knew enough to understand that any visual change might spook them. And that death-rattle sound would reassure them that it was a friendly approaching.

We got out at the same time. Mack leaned against the front end of his car, standing square. I didn't try to imitate his stance, but I kept my hands in sight.

He lit a cigarette without offering me one. If that was supposed to be a message, I didn't get it.

"I usually bring a few packs," he said, as if he'd just seen into my mind. "If I light up, they know it's okay to come out. If they want the smokes, that is."

"And they always do."

"Sure. You'll see them—"

"I saw them already. Two on my right, three on my left."

"Huh!" he grunted. Dolly had told me he was from Chicago. So, doing the kind of work he did, he would have been hard to ambush in a big city. But in this kind of place, he couldn't read trail signs.

The guy who came out first moved up on my side. Hard to tell his age, but he was some kind of young. Tall, narrow shoulders, thick reddish hair. Wearing a field jacket that didn't look so different from mine. It fit him way too loose, so I figured it was scavenged, or pulled from one of the donation bins they have all over this area.

Either he didn't know enough to keep his hands in sight—which would explain why he hadn't read my gesture for anything special—or he did, and thought he'd look more menacing with his own in the outside pockets of his jacket. Maybe that worked on some people.

The sleeves of my jacket were cut wide: the left held my stubby, carried butt-down in a pouch held closed only with a thin piece of Velcro. I knew I could pull it and empty the magazine before anyone I was likely to come across in daytime would see my hand move. The black-bladed Tanto was clipped inside the top of my right boot—one of the first lessons I'd learned in the jungle. Learned by listening to my . . . I don't have the right word for what Patrice had been to me, but I can still hear him speak, inside my head:

"If you get hit, drop! If the shooter was working single, he'll probably try and get to you while you're still alive. Curl up, like men do when they're hit bad enough so they feel the pain but not bad enough to put them out. Always keep a dagger inside the top of your boots, both sides. If it's only one man who approaches, and he bends down to admire his work, you strike! Right here," the Irishman who would never again see his treasured homeland told me, tapping his groin to make sure I understood the target area.

"Always aim there. No matter where you plant your spike, you've got a good chance at hitting an artery. And a shorter distance to reach, too."

"What if it's more than one?"

"Ah, it's always the same move, lad. With more than one of them, it's got little chance, but it's better than none at all. Probably won't work, but it'll make the bastards pull their triggers. That way, you die fast. That's a damn sight better than the way they'd want to handle it."

"Hey, Mack," the young guy said, making the words into a greeting. "Who'd you bring with you?"

"A friend of mine. Dell."

"Dell what?"

"Stop playing to the crowd, Timmy. I ever ask *you* your last name?"

"I don't like the way he's looking at me."

"You don't like the way anyone looks at you."

"I got a responsibility—"

"Me, too," Mack said. He didn't say anything more, but all kinds of kids started to come out into the open. He handed the redhead a full carton of smokes, leaving it up to him to dole them out, doing it the same way I would have with a tribal leader—giving him the best way to keep face.

The redhead dropped the carton into the side pocket of his jacket, like dealing with the cigarettes was something he'd get around to. But, for now . . .

"So. Your friend. Your friend 'Dell.' Why's he here?"

"He's trying to get Homer out of jail."

"This guy's a lawyer?"

"No, he's an astrologer."

"Okay . . ." the redhead said, thoughtfully, as if my appearance was starting to make sense to him. "What d'you want?" he said to me.

"Just to ask some questions."

"What kind of questions?"

"The kind of questions I ask. You don't want to answer

them, don't. But if you're for real, if you want to help your friend, you will."

"Just me?"

"Anyone who was around Homer when the cops took him."

"That was just about all of us. Homer started out with us that night, but after a while he took off. By the time he came back, it was real late, so most of us were asleep when the cops crashed in. But Homer, he was awake."

"How do you know?"

"Heard him shouting. Even before they lit us up."

I gave him my full attention, as if I didn't see other kids crowding closer and closer. If that bothered Mack, he didn't show it. I don't mean show it on his face—I was turned away from him. But his body didn't shift, and his breathing didn't change; I could even hear the whistle through his nose.

"They've done that before, the cops?"

"Oh, yeah," the redhead said. "Anytime a tourist makes a complaint, they do their 'Don't be here when the sun comes up!' thing. That's just for show—they know we don't mess with dope, and we don't steal, either. Only thing different was, this time they took Homer."

"That was the first time they ever did that?"

"Yeah, it was. They know the dude wasn't wasted on anything—he's just not right, you know what I mean?"

"Yes. Is he the only one?"

"The only guy who hears voices? Around here? You've got to be a stranger in town."

"I meant the only one you let hang with you."

"If they act right—no grabbing at the girls, no trying to snatch our stuff, none of that tough-guy crap—anyone's welcome. But we're not a branch of Goodwill, if you get what I'm saying."

"Sharing, that's expected. Begging's not allowed."

"On the nose. We'll share with anyone, but not more than

once. One time, they might just stumble over us. If they're hungry—hungry for food, I'm saying—we've always got something. But if they come back, they better be bringing something to share with *us*."

"What could Homer bring?"

"Hey, you'd be surprised. Homer likes the beach late at night, when there's no one else around. You're not supposed to take driftwood, but that's just a stupid rule some 'I'm *soooo* Green' made up. And tourists, that's *exactly* the kind of thing they want.

"One of the women at the art gallery, she comes by every once in a while. If we've got driftwood—specially if it's all dried out—she'll buy it from us. And sometimes Homer brings ambergris—little lumps of rock that the whales throw up, or dump out some other way. It's got this pink center, looks real pretty. This woman, she'll buy that, too."

"Homer tries to sleep through the day," Mack said. "Not many people are going to walk around after dark looking for driftwood. And if you try and take a piece in daylight, some environmentalist will call the cops."

"Makes sense," I said.

"Homer's no sponge," the kid added, just to make sure I understood. "He always tries to bring something, even if it's just old magazines."

"Sounds fair to me."

"It *is* fair," the redhead said, a little more strength in his voice. "He comes here because he knows it's safe. There aren't that many safe places for a guy like Homer to be around after it gets dark."

"That's why you're all here, right? I don't mean for the same reason, but for the same *kind* of reason."

The redhead took a small step back, like he wanted to get a better look at me. "You ever go on the run?" he finally asked.

"A long time ago. When I was a lot younger than you."

"You ever find—?"

"All I found was a way out. Nothing like what you have here."

"How would you know what we have here?" he said, quick-glancing over at Mack.

"You stand by each other," I said. "You share what you have. You stick together as best you can."

"That's all you know, and *that's* enough for you to say—?"

"That's all there *is,*" I cut him short. "All there ever is."

The redhead nodded. I couldn't see the others, but I could feel they were nodding along with him.

"Come on," he said, turning his back and walking into the deeper brush.

Mack took his own pack of smokes from a side pocket of his cargo pants.

He shook one out for himself and then placed the pack on a flat rock, together with a black metal tube. Without hesitation, the redhead tapped out a smoke for himself and gave Mack a questioning look. When Mack moved his head just enough to show he was nodding an okay, the redhead pulled the metal tube apart, stuck the tip of his smoke inside, took in a breath, turned his cigarette to assure himself it was glowing, let the smoke drift slowly out of his nose, then recapped the tube.

I hadn't seen one of those no-flash lighters in years—they were once standard issue for soldiers all over the world, especially freelancers working in places where no government would ever acknowledge them, and no family would ever claim their body. We all knew it would be closer to "when" than "if," but that's why we got paid what we did.

If any of us had a family, they never said so—those pictures of women some carried, they might claim it was a girlfriend, but never a wife. More likely, a whore they paid to pose with them while they were on leave.

Mack's gesture was clear to the redhead. Whether I smoked or not wasn't important—what was important was that I was as welcome to the cigarettes as he was. Sharing tobacco was an Indian thing. How it got to be so, I don't know. But no Indian casually passes a pack around. I took a cigarette for myself, lit it the same way the redhead had, took a single drag, then put the filter-tipped smoke flat on the rock, still burning.

"You know how Homer is," the redhead said to Mack. "When he rolls up on us, it's always before daylight comes. A lot of us, we sleep pretty late, specially if we've got a good spot. But someone always has to stay awake—that's the rule."

"Only way to work it," Mack said.

"The cops don't roust us. Not anymore, anyway. They know they'd just be wasting their time. We'd hear them coming way in front. Everybody'd be awake, waiting. If we had some dope—weed, I mean; we don't allow nothing else—they'd never find it. No guns, either. Allowed, I mean, not stashed.

"None of us is going to be on any WANTED poster. And they know if they arrested any kids who left one of those lame group homes, those same kids'd be back with us in a couple of days anyway."

"Sure," Mack said, not necessarily agreeing, more like acknowledging without passing judgment.

"I was just saying what I did before because I had to make sure the others didn't think I'd give Homer up. Some of them, they've been with us long enough, it wouldn't be a question. But we're always getting new kids coming around."

He turned to me, his face saying he was asking a question, but his lips didn't move. A test. I was used to tests, and this was easier than most.

"You've got to show that you don't 'cooperate' with the

law," I said. "You never give up a member. And you've got to see if any of the new ones are plants, too."

"Yeah? How would I know that? The last thing you said, I mean."

"A planted informer would want to get close enough to hear anything you might be saying."

"And how would I know *that*?"

"You? You'd probably have people you trust watching them, see if they tried to get closer to where we are."

"That's right," he said proudly. "But you'd never know they were there."

"Yeah, I would."

"Really?" he said, more sarcasm than question.

"Nobody's tried to get closer," I said. "And I didn't have to interview any of your people to know that."

"You sure?"

I made my voice come out tired-sounding. "Tell you what: We leave now, no more conversation. We come back tomorrow. Give you all the time you'd need to find out if I was right."

The redhead gave me the long, calculating look of the day-to-day survivor. "You got some strange friends," he said to Mack.

"Skilled ones."

"What's the difference?"

"When someone has skills that you don't, you slap labels on them. Labels like 'strange.' Labels like they slapped on *you* until you got it together enough to change your address."

"You got those skills? The ones he has?" the redhead asked Mack, tilting his head in my direction.

"Not in places like this. In a big city, yeah . . . some of them, anyway. But not here."

"I know. I mean, we all know you're from Chicago. To you, this place must look like a jungle."

"Some parts of it, sure."

"Not to you, right?" the redhead said to me.

"To me, too."

"I don't get it, then."

"Jungle doesn't look strange to me."

The redhead touched his right ear.

"That. But this, too," I told him, touching my left eye with one finger and my nose with another. I didn't have the time to explain pattern-disturbance signals to him, and I'd only scare him if I did.

Probably scare him even more if I told him I'd been within twenty meters of his band not so long ago. I periodically check the terrain all around where Dolly and I live, making sure I can blend if I have to. And not just at night: I'd been even closer to the birders—mostly old people who walk around with binoculars looking for a new species to add to what they called their "life lists."

I've got one of those myself, but it's not on a piece of paper . . . and there's no birds on it.

He gave me a look he'd been trying to learn from Mack—he had to have spent some time in institutions to learn the value of mastering that. He had it down pretty well. Not as good as Mack, but damn good for his age.

He'd have to practice a lot more years before he got close to Mack, and he'd never get close to how I'd learned—been forced to learn. His life had probably been hard enough that he'd never believe how fortune had blessed him.

"Just start at the beginning," I said.

He gave Mack a look. Just a quick glance to lock in that it was okay to talk to me. But then the understanding that Mack wouldn't have brought me unless it was hit home; he scrunched his eyes closed, trying to concentrate.

It took a minute for his screen to clear. He started speaking, like he was reciting something he'd memorized:

"We were all down for the night, except for Jesus," he said, saying it like "Hay-Zeus" so I'd know he meant the Spanish kid. "Homer had shown up around . . . I'm not sure, maybe just before five. He's always careful to be quiet so he doesn't wake anyone. This time, he just rolled out his blanket—we all pretty much have our own spots."

"When the cops came . . . ?"

"Oh, we were mostly *all* up by then. We have to make sure everything's cleaned by daylight. It's not like this spot belongs to us or anything—the old guys, they take a place and mark it, but we can't do that."

"You've got—what?—at least a dozen in your crew, maybe more than that, right?"

"So?"

"So how come you can't hold your spot against the old guys?"

"They're not like *old* old. More like, you know, adults. They've got . . . options we don't have."

"Weapons?"

"That's not it. Any crew who lives outside has blades, hammers, stuff you'd need to make a shelter. But the older guys, they're, like, permanent, you know. Not like the circuit riders. So they know we're all . . . we're not where we're supposed to be, okay? All they'd have to do . . . just one time, and we're burned."

"Do what?"

"Make a phone call. To the cops, or CPS, or anyone who's supposed to be looking for us. Then we get sent back. Sure, we don't stay, but it breaks us up, and it takes a long time to put everything back together."

"They mark their spot, you leave it alone. You try and mark

yours, they might want it for themselves. And you don't want that. Not because you're afraid of them, necessarily—it's just not worth what it could cost."

"Yeah," he confirmed.

"These 'circuit riders,' they respect the marks, too?"

"They don't respect nothing. But they don't want cops looking at them, either."

"Okay," I told him. I needed what he could tell me about Homer—I'd get Mack to explain some of what he said later.

"We saw the cops before they saw us, but, close to the underpass like we are, we just waited on them. If we booked, some of us would get away, like always. But I gave the signal to hold—I could tell by the way they came in they weren't looking for runaway kids."

I made a gesture he'd understand, asking him how he knew.

"Four cars, two unmarked. Means they're looking for someone who maybe just shot at one of them. That happens around here more than you'd think. Some guys go meth-wild. They see a cop, they get all paranoid. And everyone's got *some* kind of gun, it seems like."

"Except you guys. And maybe the ones you call 'permanent'?"

"Yeah. I mean, how stupid would that be? Anyway, sometimes all the cops are looking for is information. You know, like, did we see a man in a red coat an hour ago? We always tell them anything we know—and we don't make stuff up. It's like this contract—we do that, and they don't bring any of us in, like they didn't see us."

"So the guys you call 'permanent,' they all carry some kind of ID?"

"Yeah. They can even list their address as 'homeless,' and that's okay ... around here, anyway. But this time the cops *were* looking for someone, only they didn't have a description or anything."

"They asked you about seeing guys with tattoos? Shaved heads? Jackets with Nazi stuff on them?"

"Yeah," he said, speaking softer. "How'd you know that?"

"Just a guess."

"Sure," the kid said, side-glancing at Mack again. "Only we hadn't seen anyone at all. No strangers. But then Homer just *has* to show them this watch he found somewhere. A minute later, they're dragging him away. He starts screaming, like he always does when he wants people to back off, but it didn't work. I mean, they didn't pound on him or anything, but they wrapped him up good, tossed him in, and took off."

"When you say Homer showed the watch he found to them, how did he do that?"

"I don't get what you're—"

"Did he just hold up his wrist, or did he take it off?" Mack cut him off.

"Oh. Okay, he took it off. Carried it over to them. He was talking about how God tossed it up from the ocean so he—Homer, not God—could tell time or something. It gets so foggy around here, sometimes it's pretty hard to know when morning's coming.

"One of them—a guy wearing a suit, so he must've been a detective or something—he really looked it over. The watch, I mean. I didn't hear him say anything, but—*snap!*—they all kind of surrounded Homer. I'm not sure what they said to him, but that's when he started screaming."

"The permanent homeless the kid was talking about, those are the same ones you said had e-mail accounts?"

"Yeah. Homeless-by-choice, high coping skills."

"And they're not the kind to welcome strangers? So those 'circuit riders,' they wouldn't find a spot with them?"

"No," Mack said, not a trace of doubt in his voice. "The circuit riders aren't always the same ones, like this was a stop they make every year. Could be FTRA, or—"

I made an "I don't get it" gesture.

"Freight Train Riders of America. Pretty much what it sounds like. They live on trains, all over the country. Some of them will drop off anytime they want to, usually when they need something. Then they'll just hop the next thing smoking. Some of them know each other pretty good—the longer you've been riding, the better the chance of that."

"Hard guys?"

"Some of them, sure. And in a pack . . ."

"But they're not on the run?"

"I guess one might be, every so often. But that's not what their thing is about. If one of them jumped off in, I don't know, Salem, say, and did something he could get himself pinched for, he'd get back on the rails fast. If he was to run across guys he trusted, he might tell them. But most of the time, you're really talking about some kind of no-contact stealing. Restocking provisions, not armed robbery."

"They can't be the only ones riding."

"They're not. But if you ride alone, or even with a couple of buddies, you'd want to step off if you saw them coming."

"So this 'circuit,' it could go anywhere?"

"Sure. And there's been some guys who use the rails the same way other guys use cars, if you see where I'm going with this?"

"Serials."

"Yeah. Rapists, thrill killers, all kinds of very bad guys. But they almost always work alone. Sometimes, two do everything together—the ugly stuff, I mean, not like two pals traveling together. But that's pretty rare."

"So, no matter if it was this FTRA crew or a loner, they

wouldn't be jumping off to kill someone. Someone *specific,* I mean."

"I don't see it. I mean, you're right—the sex-kill guys, they just take whatever's available. But a big robbery, no way. That takes planning, and a place you can stash whatever you took. And a contract killing? Who'd hire guys you might never see again?"

"So, no matter how you add it up, there's no way Homer killed that Nazi?"

"None," he said, his pale-blue eyes calm but sharp-focused.

"I want to be sure I have this down right," I said.

Dolly was listening to me, but looking at Mack, hard. Waiting for him to verify it if I did. So I went on:

"The permanent homeless, the only real difference between them and anyone else is that they don't live indoors."

Mack nodded.

"That crew of youngsters, they all come from different kinds of places, but they all . . . escaped, went AWOL, or whatever they call it."

He nodded again.

"And those two groups, they don't mix."

"No."

"And the crazy ones, the ones you see walking around, they don't get together?"

"Not like the others. Some of them even say they're married. But that's two people, not a whole group. They're usually in their own world, each of them."

"So that's at least three groups the businesses who make a living off tourists wouldn't want around."

"Wouldn't want them *visible.* The permanent group, they

know that song by heart. So do the kids. The kids don't *want* to be visible, anyway.

"A tourist sees some of the permanents, he probably figures they're out on a camping trip. No big deal. But the ones who walk around drooling, talking to themselves, scratching at their faces—*they're* the ones the businesses don't want around their places. That's why they created this job. My job, I mean."

"Those circuit riders—"

"If they're any good, nobody sees them. For those, it's always hit-and-run, sometimes for no longer than just between freights."

"What about the professional beggars?"

"The ones you see in wheelchairs with signs—'Wounded Vet,' 'Will Work for Food,' 'Out of Work, Out of Luck.' Those?"

"Yeah."

"They know what they're doing. This place is way liberal on just about any issue you could come up with, but if a merchant doesn't want any pro beggars outside his place, all he has to do is make a call—the cops will move them out. Quick. There's places where it's okay for them to set up shop, and they all find out about that, sooner or later."

"The cops . . . You talked to them about Homer?"

"Talked to one I know. He told me they *had* to hold him. Homer had the dead man's watch, and, for now, that's all they got."

"He couldn't be convicted on just that, could he?" Dolly asked.

"Not by a jury, I don't think. But any lawyer they give him won't be thinking about a trial—Homer's the perfect NGI. No way he could even be competent enough to understand what's going on. No matter how this plays out, unless they find whoever took out that guy who washed up on the beach, Homer's going inside.

"Jail or a mental hospital, it'd be the same to him. The voices would come back, and they'd have to blast him with meds just to stop him screaming. Outside, he can handle it—sleep all day, only go out when it's dark; that seems to do it for him."

"Dell . . ."

"I'm not a detective," I told Mack, later.

He gave me a look. "Who said you were?"

"Sometimes, Dolly thinks I can do things. . . . You know, women, right?"

"Me, *I* don't. I never met a man who actually does. But your wife, she's not confused, is she?"

"What's that supposed to mean?"

"Whatever she 'thinks' you can do, it's because she knows you can. And not from hearing you talk about it."

"What's next?"

"Waiting," I said to Mack. "I'm sorry about this Homer guy, but without seeing what cards they're actually holding, there's no way to start. What we really want is the dead guy's rap sheet. The cops wouldn't have to investigate to get that—they ID'ed him from his prints, so you know they're holding *some* kind of paper. You wouldn't happen to have a friend on the force, would you?"

"No" was all he said.

"Place like this—this town, it's not sealed."

"Sealed?"

"Like a prison is sealed. Prison guards find a dead man, them knowing who *couldn't* have done it narrows it down. Sometimes, way down. Here, people come and go all the time.

Take the tourists out of the mix and what do you have? A little fishing village, right?"

"That's about it, yeah."

"Try it this way: take out all the businesses that don't depend on visitors, what's left?"

"Okay, I got it," he said, just enough annoyance in his tone to tell me he'd gotten it the first time.

"I know there's some wealthy people here. Has to be, to afford some of the houses you see once in a while. But people like that, they don't have to *buy* local. Maybe wouldn't even want to."

"So what you're saying, we know Homer didn't do it. Add the runaway kids to that list. And probably throw in the permanents, too. I can't see some circuit riders stopping off just to kill that particular guy. What's that leave?"

"One more thing, for starters," I said.

"What?"

"We're talking about a killing, not an accident."

"So?"

"The dead guy, he couldn't have been out of prison long."

"You're thinking a shot-caller from that same joint put out a ticket on him?" Mack said, like he was thinking out loud.

"Maybe. But I don't know of any big White Power operation anywhere around here."

"Me, neither. Eugene wouldn't be such a good place for them, either. But Vancouver—not Canada, in Washington, just the other side of the bridge from Portland—that's pretty close, only a few hours away. Or, you want to go far enough northeast of here, there's all kinds of . . ."

"Okay. But we *still* need to get a look at the dead guy's prison record. Not just what he went down for, what he got into while he was inside. Those tattoos—they'll tell us something. At least one thing, for sure."

"What?"

"Whether they were there before he went in. Or if some were there already but others got added. This isn't California—race war isn't on the menu every day."

"So?"

"So he wouldn't necessarily need a gang to stay safe while he was locked up. Guy was well put together, not a natural target. And we know 'hate crime' means he did something that would carry status with some convicts. But if he was down on the prison books as 'affiliated,' he could have been involved in something during his last stretch that'd carry past the walls."

"Revenge?"

"One kind or another, maybe. There's almost no blacks around here. Plenty of Mexicans, but I've never seen ink on any of them."

"They're not migrant laborers. They live here."

"So?"

"So how many have you seen with their shirts off?" he said, almost defensively.

"Faces and hands, I've seen. And plenty of those. No tears on their faces, no numbers on their forearms, no *pachuco* crosses."

"Okay." He shrugged. Meaning he didn't know what I was talking about, but it didn't matter.

"The dead guy might have told some stories, like I said before. Or maybe he was supposed to pick up a package and turn it into money. Could be he did that, only he kept the money for himself."

"You think that's likely around here? Meth is *the* drug—and the local stuff is supposed to be so good, people actually drive down from the north just to buy. But that's all home-brewed. Heroin is starting to make a little comeback, only not enough for a big sale, not here."

"Yeah. Any package would be powder, anyway . . . and that market's not here. Still, that'd be a reason. Maybe not the best one, but . . ."

"What?"

"If this guy had been told where a few keys were stashed, and he grabbed it for himself, he'd deny it as long as he could. This isn't a movie set—they'd have him shrieking in five minutes. Once they checked on his story—found either the powder or the cash—they'd kill him right there. Wherever they'd already taken him to.

"So why walk him out on that cliff? A gunshot would carry like a sonic boom. They couldn't rely on weather—nobody around here can—so they'd have a whole mess of porous rock to scrub down if they clubbed him to death. If they planned on dumping him in the ocean, they would have known enough to gut him first—a knife would do that, and they'd have one handy for sure.

"Except they *didn't* open him up. So the only thing we know for sure is that there was more than one man in on it. As for that porous rock, you said it yourself—it rains all the time, like a natural scrub-down. Besides, they wouldn't worry about the cops collecting anything from the spot where they finished him. Even if they somehow got the idea to check the top of that outcropping, you know how many tourists pass over that same spot every day?"

I could hear "How does this guy know so much about killing?" running thru Mack's head, but it didn't reach his eyes. "How do you know there was more than one man in on it?" is all he said.

"Whatever was used to crack through his skull, it wouldn't be something you could hide under your coat. And who turns his back on someone he thinks might be a threat? Prison alone would have taught him at least that much."

We were quiet for a couple of seconds. Then my phone rang.

"Come home" is all Dolly said.

I could tell from the tone of her voice that this wasn't some "Help!" thing. And she hadn't used any of the signals, either. So I told Mack I'd find him later. Meaning, "Drop me off and keep going."

When I walked in, Dolly pointed toward the basement and raised her eyebrows. She wouldn't go down there without me, and there wasn't enough privacy upstairs to show me whatever she wanted transferred from that camera-phone I'd given her.

"That's the skull," she said, pointing at the X-ray shot projected against a five-foot square of whiteboard I'd put up in the basement. "See the intrusion line? It was one blow, powerful enough to penetrate all the way to the brain."

"So he never saw it coming?"

"Probably not. Even the slightest movement—or even a sound like a sharp intake of breath—would have altered those intrusion lines. This looks almost . . . surgical."

"*Un piton?*" I wondered aloud. Nobody would need one to climb to the top of the promontory I'd explored . . . but nobody would look twice at one dangling from a man's belt, not around here.

"A mountain climber's spike? I guess it could be. But why would a killer use something like . . . that thing?"

"One shot; one kill."

"I'm not following you."

"A sniper only gets one shot—if he misses, or even if he just wounds the target, it's worse than if he'd never tried. Look," I said, using the arrow pointer to show her, "there's that . . . 'intrusion line' you called it . . . but the skull's missing a whole wedge, like a triangle was pulled out. Whoever took this guy out, he was good. And he'd done it before, to *get* that good."

"So they brought him up to that spot on purpose. That's where they *wanted* to kill him."

"That's what it looks like."

"That means it happened *here,* Dell."

"Happened here? Sure. But that doesn't mean the dead guy was *living* here. There's a million ways to explain why whoever killed him took him up on those rocks."

"Mack wants—"

"I don't give a damn what Mack wants. You want me to run around, sticking my nose in places, taking chances, just so some crazy man can get turned loose?"

"If you had let me finish, I would have said that Homer isn't why I have to do this. I don't care where the dead man was from. He's gone now. But if the *killers* are here—*live* here, I mean—how long is it going to be before they do the same thing to someone else?"

"Kill more Nazis? Good for them."

"Will you stop? You know exactly what I'm saying, Dell. Whoever did that . . . killing, he was good at it—you said so yourself. Someone like that, he didn't learn without practice. Maybe a lot of practice. You said *that,* too."

"Dolly, we don't even know if there are any 'people like that' around here anymore. It's much more likely that they had a job to do, got it done, and moved on."

"Then it'll be easy."

"Easy?"

"Easy for you, Dell. But—damn!—let me show you the slides of the tattoos first."

Why Dolly thought the slides would tell me anything, I don't know.

There was a lot of ink. All pointing in the same direction, sure—but that direction had been the dead man's choice. Personal. Maybe whoever took him out was doing everybody around here a favor.

"Well?" she finally demanded.

"Well, what, baby? I'm no expert on tattoos. So this guy was a Nazi, or a skinhead, or whatever they're called now. But—"

"He had those tattoos a long time, Dell. For such a young man, I mean."

"So?"

"So he got them in prison."

"Maybe," I said, not convinced. Pain tolerance varies. And motivation can give it one hell of a boost. Maybe he was out on bail, but he knew he was going to prison when his case was over, so he got his whole skin done in just a few sessions.

Dolly read my thoughts. "Look at them *close,* baby. They look pretty amateurish, don't they?"

"You're saying he got them the *first* time he went in? And, back then, he might have made a choice he couldn't walk away from later?"

"Wouldn't finding out be worth something?"

"I don't see—"

"Please."

"Dolly, honey, I could find a tattoo guy easy enough. But I wouldn't know what questions to ask. And I'm not showing anyone those close-up pictures they took in the morgue—that would put *me* too close."

I didn't have to say the rest of it: I'd take risks if I had to, but not for other people. The only "had to" in my life was Dolly.

"I know you can't ask around here. But you could find someone, Dell. I know you could."

Damn.

The man's head was shaved, with a long ponytail growing out of the back, Mongol-style.

His face was some kind of Mediterranean mix, so his hair was a style preference, not ancestor homage. But his outfit was all business: a sleeveless red smock over a black jersey shirt that didn't quite reach his elbows, chinos, and black Mephisto shoes—the kind you could stand in for hours at a time in comfort.

I dialed in closer. His ropy arms were covered in fine-art tattooing, but his hands were unmarked. And as well kept as a dermatologist's. I could see all that because I'd walked into his shop right behind him.

After watching for a week, I was reasonably sure the pattern never varied. He was the boss, so he opened the place every day, always before eight in the morning. The shop never got any real business before mid-afternoon, but he always used the empty time well: checked every station, inspected the bathroom and the refrigerator, cleaned either or both if they needed it. He turned on a bunch of different kinds of lights, some just for a test, others he left on. I knew he'd put some cash into the till he emptied when he left every night, always past midnight. Then he worked on the books, did some sketching. Even had his lunch delivered, so he never left the place.

He was always the last one out, too.

That's when I'd call Dolly on a burner cell, say, "Working," and turn it off. Then I'd smash it and drop the pieces in various spots I'd scouted during the day. If some cop ever found an excuse to run the LUDs on Dolly's phone, she'd just say the same idiot had called her every night, had some kind of weird accent, said some word she couldn't quite make out, and hung up.

Finding places to stay—places that took cash and didn't waste money on security cams—was easy enough if you weren't too fussy. I was trained better than that—you get too fussy in the field, you've got a good chance of becoming part of the ground.

The boss man looked up as I stepped in. He didn't move as I walked over to his spot. He was all the way in the back, but the corner-mounted mirrors would let him see everything that was going on.

I sat down in the reclining chair closest to him, but I left my jacket on, so he'd know I wasn't there for a tattoo. I put five hundred-dollar bills on the armrest, fanning them slightly, so he could see how many there were. When he came over, I started talking.

When I was finished, he said, "You ask a lot of questions, friend."

"I'm not your friend," I said, toning my voice to make sure that he understood I was saying it neutral. And that he wouldn't want me to move off that spot. "I'm looking for someone. All I know is that he's got a lot of tattoos. It would help me if I knew a way to tell if they were professionally done, like yours were."

The man shrugged his shoulders. "Charging money doesn't make you a professional."

"It makes me one," I told him, nodding my head toward the money I'd put down.

He nodded, too. But slowly, letting me see he was thinking it over.

"This person you're looking for, you know he didn't get the work done here."

He said it like a statement, but I could feel the question in his voice. So I said: "If I did, I'd already know the work was done by a pro. And I wouldn't need to ask you any questions to find him, either."

"Maybe you're looking for someone who works here."

"If they worked here, they'd have to leave sometime. And then I—"

"Wouldn't need to ask me any questions."

"Yeah."

He nodded again. Then he picked up the money.

"The best way to tell is the depth."

"All professional tattoos are the same depth?"

"They should be. Damn close, anyway. But just about any-one can get a license, so . . ."

"Are there any sure tells?"

He gave me a puzzled look.

"Any way to see if they *weren't* the correct depth?"

"Look at this," he said, holding up a knurled metal knob. "Watch." He pushed, and a needle popped out of the front. Just the tip of a needle, really.

"That's not a needle," he said, as if he could read what I was thinking. "A pro's set is actually several small needles—we call them 'sharps'—attached to a needle bar—what we call a 'configuration.' You use different ones depending on whether you're going for lining, shading, or solid color. And that's just where you *start:* the better the quality, the more expensive the set."

"If anyone can get a license, anyone can spend money, too."

"Fair enough. Try this, then: You can adjust the depth of a needle, but you still need to keep that as uniform as possible. Especially if all the work's being done on the same canvas."

"Skin?"

"Skin," he confirmed. "First the epidermis, then *just* into the dermis. Never more than slightly deeper than the thickness of a dime."

I didn't know what that would look like sideways, and let the confusion show on my face. He pulled a few hairs loose from his ponytail, deftly laid them together to form a single strand, then placed the result flat against a white plastic tray. "Not much more than this," he said, putting the tray on my lap.

"Got it."

"Okay. Only the very best artists work freehand. At that level, there has to be real trust between the artist and the client. People always have some kind of . . . image inside their heads. No matter what they say—you know, 'Just give me something cool,' like that—they still have a picture in their minds. That's why we use stencils, so they can see for themselves what the finished product is going to look like. Then all we have to do is make a transfer, and fill it in."

"So if it's blurry . . . ?"

"That doesn't necessarily mean a thing. Some people, they *want* blurry. The street racers love it when you fade their cars from crispy front to what we call 'moving' out back. But the quality of the work, that doesn't necessarily mean the artist even has a license. It's like anything else—there's jailhouse lawyers who know more about the law than anyone at the PD's Office."

I watched his eyes, saying nothing. So he went on: "When you say 'amateur,' you mean 'prison,' right?"

It was my turn to nod.

"That makes it easier."

"Okay," I said. I was there as a buyer, not a trader.

"You can put on a prison tat one of two ways. The hard way is just draw on the skin with a Magic Marker, dip a mini-spike in ink—you can make one out of damn near anything—and just keep planting it until the whole thing's done. But, doing it that way, you either have to go deep, or keep hitting the same spot, over and over."

"A lot of pain?"

"For some, that's what they want. Not the pain. They want proof that the tattoo was more important to them than the pain."

"And that other way?"

"You can make a machine—what we call a 'rotary.' Those actually work, if they're put together right. You just get some very fine wire—like from a transistor radio or a cassette recorder—and wrap it around any little screw you can find. Now you've got your relay, but you still need a bristle from a wire brush, the kind you use for scraping off heavy coats of paint; they always have those in one of the prison shops. You use a mechanical pencil—the best one you can get your hands on—for the cylinder, and you make an arm with anything flexible and a little magnet. Then you need another transistor radio to power it."

"Hurts less?"

"A lot less. But it's a bumpy ride—you have to be *really* skilled to use one. You can make ink out of . . . well, even ink from a ballpoint, or a melted-down piece of plastic. Checkers are better than chess for that—nobody wants white ink, but red and black, those are the big sellers.

"The *real* danger is always infection. Even if you hold the spike in flame first, dip it in alcohol, and *then* hold it under a lit match, it's still not truly sterile. Even in shops, you can't be sure. Here, we use a needle once, we're done with it. And we buy them presterilized, in individual blister packs."

"Infection? Like . . ."

"It's prison, man. Hep C, if you're lucky. HIV if you're not. Remember, in there, they use the same needles, over and over."

"Could you tell by looking at a picture of one?"

"Probably . . . But if the job was decent and the picture of it wasn't, I'd be guessing."

I took out the whole array I carried with me and spread it out on the plastic tray.

He didn't say a word. Just got up, walked over to what looked like a hand-built wooden tool chest, and came back with a rectangular magnifying glass.

"This one for sure," he said, pointing at a swastika.

"Not just because of what it is, right?"

"You think people don't walk in here and ask for that Nazi stuff? No, that doesn't mean anything. Look for yourself—see how the outline has those little 'bubbles' in some spots? If I had to guess, I'd say the outline was spiked in by hand, and the fill was with a machine. No shop would do it that way."

"What about the other ones?"

"This one's the most obvious, but none of them look like in-shop work—even a crappy shop would have better equipment. But if this here is all the tats he had, I might be able to tell you something."

"That was all."

"No spiderweb on the elbows? Probably not a skinhead, then."

"Yeah?"

"Sure. Anyone who first inked up in prison, he couldn't fly that flag—the spiderweb, I'm saying—unless he came in already wearing it."

"Want to say why?"

He shook his head. Then, in one fluid motion, he whisked the five hundreds off the chair's arm and into the side pocket of his red smock, telling me he'd already earned it.

M y plan was to walk out of the tattoo shop and disappear.

It was less than three blocks to an alley that led to the "men's hotel" where I'd spent the previous night. I didn't have to check out—I was already carrying everything I'd brought with me in a shoulder-strapped duffel.

I'd only rented the room for one night. "In advance," the clerk said, not looking up from whatever he was reading. "Checkout's at noon. You don't come back in time, the room gets padlocked. You come back later than that, costs you another night's rent to open the lock."

I'd picked that misery-smelling SRO because it had two things I needed: not only was it close to the tattoo parlor, it was also just a few blocks from the bus terminal. I didn't have any reason to suspect the needle artist would want to tell the cops a stranger had been around, asking strange questions, but taking risks you don't need to take is a stupid habit I'd avoided ever since I'd been told it was. The safest way to learn such truths is to listen to a man who'd learned them from experience.

If the cops *did* come looking for me, they'd check the outgoing bus schedule first. It wouldn't be any more helpful to them than the hotel clerk would be.

I didn't have any illusions that desk clerks on that side of town would feel some sense of solidarity with a man on the run—that was for "noir" movies, not for the world I lived in. But how cooperative could the guy be, even if he wanted to? I didn't look like anything special; he'd made an effort *not* to look at my face, and the slab of scar tissue on my left wrist was invisible under my jacket.

When I first got to that town, I'd looked around, always on foot. It's the best way to learn any city, if you have the time. London cabbies have to pass a test harder than the ones they give people who want to be lawyers—they have to know a city so full of twists and turns that a GPS signal would eventually hit a wall. So they ride around on bicycles or scooters for a solid year, minimum. One of them told me about it. During a long ride, a long time ago. He said that was why they call prepping for that exam "getting the knowledge."

Once I found that tattoo joint, I'd stayed in a different dump every night, working my way closer and closer. Then I kept watch a few more times, to be reasonably sure he'd be alone in the mornings.

The bus station being so nearby was just a piece of luck, but it had settled where I'd spend that last night.

He'd been in the background for days, so I wasn't surprised to pick him up again.

What he didn't know was that I'd spotted him the first time he'd broken the background pattern. Not much of an edge, but . . .

I didn't know his real name any more than he knew mine, but I knew his face. I'd met him a long time ago, when he was in charge of one of the "commando" units in Africa I'd just signed on with. Called himself "Brander" at the time. Dutch, I think. Or maybe a displaced Boer.

I don't remember what name I'd been using. Nobody in the field cared, and all the sign-up man would know was the numbered bank account to wire your pay into. Less than a minute after it hit that account, it would be vacuumed out. Same bank, different account number. That was before the Swiss wall of *anonymat* had started to show a few cracks.

I didn't learn until a few weeks later that what he called himself wasn't just the name he was using; it was what he did. By then, I wasn't surprised at anything mercs would do. To themselves, to the enemy . . . even to their "comrades," if they detected a weakness not masked by the killing gear we all carried.

Why a man would be insane enough to leave his personal mark on the bodies of the enemy was beyond my understanding. Still, the knowledge wasn't without value—it wouldn't be *my* mark the enemy would find. And if the outfit I signed on with promoted men as seriously bent as this one, I knew I'd have to find new work soon.

Now, another thing I knew was that he hadn't been tracking me on contract. He'd seen me several times, and I'd deliberately wandered into a filthy SRO a couple of days ago, baiting the trap in case someone was paying him for my life.

With a man like him, not many possibilities in play: if he wasn't being paid to take me out, he was looking for me to lead him to a payday.

So the only thing I had to find out was whether he'd just recognized me by accident, and kept watch to see if there was something in it for him, or if he knew who I was—who I was *now*—and planned on selling that knowledge.

When the product is knowledge, the seller wants to know its maximum depth and width before wrapping the package. If he saw me as a product, he'd want some idea of value before sale. And if someone had hired Brander, I'd need *that* name before I sent him over.

Just the thought of my Dolly's name in his mouth meant he was already dead.

I didn't know the town, so I couldn't suggest the kind of bar where people made it their business to mind their own.

And if *he* knew his way around, any suggestion he made would be a mistake—too many variables. Best not to approach him at all. Find the right spot and wait.

I know how to do that. Both parts of that.

I knew where a man like him would feel most comfortable approaching me, so I just kept on walking until I was outside the city limits.

Less than ten kilometers, judging by my normal full-pack

pace, then subtracting the much lighter weight of the duffel I was carrying.

The railway underpass was as good a spot as I'd be likely to find. Hoboes might use it for shelter at night, especially if it was raining. Winos might be there *anytime,* but it was too exposed for a crackhead to pipe up in—none of them would have the patience to wait, anyway.

Anyone looking to hop a freight would know the train schedule, but the whole area was empty, except for what was left of the man sprawled in a pool of liquid I knew wasn't water, wine, or blood.

I hunkered down against the wall, lit a distracting cigarette. If Brander was following, he'd be along soon enough.

He wasn't far behind, so he'd probably kept me in sight all the way.

No real choice about that—he could read trail signs in a jungle, but tracking a man using roads was damn near impossible, even when they were dirt.

I saw him coming. That couldn't have been a mistake on his part. He wanted to make sure he didn't spook me into rabbiting. Or shooting.

"Hey," he said, as he came close enough to speak, hands open and empty. "Remember me?"

"No. Should I?"

He casually dropped into a squat on my left side, as if I'd asked him to take a seat. "Come on, André. It's me, Brander. We served together in—"

"Okay."

"Okay what?"

"Okay, I remember you."

"I've been watching you."

"Okay."

"I figure you gotta be here for the same reason I am."

"Is that right?"

"I've been here five fucking weeks," he said. "Came in after a little stopover in Japan. The whole Triangle, that's played out now. I heard, if you wanted some action, there's people hiring here, looking for men with Darkville experience. Only, I can't find anyone to ask."

I didn't say anything.

"I need work. I'm not too old for the field," he said—so defensively that I knew everyone hadn't shared his opinion—"but what I'd really like is a nice training gig. Heard they got all these 'militia' morons out this way—good money, if you can prove you're the real thing."

"Okay."

"And I figure you heard the same thing, am I right?"

"No."

"Come on, man. We *served* together. I haven't found any of these militia guys. Not yet, anyway. But you've been here much longer than me, I'm thinking. Not in this stupid little town, in this country. So I'm just out strolling and I spot you, packing some gear. I tell myself, 'Brander, you just struck gold.' There's got to be enough for both of us. Maybe even more, if we partner up. Am I right?"

"No."

"No what?"

"No, I'm not looking for work. I've already got work. But not here. I wasn't looking for some 'militia,' or whatever you call it—I was looking for a recruiter. And I found one. Shipping out next week."

"To where?"

I just looked at him.

"It's like that, huh?"

"Why would it change?"

"Yeah, I know. But, if they're looking for men, they'd be looking for more than one. And I need the work. I checked the job board, but there's nothing. I mean, not nothing *on* the damn board; I mean the board's gone, man. Like it never existed."

I didn't say anything.

"There's supposed to be work in Honduras, some Spanish guy looking for men. But that's really low-rent. What they call 'retail kidnapping.' Not grabbing some major player for millions, just some local merchant, for, like, twenty-five K. Got to do about two of those a *day* to make any coin. No planning, just roll up and snatch. Too many ways for that to go wrong. And who'd trust those greasers, anyway?"

He was sweating. Not from the heat—Brander had worked terrain that would make this place seem like springtime in Canada. He was probably only about ten or so years older than me, but he knew he was running out of options.

Maybe he really *was* worried that this "militia" he was looking for might think he was past it, but that didn't feel right. How would they know whether any stories he told them were the truth?

No, he probably thought I'd found work but was keeping it to myself. And if there was work, he knew they'd take him on—disposable goods don't have to be the highest quality.

Maybe he hadn't put a penny aside. He'd worked long enough to have a bankroll, but any merc his age still looking for a job was more likely to be broke than greedy.

Probably never thought too far ahead, either. Any references he'd give would put his reputation out there, too. My best guess was that the modern forces weren't signing up just anyone who applied, and none of the tightly organized groups operating today would tolerate his little habits.

I cut my eyes to the side, took a closer look. Everything about him was a shade off—looked less fit than he should be, needed a haircut, and his clothes were a little *too* grubby, even if he was trying to blend in. His eyes were soft-focused, and his hands didn't look cared for. I'm not talking about some gangster manicure; I mean they didn't look . . . ready.

They weren't.

I didn't know why Brander was in that town, only what he'd told me.

But I knew he was desperate, and shrugging him off wasn't an option. If he'd already made up his mind to learn whatever he could about me, the reason didn't matter.

I didn't know what he was still capable of, but one thing for sure—he could attract attention. Dolly's face filled my mind. *Always the death math,* I thought, as I slowly got to my feet and checked the terrain as if Brander and me were a team and that was my job. He didn't move. I stretched my arms high, yawned, and spun my right knee into his forehead in the same motion. The back of his skull seemed to splatter just before a trail of fluids started flowing from his head as it slid down along the wall.

He might still know what to do, I remember thinking, as my right hand came out of my side pocket, holding a push-button tube that snapped a four-inch titanium spike out of the front. I stabbed that into his ear, then used a palm strike to drive it to full-depth penetration.

I yanked out the spike and walked away, wiping it down with an alcohol pad as I moved. Still moving, I gloved up, then squeezed out another pad and set the spike on fire. I switched hands to allow a full burn-off, then kicked it into a pile of rubbish.

If the cops found that spike, they'd know what it was, and the dead body so close by would tell them what it had been used for. But fire doesn't leave fingerprints, and homeless men kill each other all the time.

Dolly welcomed me back like she always does.

"Tell me!" always comes first.

"He got the tattoos while he was locked up. But I don't know when he was put away for the first time."

"The police—"

"They probably could get juvenile records, even from another state. But I don't think they'd bother to try."

"You don't think much of them, do you?"

"Here, you mean?"

"Yes."

"I think the same of the police everywhere. They can't be trusted. They could even know a lot more than they're saying. Or be holding back so they could trip up the killer if they ever got to question him."

"Remember that detective, the one who testified in Mary-Lou's case?"

"Sure."

"You know what he thinks of the DA's Office. I think *he'd* try. To get the records, I mean."

"Maybe. But what would I have to push him with? Wouldn't the cops already know the age of the tattoos? From the autopsy, I mean."

"No, they wouldn't," Dolly said. "Not really. I mean, tattoos do fade over time, that's true. They stretch, too. Like, if what was once muscle turns to fat. But this guy wasn't old enough for any of that. Maybe if they cut again, thin tissue slices, they could see how deep they were. Maybe that would—"

That's when I told her what I'd found out, putting in just enough detail for her to understand it didn't matter.

"**H**ow far do you want me to go?"

"Homer was functioning. Maybe he wouldn't ever hold a job, but he wasn't a danger to anyone. He shouldn't be locked up. And if they keep him too long, he'll probably just surrender to the voices."

"I wasn't asking you," I said to Mack.

"*Arrêtes-toi!*" she snapped in rapid-fire French.

"Stop what, *précieuse*? It was a reasonable question. A question I asked *you*."

"I won't risk you, Dell. I won't. But if there's a threat watching this place . . ."

"I know."

"Only if it *has* to be," Dolly said, drawing lines.

Our lines—different circles around the same place. A *légionnaire* is usually outnumbered, so he is trained to place no value on an enemy's life—and to highly value ambush as a disproportionately deadly tool. A Médecins Sans Frontières nurse would regard all human life as priceless, but not all equally so—Dolly had never forgotten the necessity of triage.

I turned to Mack. "How far are you prepared to go?"

"My job description is kind of vague."

I translated that easy enough: Mack knew all about triage, too. He wasn't going to risk all the work he was doing just to spring Homer, so I couldn't count on him to go past his self-imposed limits . . . but he had a lot of room inside those limits.

"We need all the information we can get on the dead guy."

"I already got his record," he said, putting a few papers on the butcher block.

I scanned them quick. "This is his adult record. But I'm thinking he did time before. As a juvenile, maybe."

"Those records are sealed."

"But not erased."

"Okay."

"Okay, you understand? Or okay, you can get them?"

"I haven't got a friend on the force here, like I said. But I'm not *from* here, so . . ."

It was my turn to say, "Okay."

Maybe Luc is watching, I thought.

I was Nazi-hunting. Not to kill them, not necessarily. But to find them, yes. And if some met death along the way, *que sera sera.*

Vancouver had the skinheads Mack had promised. When I asked him how he knew so much about them, he'd just said "Chicago." So I pressed him harder, trying to push his buttons.

"Nazi scum." I dismissed them all.

"Not the young ones," he said, turning his eyes to meet mine. "Those kids, they're just joining the only club that'll have them. They've got no place to go, nothing to do, no reason to . . . exist, I guess. So, when someone tells them they're special, superior, destined to rule, it strikes home. 'Home,' that's not a word that even meant anything to them before."

"Yeah. Poor kids."

He ignored the sneer in my voice. "Not all of them. Some come from middle-class families. Even wealthy ones. But they've got no identity. No sense of themselves. The only thing they know is, they don't matter."

I guess my face told him I wasn't buying it.

"Look, what's the difference between the kids in the homeless camps and skinheads? Nobody wants them, so they want each other. But if you're talking about the bosses, the ones who give the orders and never go near the front lines, that's a different game. You want scumbags? That's where you'd look."

So, once I got to Vancouver, I just strolled around aimlessly until I spotted a little house in a run-down neighborhood.

No way to miss it—they weren't hiding anything from their neighbors. It was decorated with everything their role required, down to a replica of the "88" with the pair of lightning bolts running across it that had been on God's gift to Homer.

I'd left Dolly's car in a lot in downtown Portland, and just walked across the bridge to Vancouver. But getting inside that house without being seen could be tricky, and getting out even harder . . . depending on what I ran into.

One thing for sure. I knew I'd have to leave a lot quicker than I could ever manage on foot.

I wasn't trained as a car thief. I couldn't rent a car without a credit card. And even if I used a dummy, whoever handled the rental would be likely to remember my face. I don't mean some clerk, I mean the cameras all those places have now. They weren't worried about an armed robbery; the cameras were for ID thieves who used stolen credit cards.

With gangs, it's always tricky to isolate an individual. But that's what I'd need to do if I wanted to cross that bridge in a car.

After a couple of days, I was beginning to think there were no black people in Portland.

Plenty of Latinos and Asians. But I couldn't use a low-rider, or a tricked-out tuner car. So I gave up on using some gang-banger's bland-sedan drive-by machine—I'd have to settle for a regular guy.

That wouldn't be as confusing to the cops if anyone grabbed the plate number, but there was an upside, too—the kind of guy I decided to settle on, his plates would convince the law that whoever reported them had written down the wrong number.

If the skinheads themselves could get a plate run—maybe somebody's girlfriend worked at the DMV—one look at a driver's-license photo and they'd know it hadn't been the person who owned that car who'd . . . done whatever I might end up needing to do.

This time, I left Dolly's Subaru in the long-term lot at PDX. Then I walked over to the terminal, went inside, and followed the triple-width revolving door right back out again. I had a carry-on bag with me—all I had to do was go down one flight and wait until a cab pulled up to the stand.

"The Governor," I muttered to the driver. I had checked it out on their Web site before I'd made the trip—a nice hotel, but not a new one. And way downtown. If my outfit—a heavy canvas coat with a high collar, dark jeans over black work boots, and a watch cap—surprised the cabbie, it sure didn't slow his conversation.

More like a rant, actually. I don't think I could have gotten a word in if I'd wanted to—he was one of those guys who could breathe and talk at the same time.

The seat next to him was cluttered with all kinds of paperback books, and a few notebooks of his own. I figured him for some kind of older student—probably getting his post-doctoral degree in political science. He was explaining how the last election had been "engineered from the top," whatever that meant—if it was rigged, where else *could* it be from?—when he interrupted himself to ask me, "Front or back?"

"Back," I said. Just a reflex—I didn't know the place had more than one entrance.

He pulled up on the left side of a wide one-way street. Told me the price. I paid him with five dollars on top, and was out of the car while he was still saying . . . something.

It was even better than I'd hoped—no doorman at the back entrance. No bellhop trying to snatch your bag, either. I just started walking away, aiming for one of the downtown parking lots. They weren't walled in, but there was always a roof over the whole structure.

Easy enough to scale, but too many people had nothing better to do than play with their cell-phone cameras. So I climbed the stairs to the top floor, found a pool of shadow, and sat down to wait.

It took less than an hour.

Plenty of people came in to take their cars, but either they weren't alone or they were the wrong color.

I stayed still until I saw a black man walking confidently toward his car, a dark-red Mercedes sedan. I walked soundlessly behind him, eyes on his back, ears everywhere else.

When he pushed the key fob to unlock his car, I pushed the pistol into the back of his spine.

"I need your car," I said, softly. "Not for long. I'll bring it back. I don't want to hurt you, but I will if you make me."

"Just take it easy," he said. It wasn't the words, it was how he spoke them that told me he knew how an amateur might panic and jerk the trigger.

"Good advice," I told him, holding the door open and gesturing for him to get behind the wheel. As he turned his face back toward me, I hit him with a full shot of the mist. Opening his mouth to scream didn't help—it only made him take in a lot more.

I looked around. We were still alone. I pushed the button to start the car, just in case he had some kind of alarm hooked up. No.

Another button on the key fob popped the trunk. I put him inside, closed it shut, and drove down the circular ramps until I got to the place where you had to pay. His wallet had the plastic card I thought a man who drove a Mercedes, wore a suit to work, and put in long hours would have handy.

I just slipped the card into the slot, waited for the gate to lift, and was outside and rolling toward the bridge in a few seconds.

I wasn't trained as a spy; I'm not a scientist, either.

So, when I can't make the tool I need for work, I have to pay for it. What I do know is how to pay for those kinds of tools without the buyer and the seller having to meet in person.

The man I got the mist-spray canister from said it would be good for at least ten years, provided I kept it refrigerated between uses. It was guaranteed to immobilize, but when I asked if it would kill, the man who welcomed the alley's darkness shrugged his padded shoulders and launched into a long list of what he called "variables." If the target had asthma, or a bad heart; if I used too much of the mist . . .

I was trained against killing noncombatants. Nothing to do with morals; it's just that it's stupid. Makes more problems than it ever solves. But when there's really no choice, you have to chance it.

I got over the bridge, found some shadows, and pulled in, firing a quick burst from the megawatt spotlight as I did.

For a tick less than a full second, the whole area was as clear as an HD television screen. Nothing moved. So either that spot was empty, or whoever was there knew they were safe behind cover. I didn't have the time to outwait anyone, so I gambled on "empty."

Even if it wasn't, maybe somebody would see a man they'd never be able to ID pop the trunk, get out from behind the wheel, and wrap a still-unconscious body in a dark shroud, with his hands at his sides. When I flipped the toggle switch, the shroud inflated. Not tight enough to close down his lungs, but way too tight for him even to try and claw his way free.

With his mouth wrapped in a taped-over foam pad, and the kind of nosepieces you see in hospital wards inserted, he'd stay put even if he came around from the misting.

Timing a home invasion is easy enough, but only if you're holed up somewhere with a good sight picture, so you can study the landscape for a while.

How many people live there? Is there a dog? Any pattern to the comings and goings? Children? Alarm systems?

But I couldn't waste that kind of time, and everything Mack had told me about skinheads said they'd sleep late and be gone by midnight, or even earlier.

Of course, if they were hosting some kind of meeting—or even decided they'd stay home that night and just get drunk—I could be walking into more of them than I wanted to. But drunks aren't quiet, and the music Mack had played for me off a CD he had was so loud even on the lowest setting that I knew I'd hear it way before I got too close to back out.

I say "music" because I don't know what else to call it—it was just some guitar chords and drums with a lot of screaming. I could make out "niggers" and "kikes" and "muds" . . . not much else. "Power!" was a word they repeated a lot. It made what kids called "rap music" sound like a trained choir backed up by a symphony orchestra.

I had to keep the Mercedes close by, in case I had to leave in a hurry. The lot next to theirs was empty, except for the charred remains of what I guessed had once been a house. Dogs were barking, but it wasn't because I'd set them off—they hadn't stopped once during the three times I'd circled the block.

For whatever reason, all the dogs were chained to stakes

in the front yard. Like they were there for display, not for protection.

I opened my carry-on and took out a pair of mechanic's gloves, black mesh, slightly padded. They slid on over the transparent latex I'd never removed, then Velcro-closed. The matte black jumpsuit slipped over the unpolished boots I was already wearing. The watch cap could be pulled down into a ski mask. All I had to do was screw the silencer into the front of the pistol and strap it to my chest, and I was ready.

I would have used the suppressor for what I wanted, even if noise wouldn't matter. My Beretta Star Px4 cost a fortune and was well worth it—perfect for carrying concealed, with a 10-round .40-caliber magazine. But it's *so* short that it wouldn't look menacing enough for the kind of men who would be in that basement.

The windows were dark, like nobody was home, but the back door wasn't even locked. I stepped inside, breathing very shallow, counting to one eighty in my head. Voices from below. A basement, maybe?

I moved in that direction; the thin, removable, no-pattern crepe soles on my boots kept me soundless. A dog would have picked up on my scent, so I guessed they were all still outside. Anyway, a barking dog's no warning signal if it never *stops* barking.

I didn't need a dog's nose to smell the marijuana. A light of some kind was coming from the basement, and I could hear voices. More than one.

My training was screaming at me: *Attendez!* The enemy had not detected my presence—I could line up the targets before they knew they *were* targets.

But I couldn't know when others might come. And if they came in the same way I had, they'd be behind me.

Okay, then.

I padded all the way to the bottom step. Three men. Young

men. Smoking dope. The light was from a big TV screen—no sound, but none needed for what it was showing. They never even looked in my direction. Most of the basement was shadowy. Could be more than the three I'd already seen—I didn't have night-vision goggles. Maybe zonked out?

I'd already done too much thinking. I stepped out onto a linoleum floor, the pistol extended to make sure they could see it. "Don't make a sound" was all I said.

They didn't. Maybe they were all muzzy from the dope, or maybe they were smarter than they looked.

"Keep your hands where I can see them."

They did that, too.

"I'm looking for a man," I said, tonelessly. "I think you might know where I can find him. Here!" I finished, flicking a rolled-up and rubber-banded photo of the dead Nazi's face in their general direction. "Pull off the band. Unroll it, I'm saying. Then take a look. A close look."

"How do we know—?"

"You don't ask questions. You just give answers. I get the answers, I'm gone. I don't, then *you* are. All of you."

They looked in my direction. Not trying to ID me, trying to measure their chances. They couldn't have liked them much—silencers scare people more than pistols. The one in the middle took the rubber band off, held up the blown-up mug shot, and squinted at it.

I tossed a blue aluminum-cased flashlight at them. The one on the far right flinched. The one in the middle gave him a "don't act like such a punk" look. Then he picked it off the couch, and played with it until he figured out he had to twist the front to turn it on.

"This is like an old guy, man," he said. "He wouldn't be hanging with us."

"I didn't say he was one of you. But I know you've seen him," I said, my voice carrying a certainty I didn't feel.

It was quiet for a second.

"One quick *pop-pop-pop!* Nobody'd even find your bodies for days. Want me to just pick one of you, prove I'm not playing to the two of you that *don't* die?"

"Bullshit, man! You think we're the only ones—?"

The guy in the middle must have elbowed him—he stopped cold like his voice box had suddenly given out.

"So I've got even less time than I thought, right?"

None of them said a word.

"Okay, then, here's how it goes. Either somebody tells me about this guy—right now—or one of you gets shot in the head. It's that fucking simple."

"We've seen him," the guy in the middle said quickly. "But he was just moving through. Needed some traveling money. And he had rank, man."

I kept the gun leveled, as if I was expecting more.

I wasn't, but it came, anyway.

"We told the other guys that!" the one on my far left blurted out. "We're righteous, wood. RAHOWA, ATW! You don't need to be . . . you know."

I put it together so quickly it was like watching a speeded-up movie.

"The other guys didn't show you any weapons. And they let you see their faces."

"Yeah! I mean, we already told *them,* right? And we even got a number to call if we see him again."

"This ain't right," the one in the middle said, sulking like a kid who wasn't allowed to go to a party. "How were we supposed to know anything? The first guys, *they* passed us, okay? And they had rank, too. *High* rank."

Speeding inside my head: The dead guy had been on the move, and he was well ahead of whoever was following him. He wouldn't have chanced stopping at this place if he wasn't sure of that.

I couldn't think of a way to ask the punks on the couch for the number the trackers had left for them to call—it would be the same as admitting *I* didn't know it.

"Passed you?" I said. "Why do you think I'm here? Me, I'm the final exam."

"But—"

"Shut up. Look on the back of the photo."

The one in the middle turned it over. "It's just a—"

"Different number," I cut him off. "The old one—the one they gave you to call—that's burned. You call it now, you'll be talking to the FBI."

"But . . ."

"My job is to find who *got* it burned. See what I'm saying? You call that number, there's gonna be people listening. Not *our* people. Get it *now*?"

"It wasn't us!" Sounded like all three spoke at the same time.

"Any of you got pending cases?"

"No, man," the one in the middle said. "The only one in our crew who had a case on him was Otto. You know, for that 'triple threat' thing they're calling it on our Web site? A mud who's also a queer, walking right out of that bar with a white girl—no way to pass that up. And Otto's been locked up for months now."

Time running out, I thought. *Take the chance.*

"The DA's having a little trouble with one of the witnesses," I said. "And if they keep delaying the trial long enough, he might have trouble with the rest of them."

Their silence told me all I needed. They bought it. The masked assassin holding them at gunpoint was going to take out the witnesses against Otto. But why go near them? I had to have a reason, so . . .

"Nobody visits the jail," I said. "Nobody accepts collect calls. No notes get sent in. And nobody calls the number the three guys gave you—only the one on the back of that picture you're holding. Everybody understand? Everybody know who sent me, and what they sent me for? Everybody know *now*?"

"RAHOWA!" they all chanted again. Trying to sound strong and keep it soft at the same time.

They only got the last part right.

I didn't want to pop the trunk and leave the black guy all buzzed from the anesthetic in a neighborhood where he'd get hurt.

Or in a neighborhood where I could get seen doing it, either. So I drove the Mercedes back to where it belonged.

Some parking garages have cameras, but unless they'd gone way over the top, like with infrared, it was too dark in this one for them to be much use.

The parking slot the black guy had used earlier was as empty as I'd left it. So was most of the garage. I pulled down the mask, slid the Mercedes into the waiting slot, popped the trunk, hit the button to deflate the bag, snatched the nose plugs out. He was still breathing.

I positioned him behind the wheel, stuffed five hundreds into his wallet, and put it back inside his suit. When I got down to the next floor, I pulled off my invader's gear, stuffed everything into my carry-on, and walked away.

The airport was too far to walk without attracting attention; I'd have to get some joint to call a cab for me.

A strip bar would be better than a hotel for that—I wouldn't have to risk pretending I was a hotel guest—but strip bars pay way too much attention to their customers.

I was walking toward what looked liked an expensive hotel—new and kind of Asian-influenced in the well-lit lobby. Except for the boots, I was dressed okay, and a French accent usually passed for upper-class in four-star places that didn't speak the language. I was getting ready to be a pretend-guest when a cab rounded the corner. I hailed it.

It pulled to the curb. The driver was an older guy, probably wanted to make some off-books cash, but smart enough to make sure he wasn't going to lose any first.

"The airport," I said, holding up my carry-on. "They change my flight so late and now I must go on the first one. At six in the morning, it leaves! The hotel, it—"

"Get in the back, buddy."

Bless that French accent.

He was like most people who say they like to talk.

That's supposed to mean they like conversation, but it actually means just what they say it does. I didn't have to contribute much until he asked me what airline I wanted.

"United," I said, fumbling with my wallet for a fifty. "This is enough, American money, yes?"

"Sure," the driver said. From the way he moved out, I guess I'd overpaid a little.

Fifteen minutes later, I was back in Dolly's car, headed home.

"**D**ell! I was starting to—"

"I have to sleep," I told her, kissing her cheek to let her know I was okay: no wounds, inside or out. "When I get up, we'll talk."

"**I**s that one of them?" I asked Mack, as we passed a man pushing what looked like a three-story tower erected inside one of those metal-mesh pushcarts they have in supermarkets.

"That's Billy. He's happier outside, on his own. Not on the register, so he doesn't get a check."

"One of the ones who . . . cope, right? Only he doesn't hang with anyone?"

"That's about right. But you have to look close to be sure. You see a guy carrying around everything he owns, probably he's in that slot. But . . . Well, you can't tell anything from the clothes. Or even how he moves. There's a lot of older guys around here, especially near the beach. Not crazy, retired. Guys with money who spend a lot of time putting their outfits together. So they look what they think is 'rough and ready,' you know?"

"The shoes."

"Yeah," he said, unable to keep the surprise from his voice. "That's the cue: the ones who go for walks in the morning. Probably have a cabinet-full of vitamins, too. They'll wear old clothes, but no way they're going to take a chance of turning an ankle."

"Homer didn't kill that guy."

"I fucking *know* that. There probably isn't anyone around who doesn't. But getting him off at a trial isn't going to accomplish anything. Like I said before, we have to get him kicked loose, out of *any* confinement, no matter what they call it. So he can go back to the way he was before."

"He could do that? Even after all this?"

"Homer? Sure. I see him pretty much every day. Or night. He's on his meds, and that isolation unit suits him fine, now that I got the staff to keep the lights off at night. But a trial . . ."

"I got it. As long as they think they got the killing solved, they won't even be looking anymore."

"Yeah."

How much can I trust this guy? "What if they got a phone tip, or something like that?"

"Wouldn't do a thing. Far as the people around here're concerned, Homer solves everybody's problems. Cops're happy, DA's happy, City Council's happy, Chamber of Commerce . . . happy. And it's not like there's going to be some nosy reporter sniffing around, either."

"Okay."

"Okay what? If we don't solve the case—prove someone else did it—nothing's going to change. They'll all just stand pat."

He took one of his deep, whistling nose-breaths. "Look, here's what it comes down to: The liberals, they'll go along with a mental-health commitment. I mean, what's the issue— that Homer's *not* loco? And everyone else will get what they want, too—crime solved, streets cleaned, and the guy who got himself killed, nobody's going to miss him. Remember, the dead guy wasn't a local—that means a lot. All Homer can tell anyone is what he told the cops. That body could have floated miles from where the killing happened."

"We already know that's not true. He had to be killed by either at least two men, or by one he trusted enough to turn his back on. Either way, the killer was good at what he did. You have to be skilled *and* strong to execute that move: drive your knee into the target's spine at the same time you plant the spike. That keeps it planted. So, if the whole chunk doesn't come out, you can ride him all the way down. Finish the job on the ground."

He just looked at me like he was waiting for more. Okay, I could do that:

"And there's the time line, too: That photo that was in the papers? I know who took it. And when."

Mack listened to everything I'd learned from the video ninja.

"He'd never testify."

"He wouldn't *want* to testify. But . . ."

"You mean, get some lawyer to try it on the facts?"

"Why not?"

"Because Homer *would* want to testify. They couldn't stop him. If they tried, he'd start his screaming thing. And once he did, no way he stays out of the state hospital, even if some jury bought the idea that he wasn't the guy who did the killing."

"There could be another way."

"What?"

"I'll have to check on a few things first."

"**D**on't you have any opinion of your own?" my wife demanded. Hands on her hips, a sure sign she wasn't playing around.

"If I had to guess, I'd say, yeah, he'd keep quiet if he knew something happened. But would he actually help *make* something happen? There's only one way to tell, Dolly."

"I am not asking about Mack," she said, the muscles in her arms tightening, like she was getting ready to throw a punch at anything that might be a threat to me. "I'm asking you."

"It's the most logical tactic."

"Murder is the most logical tactic?"

"You want them to kick Homer loose, there's only two ways: find out who killed that Nazi—find out *and* put together a case so strong that the cops would grab it *and* convince the DA to go along—or kill another one. Homer, he'd have the best alibi that could ever be."

"Just like that."

"It's not exactly blowing up a day-care center."

"Dell . . . Most of them—the young ones, I mean—they're just . . . trying to find themselves . . . or find a place where they could fit in, maybe. This town, it's ultra-tolerant of gays, Mexicans, almost anyone you can think of. Except what they call 'trailer trash.' White kids who don't have working parents. And aren't that smart, or good at sports, or . . . I don't know. But *you* know what a young man does if nobody wants him. Better than most. Why hate them so?"

"It wasn't just Jews they sent to the ovens, Dolly. A *gitan* would always be first on that line. You ever hear a Sabra talk about his 'homeland'? That's Israel. The place where the 'wandering Jews' could settle down. Gypsies are never going to have a homeland, never going to stop 'wandering.' They can't. When you say 'Rom,' people think of Hungary, right? Okay, remember what we saw on the BBC last week, about this swine Orbán, their Prime Minister. I plugged his name in, took about five seconds to find this. I even printed it out:

Zsolt Bayer, a prominent right-wing commentator with close ties to the ruling Fidesz government and its controversial Prime Minister, Viktor Orbán, recently had this to say about the country's Gypsy minority:

"A significant part of the Roma are unfit for coexistence. They are not fit to live among people. These Roma are animals, and they behave like animals. When they meet with resistance, they commit murder. They are incapable of human communication. Inarticulate sounds pour out of their bestial skulls. At the same time, these Gypsies understand how to exploit the 'achievements' of the idiotic Western world. But one must retaliate rather than tolerate. These animals shouldn't be allowed to exist. In no way. That needs to be solved—immediately and regardless of the method."

"*Der Spiegel* ran this editorial saying how 'shocked' they were. And if anyone would know an undercover Nazi agenda, who better? When this filth says 'not fit to live among people,' you think he's *not* saying unfit to live, period?"

"Dell, you don't even know if you're a—" Dolly cut herself off before she cut even more deeply.

"You put me back there," I told the only person I loved.

"Dell, I'm sorry. I wouldn't ever—"

"Sssshh, precious," I whispered, holding her against my chest. "I'll get it done."

"I don't care about it! Not anymore, Dell. I swear."

"Okay. I'll give Mack what I found out, and let him take it from there."

"Promise?" my sweetheart said, very softly.

"Yes," I lied.

It wouldn't be the first time I'd hopped a freight.

And I hadn't learned about the existence of the FTRA from Mack. I'd let him think that, because it was the only way to make sure Dolly thought that, too.

It wasn't so long ago that I had needed a way to get in and out of Denver without leaving tracks. Not that "paper trail" nonsense TV is always bleating about—if you stayed off airplanes, didn't use credit cards when you needed gas, and didn't pose for convenience-store cameras, that part would be easy enough. What I'd needed was a way to *float* through, moving like the mountain breezes they take for granted that high up.

I had to go to Denver to keep my promise to MaryLou McCoy. I had promised to take a life in return for her promise to fight for her own. Up to that moment, she'd been a block of stone. Whatever was coming, let it come. She wasn't going to move toward it . . . and she wasn't going to step aside.

"What do you think is going to happen if you won't let us help you?" the lawyer we'd hired for her had asked.

MaryLou's pale eyes were as empty as her response: "It's already happened."

That's when I saw it clearly, instantly translating her whole attitude into the obedience the Legion had drummed into us: *La mission est sacrée.* MaryLou had been supposed to leave town the next day for summer softball camp, a showcase that would let her pick from the bouquet of scholarship offers they'd be handing her. But she'd had a higher mission—protecting her baby sister, Danielle, from a fate she was sure awaited the child if MaryLou left her.

She never knew the truth until the fourteen-year-old viper she'd thrown away her own life to protect took the witness stand . . . as a witness for the prosecution.

"I'm not like them," Danielle told the jury, distancing her-self from all those girls who had told how they had been gang-raped before being dumped outside the ER like bags of garbage. The girls who'd lacked Danielle's beauty and physical endow-ments. Making it clear that nobody had raped her. No, she'd been "initiated" into a special society, run by a special man, a man who loved her with all his heart. A man named Cameron Taft. "All the girls were after him," she crowed.

"So your sister was jealous of you?" MaryLou's lawyer asked, keeping his voice empty of inflection.

"Look at her." Danielle pointed. "And look at me. What do you think?*"

By then, I knew that the founder of Tiger Ko Khai was a man named Ryan Teller, a "combat vet" who'd been kicked out of the military years before. I was already sure he'd never return. Three of his acolytes had stopped by their hangout, but only two of them left alive. I was confident they'd deliver *that* message to their Supreme Leader.

But I'd had to make MaryLou trust me. And get her to under-stand that, no matter the outcome of the trial, she hadn't sac-rificed for nothing. Ryan Teller was a human virus, and other places wouldn't have been vaccinated against him. The only way to stop him from spreading was to make him dead.

Hopping a freight wasn't hard. I sure wasn't the only one riding that way, and I looked right for the part. Everything I wore was "used," and my face fit my clothes.

Anyone who looked in my duffel would have known I wasn't a hobo—if the equipment hadn't tipped them, the cash would have.

But nobody was going to take that look. A couple of men caught the same car I was riding. A working team—I could tell from the way they ran through their routine: check the car for occupants, then evaluate potential targets. I was the only one in that car. Sprawled in the corner, the duffel's strap looped over my left arm as if I was asleep and wanted to protect whatever was in there against a sneak thief.

They came up on me quiet. Not like experienced soldiers would, just without talking.

I had the pistol out while they were still closing on me. When they got near enough for whatever they wanted, they saw what they didn't.

"Not me," I said, keeping my voice polite, so they could back off without losing face.

They put their hands up together, as if they were marionettes.

"I'm not law," I said. "I don't want you. I don't know you. I never saw you. And you didn't see me."

They nodded. Message received. Whether I was an escaped convict or a traveling psychotic didn't matter—what mattered was getting out of that car as soon as they could.

When the train slowed down for a sweeping curve, they bailed out as smoothly as a pair of acrobats.

The FTRA guys were a different breed.

They made no secret of their brotherhood as they gathered in the farthest corner of the car, speaking too low for me to hear.

They were smarter, too. We never exchanged words, but they could tell the only thing I'd be willing to "share" with them was some bullets.

Now I thought about all that.

Easy to miss what you're not looking for. And all I was looking for on those freights to Denver was to be left alone.

So I replayed the memory tapes. I hadn't seen anyone flying Nazi flags on those trains. Some had a little ink, but it wasn't anything they showed off. The Master Race on the rails was the FTRA, and all the other nonpaying passengers seemed to know it.

So I scratched my first idea. Not only couldn't I be sure of finding the right men on a freight, I was even less sure of finding one alone.

I had the equipment—a spiked tool mountain climbers call a rock hammer—and I had the plan: kill another heavy-inked Nazi somewhere down the line, let the law think some maniac was riding around, taking them out one by one, always the same way. Once the locals had their "profile," Homer would be off the hook—a serial killer had passed through their town and moved on, nothing to discourage tourists from visiting. Might even bring some new ones, "researching" the porno printed in paperback as "true crime" so supermarkets could rack it without getting complaints.

But it was too complicated. Too risky. And too likely to flop. Even if I managed to get one of them alone and finish him the exact same way, who knew what would happen after that? For what I needed, even as few as two possible outcomes was one over the limit.

"**A** lot of people you see around here in the daytime, they might act crazy—talk to themselves, even have arguments with themselves—or they might be carrying everything they own around with them . . . but that doesn't mean they're homeless."

"You mean the shelter?" Dolly asked Mack.

"That's been closed for a while. But there's that flophouse they call a 'residential rehab.' It's on the far side of 101, in a little . . . valley, I guess you'd call it. Nothing but rock there. Some idiot once thought it would be a perfect place to build a motel. The town bought it for pennies on the dollar when they hired me—I told them if they wanted to keep people off the street, especially at night, they had to give them a safe place to sleep."

"You said some of them—the homeless, I mean—they *never* go indoors," my wife narrowed it down.

"Oh, they all go indoors when they need to—sometimes to use . . . the facilities. Sometimes to steal, sometimes just to get out of the rain. The ones who never go inside no matter what the weather, they're never more than a step away from hospitalization.

"The ones with high coping skills, they know where to camp for the night. Every night. The . . . more disturbed ones, they have to . . . be shown, you know? Otherwise, they'd just keep staggering around. That leaves the kids. You met them," he said, nodding in my direction, "the homeless-by-choice crowd, and the circuit riders."

"None of them killed that guy who was found on the beach," I said.

He gave me a long, measuring look. "You're sure of that?"

"Yeah."

"Because . . . ?"

"All the cops have is a body. By now, they've gone through everything that package came wrapped in. They even know the approximate time it washed up. But that adds up to nothing but guesses. So the easiest road for them is to talk about tides and shifting currents . . . anything *nobody* can be sure about."

"So it didn't necessarily happen around here at all?" Dolly said, an encouraging tone in her voice. "The man could have been murdered *way* offshore . . . like, miles, even."

"They've got something else," Mack said, quietly.

"What?"

"They've got Homer."

"I want to make sure this is where you stand," I told Mack once we were alone. "You don't want Homer found not guilty of killing that Nazi; that wouldn't change anything for him. You want him kicked loose, right? Put back on the street, like none of this ever happened?"

We were parked in that excuse for a car of his, looking through the windshield at the ocean.

"He has to be," the young man said. His voice was absolutely flat-lined, all content, no tone. "Forget a verdict; he'd never be found fit to stand trial at all. Even if one of the half-ass clowns who make a living pretending to be lawyers tried to use an insanity defense—and what the hell else *could* they use?—no judge would let it get that far. You don't need a psychiatrist to see Homer's on another planet."

"But on the street he's harmless?"

"On the street, he's a target. If anyone asked him for anything Homer had, he'd just give it to them. He wouldn't even defend himself from any kind of assault. The best he can do is scream."

"What's the point, then?"

"What's the point of what?" he asked, his tone saying he took what I'd said as some kind of personal attack.

"I guess . . . Look, I don't know anything about this stuff.

You don't want him locked up in a mental hospital because he wouldn't be free. Okay, I get that. But if he has to be on all those drugs anyway . . ."

"That's today," he said, his voice sliding from hot to medium. "Today isn't always forever."

"You got some . . . people like Homer, you got them so they could live like regular people?"

"Oh, *hell,* yes. That's one of the good things about living around here—there's always some kind of work that needs doing. Maybe being a 'barista' isn't an option for all of them—the nasty way some customers talk might set them off—but there's always some manual laboring jobs, all different kinds. And, sometimes, you move one of them off where they were stuck, you find out there's things they're really good at. You ever been to the Lead Sled Shed?"

"That's the custom-car place?"

"Yeah."

"No," I said, thinking that the last thing I'd ever want would be to ride around in a car people would remember.

"You stop in there anytime, you'll always find a guy they call 'Fineline' working. That's because he's the best freehand pinstriper on the entire coast. Maybe in the whole state. Some of his work, it's so delicate, you have to look at it a couple of times to even see it."

"And he was—?"

"Not *was,*" he cut me off, "*is.* He's always going to be schizophrenic, so he has to take his meds every day, or he'll decompensate. But he's got a full-time job, gets paid good, stays in a *nice* rooming house—walking distance from where he works. And people around there . . . well, they understand him, you know?"

"No, I don't know. Look, I'm not playing with you. If I say I don't know something, it's because I don't. If I say I need to understand something, it's because I do."

"And if you say you're gonna hurt someone, you'll—"

"I'd never say anything like that"—cutting him off quick and sharp, so he wouldn't mistake my meaning.

He was quiet for a couple of moments.

I didn't break the silence.

Finally, he said, "Schizophrenia is a permanent state of delusion; it may vary in intensity, but it's always ready to come when it's called. It's embedded, but it—"

"Embedded—that's like you're born with it?"

"The brain doesn't work that way. You can be born with some things, like the extra chromosome in Down syndrome. And there's plenty who'll tell you schizophrenia *is* congenital. There's even a movement that's claiming you can be born a psychopath. But the latest research—scientific research—is all going the other way: there's a clear connection to early-childhood abuse."

"What's the difference between 'scientific' research and any other kind? I thought all research was . . . research, you know?"

"Three words," Mack said. "Theoretical, cumulative, and nonethical."

"What?"

He lit a cigarette and blew a stream of smoke out his window, away from me. "You start with a theory. Any theory, it doesn't matter what. Then you test that theory. Usually, you publish the results. Then other people—people you don't know—they test the same theory, to see if they get the same results themselves. Finally, enough evidence accumulates from different trial runs to make a judgment. That judgment becomes 'factual' . . . until some new body of research disproves it, or finds some flaw in the methodology."

"What's unethical about that?"

"Not *un*ethical, *non*ethical. You have to start with a question, not the answer. No opinion one way or the other. No belief system driving the research. A blank slate, see?"

"Yeah. I think so, anyway. You're saying, when it comes to schizophrenia, kids who get beat up are more—?"

"It's not that simple. Not even close. Physical abuse, that's probably not even a factor when it comes to causality. Neglect, that makes it most probable. And when early neglect coexists with emotional abuse, schizophrenia is most likely to show up. But you almost never see it before puberty."

"Why not before then?"

"We don't know. But it usually doesn't get florid—to the point where everyone knows there's something off—until at least adolescence. The hormone bomb could be the last straw, too much stress. But even then, it's not always recognized. Kids don't pick up on 'symptoms' when they know plenty of others who act the same way. When they say 'party,' they mean get drunk. Or high. Or both.

"A lot of young people act crazy when they're messed up. So they could have a schizophrenic as part of their crowd, and never see him for what he is. It's not like they all live together, or see each other all the time. Understand? Even if every time they see . . . whoever, he's acting all fucked up, they just figure it's from the same things that fuck *them* up. Again.

"What it really depends on isn't the disease, it's the *type* of it. The kind I'm talking about, that's a disorganized schizophrenic. Talks to himself, thinks he's the king of some country that doesn't exist. Or even one that does, it's just that other people don't know it. Or won't admit they know it.

"They all hear voices inside their heads, but it's not the *same* voice—frequency, volume, even the commands themselves, those vary. But that doesn't necessarily make them dangerous to other people, even if you wouldn't invite them over for dinner. The thing is, schizophrenia may not make them dangerous to you, but it *always* makes them a danger to themselves. If the voices keep telling them to do things they don't want to do, they might do anything to make them stop. Stab a pencil into their ear to write something different, smoke crack, drink canned heat, bang their head against a wall . . .

"That's what I was saying before, about not being born with the damn disease. Emotional abuse, it won't leave marks on the skin, but it digs in the deepest. There's only one thing they all have in common—there's nothing they won't do to make those voices *stop.*

"Some go catatonic. Some go mute. Some just make sounds. Some freeze their facial muscles. But the ones who *really* terrify people are the paranoids. Not the kind of paranoia that makes you think everyone's plotting against you, the kind people make jokes about. You'd have to take that level of paranoia, multiply it by a hundred, throw in some magical thinking . . . and you've got some serious trouble."

"How could they tell what something 'really' means?" I asked him.

"That's what we call 'ideas of reference.' Like, if they stumble over a curb just before it starts to rain, they think their stumble *caused* the rain.

"But the true danger is always the 'voices,' the ones only they can hear. A paranoid schizophrenic is perfectly capable of picking up an ax and chopping his way through a whole school bus full of kids, because that's what the voices ordered him to do. They may *look* like kids, but they can't fool the voices—*the voices* know those kids are really all lizards under their skin. Poisonous lizards. So he has to cut them open to see for himself."

"Christ."

"Yeah. This has got nothing to do with intelligence. There've been geniuses with schizophrenia, but the life they live keeps it at bay. Bobby Fischer was the greatest chess player on the planet until the voices got so strong that they took over his life. He was always 'eccentric' and 'demanding' and . . . well, pick any label you like. Then he suddenly stopped playing chess, started muttering about Zionist conspiracies—all out to get him, of course—before he died."

"And if the family has enough money . . ."

"Sure. That'd do it. Instead of throwing him in some dungeon, they could keep him on an M&M diet."

I just looked at him.

"Medication and maintenance," he explained. "But the ones who don't have a dime, they get their meds from the government."

"Those don't work?"

"The sad thing is that some of them work almost *too* well. Say nobody figures out that a brilliant college student's a schizophrenic until his delusions get out of control. He goes on meds in some hospital, stabilizes . . . and they cut him loose. With a scrip if his family's got money, with a Medicaid card if they don't. What happens—especially with the highest-IQ ones—they figure they're doing so good—you know, back in school, getting good grades—they convince themselves they're 'cured.' They don't need the meds anymore. And they hate the side effects, anyway. Doesn't take too long after that before they're back in some hospital. Or prison, depending on what the voices tell them to do. And some of those voices tell them to kill themselves . . . but not until *after* they've gunned down the whole audience at a movie."

"Jesus. But, once they're back to doing okay, can't you tell them that they need the meds to *stay* that way? Wouldn't they be able to understand what's happening then?"

"You can *tell* them, sure. And we do. But, like I said, there's so many really unpleasant side effects—to the meds, I mean— that they're all eager as hell to come up with any excuse to stop taking them."

"Side effects like what?"

"Tardive dyskinesia, that's the most common. Those weird movements you see in some of the walking wounded around here. Like they can't control the muscles in their face, or their arms. It's embarrassing, and it's painful. All the meds for schizophrenia are some form of neuroleptic—and the longer you use them, the more ingrained the side effects become. The meds designed to counteract the side effects only go so far."

"And they have to be on them for life?"

"Pretty much."

"Nice choices."

"Choices? Drug addicts, alcoholics, they've got choices. They know if they don't stop they're gonna die. And that last choice—too many make it anyway. For a schizophrenic, the only way they even understand there *is* a choice is when they've been stabilized on the antipsychotic meds."

"You're saying you've only got the choices you *think* you have?"

"Yeah. But the intensity varies with the individual. 'Fine-line' used to cut himself. They had him down as a cutter—self-mutilation isn't uncommon in borderlines. But we noticed he always preferred the most precise instruments he could find—he wasn't cutting himself to *feel* something, like true cutters do; he was *drawing.* That's when we realized what was really going on.

"Now he's okay about taking his meds. We don't know why they don't make his hands shake, and neither does he. But he doesn't care. What he *wants* to do, the meds *let* him do, so he looks at them the same way a diabetic looks at insulin.

"Truth is, there's a *lot* we don't know. Mental health is really in an infancy stage—there's a lot more emphasis on what to call things than on how to treat them."

"Why?"

"For the billing," he said, with a laugh you wouldn't want to touch with your fingertips. "A good coding-and-billing person can earn a better living than anyone doing my kind of work does. But when I'm paid by a program that's run by any kind of agency—or even a whole county, like out here—they can bill my time out. *I* get freedom from paperwork, health coverage, a two-bit 403(b), and enough life insurance to bury me. *They* get enough to hire a dozen of their pals as 'administrators,' or whatever title they want to give them. A good grant-writer can turn a whole town's problem into a financial surplus, depending on what's fashionable."

"How can one kind of crazy be more fashionable than another?"

"It depends on the area, for one thing. There's so-called programs that say they 'cure' homosexuality. Now, *that's* as crazy as any other delusion, but that doesn't stop people from making the claim. Once they give some behavior a mental-health *name,* the government will help fund any state program that says it's 'curing' it. Like ... say, 'pedophilia.' That's a crock. Even if a person could be diagnosed with 'pedophilia,' nobody would give a damn unless they actually *did* something. Sex offenders are scary, so 'treatment' programs for them always get money—probably every prison in America has one."

"Always comes down to the money, then?"

"Yeah. That's why, for this county, the most important thing I do in *their* eyes is getting my documentation in on time."

"Like a time clock?"

"No. This isn't punch-in, punch-out. I have to keep records of every interaction with every client, chart goals, progress ... damn near enough to turn some of my clients into actual human beings instead of numbers."

"But not quite."

"No," he said, back to that arctic voice. "Not quite."

Back at our house, alone with Dolly, I knew I had to decide, right then and there.

This part of the coast, there's no shortage of people who claim they can read your "aura," tell you all kinds of things about yourself. I can't do that. And knowing they can't, either, isn't worth anything to me.

But I've always relied on trust—my trust. Not "voices" in my head, something that's been in me ever since I can remember. All my life, I trusted whatever it was that told me "Run!" Or "Hide!" Or later, when I learned how . . . "Kill!"

A working merc proves he's passed all those tests just by saying where he's been, and being alive to say it. It took me much longer to be able to listen and trust the one command I'd never heard before about a woman: "Love."

From the moment I first saw Dolly, she had a kind of rose-tinted glow around her face. I could see it even when I was nothing to her but a wounded soldier fighting for money, and she was a nurse who hated all war.

I thought it must have been the knockout shot they'd given me when they had to cut into my leg, but when I saw her years later, it was still there. It took me longer than that to realize Dolly didn't have an "aura." The soft rosy tint was the way *my* eyes saw her.

Now my eyes can still see that glow around her face . . . and I can see when it changes color, too.

If Dolly had said what she wanted me to do, I would have done it. But the only things she ever pushes on me to do are things to protect myself—those leafy vegetables, that's an example.

I knew asking her would always get me the same answer: only if I could pull it off without endangering myself. So—no answer at all.

Okay, then.

"The Nazi who got himself killed, he was on the run," I told her.

"From what?"

"Other Nazis."

"You're sure?"

"Yeah."

"You know why?"

"No. But he was moving *down* the coast. Picked up some traveling cash from a crew of skinheads in Vancouver. After he left, three others showed up. A team, looking for him."

"So they were chasing him?"

"No doubt."

"And they got their work done, so they're not around anymore?"

"Why would they be?"

"How does this help Homer?"

"It doesn't. But if we find the men who killed him—even one of them, so long as he wasn't a local—they wouldn't be able to prosecute Homer."

"And then they'd kick him loose, you're saying?"

"You been around here for a while. This excuse for a DA we've got here, he's going to need a rock-solid case—a case he *can't* lose—before he'll let Homer go."

"I know he's weak, but—"

"He's fifty kilos below 'weak.' He knows this is all about how things *look.* Nobody wants Nazis around here—not visible ones, anyway—and nobody wants crazy people, either. He prosecutes Homer now, he can't lose—see?"

My wife said nothing, but the grim line of her lips told me what she felt.

"You're sure these will hold?" I asked Dolly.

She looked up from where she was blotting a transfer screen of a swastika to the left side of Mack's chest. He'd tried to refuse the hypo full of freeze juice—it was just a local, but he was going first, and he wanted to come across just as tough as he guessed I would. Dolly ignored him.

And she didn't even ask me about the injection. The ability to bear pain is something you can learn—but practicing the techniques can get you dead. I'd had no choice about learning, La Légion called it *"entraînement."* It wasn't until I got into the field that I learned that the techniques of pain tolerance are only useful for pain you can't avoid.

"These patches have to be kept moist," she warned, handing over a bunch of individually sealed packets. "They'll remove every trace, but they'll leave a lightened area of skin behind, so have some dirt or mud or something like that handy before you start to scrub. You especially, Dell—a whitened area would show up on you much more than on Mack."

When Dolly was done, Mack and I looked like what we were supposed to be—a pair of hunters, tracking down a traitor.

Mack vaulted into the open boxcar with ease—the train was crawling around the curve where we'd been waiting, barely moving. I tossed both duffels up to him, then jumped in myself.

The car wasn't empty. Three men, one woman. All in the corner opposite ours. Too dark to tell much more.

Mack held a drop-point knife in his right hand—an all-black Böker I'd handed him before we started our ride, easier to handle than a Tanto. My hands were empty, but my jacket was open.

The rules are simple: You don't close ground unless you're sure. Or desperate.

They stayed where they were. I could tell they were talking, but I couldn't pull out any words. As the train picked up speed, it got too noisy to even try.

It was about twenty minutes before one of them stood up and started toward us.

"Not unless you have to," I whispered to Mack. Repeating what I'd told him while we were waiting for the freight to show.

The guy was big. Tall and beefy. Could've used a haircut, but he was too clean to have been riding long.

"You guys going far?"

Neither of us said anything, both of us watching his hands.

"We were thinking, maybe you got some stuff you want to trade?"

"We're good," Mack said. Meaning the big guy was welcome to take that any way he wanted.

"You like to meet the rest of us?"

"No" is all I answered.

"Hey, look, man, we're all riding together. Just thought I'd be friendly."

Neither Mack nor I said anything.

He stepped closer.

"That's enough," I told him. There was more than enough daylight coming into the car for him to see the pistol he hadn't seen me pull out.

He jumped back like a cat who'd just seen a mouse turn into a rat. A hungry one.

All four of them hopped down as soon as the freight slowed enough.

"Now what do we do?"

"Now we wait," I told Mack. "We're looking for circuit riders, not hoboes."

We didn't find what we needed.

So we jumped off, waited, and boarded a car heading back

the way we came. This time, it wasn't a long wait. Five of them. All male. They hopped on, checked the car, saw us, and flowed themselves into a loose semicircle.

"You know what this is?" said a skinny guy wearing a faded red T-shirt, showing us his tattoo: the letters "FTRA" separated vertically and placed within the boxes created by a string of railroad tracks. He was wearing a bandanna, but it was too dark for me to make out its color.

"Yeah," Mack answered, pulling his own tee up to show the swastika. "You know what this is?"

The five of them exchanged looks.

"This is our car," the skinny guy said. I guessed he was the spokesman. Nobody else seemed eager to say anything. None of them smelled of liquor. None of them looked nervous. In the world I'd left behind, "professional" meant you got paid for what you did. And you had to be good enough at it to keep doing it.

"Okay," I said, keeping my hand inside my jacket. "Your car. We get it. We're not pro riders like you are. We're looking for someone, and we got word he might be trying a freight, so we thought we'd check for ourselves. A long shot, but sometimes you get lucky."

"We're not—"

"We know," I cut him off. "We know *now,* anyway. The man we want wouldn't be riding with a crew. And he wouldn't have your ink, either."

"How bad you want this guy?"

"Bad enough."

"Bad enough to pay?"

"Bad enough to pay what something's worth. You guys, you've got a reputation. We respect that—and we'll be jumping off next chance we get. Like you said, your car. But don't think telling us you saw some guy a while back is gonna make you any money."

"How much money are we talking about here?"

"Budget is seven. One for seeing him recently—that'd point us in the right direction. Another if that was *real* recently, so we'd have some chance of catching up. Three for where he is now, right this minute. And the whole bankroll for taking us to him."

They kind of looked at each other. Long enough for me to tell they were making up their minds about something. But about what? Try and fob us off with some bogus info? Rob us for the seven bills I said I was holding? What I knew they *couldn't* do was take us to a dead man. So, if they offered to do that, I wouldn't have much choice—wasting a couple of hundred would certainly be smarter than wasting their whole crew.

"What if we ran across some guys looking for the same one you are?"

"Be worth something," I said. "*Maybe* worth something. Easy enough to tell."

"Yeah? How would you do that?"

"If they were looking for the same guy we are, they would have told you what he looked like. Even showed you a picture. Maybe one like this," I said, flicking at the FTRA boss the same rolled-up and rubber-banded photo I had of the dead Nazi.

He caught it deftly. I didn't have to tell him how to open it—he wasn't scared the way the Vancouver boys had been. And he was going to do things the way he wanted, no matter what anyone told him.

Whoever these guys were, they didn't play games. The skinny guy didn't even pass the photo around. He rolled it up, banded it, and tossed it back.

"You got seven bills, I'll tell you exactly where you can find him."

"Not what I offered. The seven is to take us to him."

"Money-back guarantee."

"Uh-huh."

"Okay. Hand over five, and we'll tell you where he is. Right this minute. How's that?"

Mack opened his flashlight, played the beam way off to the side.

"Understand?" I said.

The skinny guy nodded. "Go for it."

Mack put the light on each of them. Face by face. The light was so soft it didn't even make them blink. I'm not sure my pistol would have, either. But if they made me go that way, they wouldn't have time to do much blinking.

I reached in my pocket, used my fingers to pluck out the separately banded rolls of fifties, and tossed five hundred his way.

"You came prepared, huh?"

"I try to always carry what I might need."

"Okay, pal. Here's where this guy you're looking for is: go back in the opposite direction this car's headed, cross the border to the next county, and that's where he is. And he's not going anywhere. The county morgue's got him. His body, I mean."

"How do you know?"

"You guys, whatever else you are, you're not riders. Any rider would know—you stop off anyplace, first thing, you grab yourself a newspaper or two."

"You're saying he's dead?"

"I said he was in the morgue. You think he was just visiting?"

"How far back?"

"The paper was almost a week old when we read it. And that was a few weeks ago."

"And the other guys looking for him?"

"Nobody rides for free. But you know that already, don't you?"

"You know the budget. Two hundred is all that's left. You

want it for what you know, it's yours. You want more, you're out of luck—I'm guessing you don't take IOUs."

The skinny guy looked to his right, as if he was silently consulting his crew. Then he said, "Three men. About his age"—moving his head in Mack's direction; easy enough for him, since his neck was as long as a swan's—"all with the same marks as yours. Way north of here."

"What line?"

"No line. We were camped; they came up on us."

"Friendly?"

"Oh yeah. Real nice. But they made a mistake."

"Yeah?"

"Yeah. They figured we was down with them," he said.

"All white, all right?"

"That's about . . . Yeah, that *is* what they thought."

"Nobody rides for free."

"You catch on quick. They didn't offer anything. One of them showed us he had a knife."

"Imagine that."

The skinny guy chuckled.

"For that other two in the budget, what'd they look like?"

"Already told you that."

"You said 'white.' And ink. There's more. I know you don't miss much, any of you."

The skinny guy looked at his pack again. Nodded as if agreeing with them. Said: "The boss was short. Stocky. He was the only one who did any talking. The others were younger than him. With those shaved heads. One had inked up the whole side of his head. Otherwise, they looked almost like twins."

"Which one showed you he had a knife?"

"The fool with the ink on his head."

I tossed the last two rolls—four fifties. Then I told him, "We could find you again."

He shrugged. "Maybe. Maybe not. Doesn't matter—what I just told you is gospel. And I'll throw this in for free: We're only about fifteen minutes out from the next slowdown. Hop off and lay low until dark. That's when the next one's coming through, going back the way you want to go."

Mack and I found a nice spot to wait.

Not for some incoming freight that wouldn't be around for a good ten hours—for Dolly to come and pick us up.

We used the time to let those removal patches do their work. I didn't mind the Nazi ink. Camouflage is camouflage. I didn't like rolling myself in jungle-dropped dung years ago, but I'd done it. A merc I worked with once explained about stillness—it's not enough to slow down your heart, take only shallow breaths through your nose, and cover yourself with vegetation; you have to blend in so deep that you're not giving off human spoor. But I could see Mack couldn't wait to get that foul ink off his body.

"He was running," I told Dolly. "And the people chasing him were the same ones who visited the skinheads in Vancouver.

"So he was moving south, and they must have caught up with him somewhere close to here. Done the job here, anyway. I said it'd take at least two; three would have made it easier."

"You know what they look like now?"

"Nothing worthwhile. The description we got would fit damn near any of them. Even the guy who inked the side of his head—there's plenty who do that."

"They could be anywhere by now," Mack said. "Probably north or east of here, but even that's not any sure thing."

"This is," I said. "They were chasing the dead guy. And when they found him, they killed him. It doesn't sound personal."

"They weren't bounty hunters," Mack said. "Not with all that—"

"No, they weren't working for money. But they did sound like a specialized team."

"I think so, too," Dolly added.

"Why?" Mack asked her. I could hear the surprise in his voice—surprise that Dolly would know anything about hunter-killer teams.

"They put in a lot of miles chasing him," she explained, ticking points off on her fingertips. "A lot of time, too. If they had a car, it was one they could drop off and pick up later. That's teamwork, right there—because, every time they made an appearance, it was all three of them, okay? But the *way* they killed him, that's really the key."

"Bashing his head in?"

"They didn't bash his head in," Dolly said, firmly. "It was a single strike. Very precise, and absolutely silent. And they used a weapon that's not illegal to carry around, so even if they were stopped they couldn't be held."

"They could be if one of them had wants or warrants out," Mack said, like Dolly wouldn't know that.

"Which means they didn't," I said—quickly, before my wife got . . . the way she can get sometimes, even with people she liked. "And what I said before, about them pretty much looking like a thousand others, that's a blend-in they'd *need* if they're really that specialized," I added.

"So they got the job done and—what?—split up?"

"Or stayed together," I told him. "It doesn't matter. What we know they *didn't* do was stick around. And you can bet your life they all have alibis covering them before, during, and after."

"Fuck!" Mack muttered.

I didn't have anything to add to his bleak summary.

"**W**e're not giving up," Dolly said.

Mack waited until he'd swallowed another bite from the sandwiches Dolly made us eat. She'd taken a fresh baguette, cut off the ends, scooped out the insides, and stuffed them full of this salad she makes out of fresh-caught tuna, leafy greens, and red onions.

"Then . . . what?" is all he said.

Dolly kind of wheeled in my direction. Meaning I'd better come up with something. Quick.

Thing is, I had. All I did was say it out loud: "Isn't there a cop, a detective? Lancer, I think his name is."

"Yes," my wife said. Meaning: Yes, there was a cop she trusted.

"With Mack's knowledge—about Homer, knowing him personally, I'm saying—and some reconstruction work, maybe we can convince him that they're holding the wrong man."

"You know this place," Dolly said. "The DA's already had his little press conference. We'd need more than one cop who—"

"Lancer doesn't like that piece of weak pastry," I cut her off. "He'd go on record saying Homer couldn't have done it. If we really convinced him, that is."

"He would," she agreed. "The cops don't have much use for the DA generally, and they all respect Lancer. But that *still* wouldn't get Homer out."

"I don't think so, either."

"Then . . . ?" she said, struggling to keep her hands off her hips in front of company.

"If this wasn't personal, the team hunting the dead guy, somebody had to send them."

"What, Skinhead Central?" Mack said, just slightly to the side of sarcasm.

"I did some reading," I said, ignoring his tone. "On the library computer. There was a killing in Portland quite a while back, maybe twenty-five years ago. Some kind of new-style Nazis beat a black guy to death. For no reason, just to fly their flag. The guy they killed was from Ethiopia, but this was before all this 'blame the immigrants for everything' stuff made it over here; the killing was just about his color.

"They all pleaded guilty. Anyway, the man who set them in motion, he wasn't even in the state when it went down. And when I say 'man,' I mean a guy twice their age."

"Did he go on trial with them?"

"No. They all took pleas. The one who got the longest sentence died in prison. Not the way you might think—some disease he picked up.

"A few years later, one of this older guy's followers testified that it was him—the older guy, I mean—who had pretty much told them what they had to do. That turned into a different trial. A civil lawsuit. The family of the man who was killed, they sued him. And the jury ruled against him. Couldn't put him in jail, but they bankrupted him, even took the house he owned."

"Okay . . ." Mack said, slowly. "But even if there's some kind of big boss who sent those three guys out to hunt this guy down, you're saying we'd have to not only catch those guys, we'd have to prove they did it. We wouldn't need any lawsuit to—"

"That lawsuit was enough to show the feds somebody was pulling the strings."

"So what?"

"So it's something they'd file away and remember. The feds have limits to their jurisdiction—they can only work inside America. Sometimes that helps them. The World Trade Center, they made sure the CIA took the blame for that. Bad intel, they should have seen it coming . . . whatever."

"That's a pile of—"

"What difference? You think the CIA didn't blame the FBI

for Oklahoma City? But that backfired—they haven't had so many politicians looking the other way since Hoover. Home-grown terrorists, they scare the hell out of people—people who vote. It'd be a lot easier for the FBI to infiltrate some White Power organization than any Muslim one, so funding for that *alone* has to be way up, and they'd do just about anything to keep that faucet flowing. But they haven't shown much return on the investment, and they could be getting desperate."

"Still, so what? It's not like we could just go to the nearest FBI office and ask them if they heard anything about a murder in some little town. I mean, we could, but no way they'd talk to us."

"I might know somebody," I said, feeling my wife's hands on my shoulders.

```
|>White Power org, prob West Coast. Identifiable
leader. Financed well. Source unknown. Seeking
hunter-killer team, mission just completed, this
area. If org already infiltrated, traffic intercept
possible?<|
```

When I'd first started getting buy-or-sell instructions on gold futures, whoever was sending the messages had been plugged in everywhere. All he'd ever asked of me—and that was years after getting the financial instructions that made it unnecessary for me to work—was to go back to work. One job only.

Refusal was out of the question. Not because this man was connected to the ID genius who'd made a past life for me and Dolly both. No, in my mind—maybe in my heart—it was as if Luc was calling out to me.

"They're gone," I told Dolly, when I sat down in the kitchen. "And they won't be back."

"You're sure?" she asked, the way she held her head telling me she wasn't expecting Mack to answer the question.

"I am," I told her. "They were tracking that guy whose body washed up on the beach. I don't know where he started from, but for sure he passed through Vancouver, heading south. I think he got way past here—maybe even down to California. But then turned around and came back this way. I don't know if he was trying to shake off his pursuit, or found he wasn't welcome where he first stopped."

"So there's nothing special about it happening here? This is just where they caught up to him?"

"That's right. So why would they stay around? They could be anyplace by now. Maybe even split up. Depends on whether they're a working team or just three different men recruited for this one job."

"So what do we—?"

"Can you get hold of a few skulls?"

"Like . . . specimens, you mean?"

"No. I know you can just buy those. But if you're going to try and sell Lancer on a reconstruction, they wouldn't be any good."

"How come?"

"The skulls you can buy, they come bleached. That's okay, but they also come hollow. So if you hit them with that mountain ax . . ."

"They'd shatter. Okay, I see what you're saying, but . . ."

"We'd need a cadaver."

"Dell," she said, very softly.

"What?"

"I trust Lancer enough to say he's an honest cop. One with

a conscience, too. But the key word is still 'cop.' And I don't trust him *that* much."

"I wasn't going to bring him a new body, baby."

"What, then? Go grave-robbing?"

"No. That's too much risk. But the coroner's office—"

"Even if you could get in, what if the dead man's family wanted to bury him? You know, have a ceremony and everything? If the corpse turned up missing . . ."

"Couldn't we find out which ones don't have family? Or the ones supposed to be cremated?"

"Maybe . . . But that's almost as big a risk. Just asking around, I mean."

"No, it's not," Mack said. His voice was lower-pitched than Dolly's, but no louder. "The morgue attendant, the guy who works nights, he's . . . bent."

"You mean he'd take money to—"

"No." His cut-off was knife-edged. "I mean he . . . he plays with the bodies."

"How could you know that?"

"I'm not supposed to. But remember, I've got a private practice, too."

Dolly and I waited, long enough to be sure Mack wasn't going to add anything. We could take his word or not—and he'd already shown enough to erase the "not."

I knew Dolly trusted Mack, or this whole mess never would have started.

But I didn't know how deep that trust ran, and it was past midnight before I could ask her.

We were in bed. Rascal was in his spot, just outside the door that we never closed. Perfect guard position. I'd like to say I'd trained him to do that, but he'd picked it himself. Even when I got him a beautiful piece of sheepskin to sleep on and placed it near the bed, he'd just picked it up in his teeth and dragged it over to where *he* wanted it.

That shelter-rescue mutt was the second-most-stubborn thing in our house.

The bedroom was at the end of a long corridor, behind two corners. Its row of long and narrow windows were all above us, on the slanting roof. We could open them by pushing buttons, and they had screens, so we almost always had perfect ventilation.

The windows were too narrow for a man to climb inside, but plenty wide enough to shoot through. And even if someone managed to get past all the other stuff I had in place, the only way to reach the windows would be to get up on the roof from the other side and then move down. No way to do that quietly, or without tripping the sensors. And what looked like cedar-shake shingles just above those slotted windows were slicker than greased Teflon.

The *most* stubborn didn't make an appearance until I put a couple of baseball grenades on a little shelf next to my side of the bed—the one closer to the door.

"No" was all Dolly said.

"They're just in case—"

"I know what they're for, Dell. And I can live with everything else you've got stacked around here. But if a whole squad charged down the corridor, and you . . . used those things, Rascal would get blown to bits, too."

"He's a soldier, honey. He's got to do his job. You see the way he keeps moving back into position, no matter what I do."

"No."

I hadn't wasted my breath trying for the third "no." Dolly had every kind of animal you could imagine out back—thuggish jays, crow-raven hybrids, chipmunks the size of squirrels, at least one covey of quail every season, a mated pair of white doves, even a damn woodpecker that kept trying to hammer his way into the wooden beam between the roof and the walls until I built him a few nesting boxes in self-defense. It was like a game preserve out there, everything growing wild.

But this alone wouldn't have been enough to attract all those different creatures. Dolly and Rascal split that job. Dolly threw buckets of peanuts—what she called "slopping the jays"—kept dozen of feeders full, even planted butterfly bushes and separate clumps of fuchsia so the hummingbirds had enough room to set up their territories without buzz-bombing each other. Dolly hated it when any of the creatures got into fights.

Rascal only had one day-job: keep the place a cat-free zone. Even if he was snoozing in the condo-sized doghouse I'd built for him, the instant he heard the birds screech a certain way, he'd bolt out like a feline-seeking missile.

That mutt was equal-opportunity homicidal. He'd treat a feral cat skulking the same as he would some fancy-breed thing prancing around like royalty—if Rascal nailed it, it was a goner. I couldn't tell one jay's screech from another, but Rascal could. Dolly, too, kind of—she'd ignore them when they just wanted more food, but she'd be outside in a second if she heard them going at each other.

The night cats weren't Rascal's problem. Around here, you could find any of those, from a lynx to a mountain lion. But Rascal wouldn't budge when they howled. Maybe he figured the smaller creatures knew how to look out for themselves after dark, but, me, I didn't think he gave a damn. His job was to protect the birds in daylight, and protect Dolly at night. And no matter what Dolly said, I knew his truth: Rascal was a soldier, and his mission was no less sacred to him than La Légion had demanded of us.

I closed my eyes and tried to put my mind in a place where I could decide if Mack was the same.

"**D**ell . . ." A sweet, soft whisper.

But this time, she didn't snuggle into me and fall asleep like she'd just been hit with an anesthetic. "What is it?" she asked.

"I'm just thinking, honey."

"About me?"

"I always do."

"I mean, right after we . . ."

"I don't know what I think about then. I guess I don't think at all."

"Your heartbeat is the same," she said, one side of her head against my chest. "But that doesn't tell me much, not with you."

"It's possible . . . just *possible,* okay?"

"What is?"

"That I could find out who killed that Nazi. But that might take too long."

"I don't understand."

"We know Homer didn't kill that guy. The cops have to know that, too. But what're they supposed to do? The DA isn't going to let Homer loose. You know how he is—all he wants to do is keep people happy."

"They couldn't convict him; you said that yourself."

"And Mack said Homer wouldn't last long in a mental hospital—that's got to be a dangerous place for a guy like him."

"But the only way they boot him out of jail is if—"

"That's why I'm telling you it would take too long, *ma chérie.* Even with Mack visiting him, Homer's not going to keep it together where they've got him now, not for months and months."

"But he won't have to," my wife said. "The DA will just hold a press conference and say the crazy man who did that terrible thing has been removed from the community. Who's going to question that?"

"By now, they know this 'Welter' guy they found on the

beach was an ex-con, with White Power tattoos. Probably a lot of people had a reason to kill him. And it's not like there's any outsider looking close. The papers here, they just print whatever that little weasel hands out."

"That's what you mean by solving it?"

"Yes. The guy who got killed, he'd only been out of jail for— Damn!" I snarled at myself. "Dolly, I'll be back in a few minutes."

"It's the middle of the—"

"I'm only going downstairs, honey."

"Oh."

```
|>No longer seeking team. Their mission com-
pleted. Target: Welter Thom Jordan, 33, M/W. 2
prison terms, assault, last one "hate crime." Only
questions now: (1) Infiltrated? (2) Info + Traffic
Intercept?<|
```

"See?" I said to Dolly as I got back into bed a few minutes later.

"What's next, Dell?"

"Depending on what I get—what I find out, I mean—I'll know how fast we can solve this . . . or even if it can be solved."

"And if . . . ?"

"There's one sure way to prove Homer didn't kill that guy he found on the beach. Only one sure way to stop the DA from holding that press conference."

"I don't understand."

"Yeah, I think you do. You just don't like it."

"If you're saying—"

"Here's what I'm saying, *ma petite.* You think Mack's important to this whole . . . 'community' or whatever you call it, yes?"

"He's vital."

"Because of what he does. And who he does it with, yes?"

"Yes."

"So, if he's not here, the town deals with all these homeless people different, right? They leave all that to Mack, instead of just rounding them up and shipping them off."

"There's plenty that still want to do that. If they can say one of those people Mack was . . . handling, I guess you'd call it—if they can say one of them turned out to be a killer, a crazy killer, they'd *start* with them . . . and I don't know where they'd stop."

"And, personally, you consider him *un homme d'honneur*?"

"*Oui.*"

"Depending on what I . . . what I find out, we may have to see if that's true."

"**Y**ou're my friend," Mack said to me the next morning. "That's why you're with me. Just hanging out."

"What's my name?"

"It doesn't matter. You'll see what I mean, soon as Khaki shows up."

"Khaki?"

"That's what he calls himself, so that's what we call him."

"And you're sure he's going to—"

"This is Thursday. Soon as the sun moves a little more west, he'll be by. This is his route—he's locked into it."

I didn't say anything. Mack didn't know me well enough to understand that when I don't have anything to say, I just go quiet. "He's not dangerous," he assured me. I got the impression it was something he said a lot. *Had* to say a lot.

"Okay."

"I'm serious. I wouldn't want you to misinterpret—"

"You're in charge."

"Sure. Only, I could feel you go into—I don't know what to call it—some state of calm, like when people meditate. But I know you weren't doing that."

"I'm just relaxed."

"No, you're not. I've never seen you relax. But, like on that freight, you were in a different . . . mode, is the only word I can think of."

Dolly said he'd never been a soldier, I thought. *Still, he picks up on where I go when I don't know what's coming but I know I might have to kill it.*

Before I could say anything, Mack's chin moved up slightly, just enough to tell me he'd spotted the man we were waiting for.

He looked pretty normal to me, except he was a tick off everywhere: wearing what looked like moccasins, blue jeans, a khaki jacket . . . and some kind of flimsy pink scarf tied around his neck. He walked purposefully, but his hands weren't in sync with his feet. The right hand especially—it was twitching like an electric current was passing through his arm.

Mack stood up, so I did, too.

"Hey, Khaki," Mack called out.

The man came right up to us. "Hey, Face," he said. It took me a second to register that this was his name for Mack.

"This is my—"

"Commanding officer," he finished the sentence. "I know who Major Hannibal is."

I started to stick out my hand for him to shake, but his right hand flew into a military salute. What could I do but return it? His eyes were like dots of brown mud. And his right hand had stopped twitching. I snapped my hand down first. Protocol.

Mack sat on the grass, folding himself into a lotus position the crazy guy did his best to imitate. I didn't know whether to side with him or with Mack, so I acted as if I couldn't get the position right, either.

To this guy, Mack wasn't military—or at least not an officer—so no salute for him. I went along with whatever connection the crazy man thought we had between us.

I guess it worked. I could feel him ease into our triangle.

"How's the new place working out?" Mack asked.

"It's a lot nicer," Khaki assured him. "I still hear them, but it's like they're . . . coming from farther away now."

"Quieter, too?"

"I . . . guess. It's hard to tell. I mean, they never shouted, even . . . before. But they don't . . . I mean, they still tell me the same things, but they don't come in so . . . frequently, maybe?"

"On their way out, maybe?"

"Maybe . . . but they still hate me."

"Is that what they say?"

"Say? Oh . . . no. No, they don't have to say it. I mean, when they're always telling you that you're so disgusting it would be better if you . . . You know."

"But you haven't even tried, Khaki. Not for a long time now."

"I'm not gonna, either, Face. What you said, right? If they hate me, why should I do what *they* want?"

"That's part of it."

"I know. There's the medicine, too. I have to take it to keep them from getting all the way inside my head. I can still hear them, but not from the inside, like before."

"That's what not being so close means, Khaki. Didn't I tell you it would be like that?"

"Yep."

"And remember, every time they move even a tiny bit more away, the harder it is for them to come back. They're already outside your head; you can only pick them up with your ears. You keep this up, and someday you won't be able to hear them at all."

"I know! It's like a . . . I don't know what to call it. When I first heard the voices, my family didn't know what to do, but I could see how afraid of me they got. I tried to tell them. I tried to tell them a thousand times—it was in my head. But they didn't understand. They just sent me to a doctor. I thought that was so I could go back to college, but it was a trick! I ended up in that—"

"You're not there, anymore," Mack cut him off. "You're with me." Then he took in a deep breath through his nose—I could hear the whistle, but I couldn't tell if the other guy did—held it for a few seconds, then made a kind of humming sound as he let it come back out.

Khaki immediately did the same thing. Whatever it was, the pressure dial on his speech—the one that I could hear getting close to the redline—moved back down.

"I'm not in any hospital now," he said, proudly.

"And you're not going to be again, either," Mack said, not in a soothing tone, just a man stating a fact. "All we have to do is keep working. Remember—"

"If you're moving forward, you can't be moving back." Khaki stepped in, even prouder than he was before.

Mack extended his fist. Khaki tapped it with his own.

Mack got to his feet. Khaki and I followed.

Mack took a cell phone out of his pocket, held it up.

"I know," Khaki said, touching the chest of his jacket. He turned to me, said, "Major!" and threw another salute.

I returned it. Then pulled it back and said "Dismissed!," hitting the second syllable a little harder.

Khaki executed a nice about-face and marched off.

"Face?" I said to Mack.

"From *The A-Team*."

I gave him a blank look. I wasn't faking it.

"It's a movie. Before that, it was a TV show. 'Face' is a part of this team of do-gooder mercenaries. There's four of them: a lunatic who can fly anything, a black guy who's seriously strong, a good-looking guy who works all kind of scams. And the man in charge, the Major, his name is 'Hannibal.'

"Khaki's been calling me 'Face' for a long time. Ever since we got him stabilized. I guess he named you, too."

"There's some logic to all that, right? I'm older than you. I'm not black. And I don't act like a lunatic. So what's left?"

"You just hit on it," Mack said, half smiling. "Khaki doesn't act like a lunatic, either. Not anymore, he doesn't."

"So moving those voices farther away, it's like taking territory?"

"Taking it is one thing," he said, not smiling anymore. "What Khaki has to learn is how to *hold* it. He was a junior in the honors program at RPI before his symptoms got too strong to disguise. He's in his late thirties now. He moved as far away from the voices as he could—his family's all in New York. His major was engineering, so physical distance made sense to him."

"But the voices came along."

"Yeah. When they were inside his head, how could they not? But you know what? At some level, he knew the truth."

"You lost me."

"His family has plenty of money. After he was hospitalized over and over without any lasting change—he'd go off his meds pretty quick—they made this deal with him: he'd go away, they didn't much care where, and they'd pay his rent and whatever else he needed—but he had to *stay* away."

"I still don't get what this 'truth' is, the one that he kind of knew about."

"I spoke with his mother. Just on the phone, but that was enough," Mack said, back to that flat tone. "I don't know what they did to him when he was a kid, but I don't think it was physical. Or sexual. Probably thought they were 'motivating' him. You know, 'to live up to his potential,' right? But they cut into him—the words cut into him—so deep that they took root. Even when his parents weren't around, he could always hear the voices. When he started doing bizarre things to make the voices stop, he got his diagnosis."

"Schizophrenic?" I guessed. Actually, it was the only diagnosis I'd heard for any of Mack's clients.

"Yeah. And he is. Now and forever. But that doesn't mean he can't live a close-to-normal life. He's smart, and he can learn. He's already moved a hell of a distance. We just have to be patient."

"And relentless."

"That's my work summed up, right there," Mack said.

Back in his car, neither of us spoke for a while.

That didn't make him uncomfortable, like it does most. After a few miles passed, he said: "You know, you said something before that's been kind of eating at me. Something about how this whole 'kick out the immigrant invaders' thing didn't start here, right? Which means it was going on somewhere else before 9/11. So where was that?"

"You know *The Turner Diaries*?"

"The red book? Sure. A lot of people consider it the White Power bible. I read it, cover to cover. Starts off with what sounds like a government plot to disarm all citizens—that'd be more than enough to set off the gun people all by itself—you know, that 'registration is just a cover up for confiscation' crap. But then it turns into this whole Jewish scheme to kill all white people and turn the country over to blacks. They're just apes, so the whites who survived, they'd end up in charge.

"That book, it didn't really get much attention until they found a copy on the guy who blew up that federal building in Oklahoma City."

"When did it come out? The book, I mean," I asked him.

"I don't know—the seventies, sometime in there."

"Before that, there was this book, *Le Camp des saints,* over in France. All about how immigrants take over the French Riviera and spread out from there—all the way over here—until they're ready to rule the world. The American book, it sounds like the same theme, just put in different words."

"All this to say . . . what?"

"This is a strange place. When the French book came out, it was translated into English. A lot of . . . 'commentators,' maybe . . . said it was racist and all that, but worthy of what the French call *l'art de la discussion.* I don't read all this 'critique' stuff, but I remember hearing people—in France, I'm saying—they thought the book was about how letting immigrants come in was the ticket to Hell.

"Brigitte Bardot was on that team. *Les intellectuels* had a good laugh at that. Plenty of French people support blocking immigration by anyone, Arabs especially. They even have a whole political party with that for a platform. And all you have to do is look at how quick the French army was dispatched to restore democracy in Mali—they say Al Qaeda overthrew that government—then look at a map and see how Mali borders on Algeria. . . . You can do the math."

"You know a lot about France."

"Not so much," I said, confident I had given nothing away—it would be no secret to anyone Dolly trusted that she was fluent in French, or that she'd served with Médecins Sans Frontières. He probably assumed that she'd met me someplace in France.

You can't rely on much from people, but you'll most likely be on the safe side if you float a vague story out there and let everyone fill in the blanks for themselves.

For the teenage girls who always seemed to be around the house, I was kind of a . . . presence. If they thought about me at all, it would be to wonder why a woman like Dolly would have involved herself with an older man, and let the rhyme of "France" and "Romance" work itself through their heads.

As for the teenage boys, they were an inevitability Dolly didn't try to sidestep, but she had rules. Hard, clear rules. If you brought in anything she considered negative—including yourself—you weren't welcome.

The boys usually decided I'd been some kind of soldier. I didn't look old enough to be a Vietnam vet, but I had enough miles on my odometer and enough visible scar tissue that they probably thought I'd been there.

Funny thing is that I actually was. Long after America officially left. But the need for reliable info hadn't gone away just because the uniformed military had.

As we were driving away in that rolling malfunction he called his car, I thought about how Mack had some of the same field skills I did.

Not as fully developed, but I wouldn't have expected them to be—his training couldn't have started as early as mine had.

I remember as if it was yesterday. I'd stepped up to an indifferent man sitting behind a battered wooden desk, politely waited for him to take another drag of his cigarette, and then said, "Is this where I can join?"

He raised droopy eyelids, said, *"Ton âge?"* When I gave him a blank look, he said, *"Dix-huit?,"* making it clear what response he expected. When I nodded, he was all finished with the interview, exactly as Luc had predicted.

Without looking up, the man pulled a bound sheaf of papers from a drawer and tossed them over to me. *"Tu signes là où y a les flèches rouges,"* pointing at the various red arrows and making the gesture for "writing" as he did. After all, I didn't speak French—certainly not *native* French—and he wasn't about to defer to my ignorance.

Thanks to the training I was put through soon after that, I could stay in the same position for many hours, not even my body-smell conflicting with my surroundings. Always waiting, but not always for the same reason. Maybe to satisfy myself it was safe to move. Maybe for the enemy to saunter past, never knowing I was waiting for them, my jungle-length bullpup set to "spray."

And, sometimes, just waiting for my next move to reveal itself to me. Timing was everything—leaving the spot I'd found too soon could be fatal, and leaving too late certainly would be.

For less than a second, I wondered if many other social workers were like Mack. But I already knew the answer: If a soldier couldn't learn those skills, he stopped being a soldier pretty quick. Stopped being, period. But if a social worker couldn't learn them, how would anyone tell? If they never left their offices, how much danger could they ever be facing? And, considering who they worked with, who would give a damn, anyway?

We were on the road, because I'd finally convinced Dolly that all the alternatives were ruled out.

"You said the only way you could convince this detective that Homer couldn't possibly be the killer was to have a cadaver to demonstrate on, yes?"

I just nodded at my wife's question.

"Can you tell me how you would do that? Convince him, I mean."

"It's . . . mechanics. Or kinetics. I'm not sure what label fits, but we know this for sure: Homer is much shorter than the man who was killed. And he's frail as well. For the spike to have penetrated so deeply from a single blow, it would have to be delivered by a man pretty close to the same height as the victim. And to pull it *up* after the strike, by a very powerful man as well. But those are . . . obstacles that could be overcome, so I don't think it would work."

"Why?" she half demanded, as if we already had a cadaver in the freezer, ready for a demonstration.

"An assassin—a trained assassin—could strike from behind a target walking down a flight of stairs. That would both give him the height and also add extra force."

"Homer's not a trained assassin," Dolly said. Stating the obvious, so there had to be another reason for her speaking to me in such a way.

"Homer's insane. An insane person can leap into the air and strike on his way down."

"Dell—"

"How is this not true, *mon cœur*? You have seen for yourself the crazy boys running at machine-gun fire because chemicals have made them believe bullets would pass through them as harmlessly as a butterfly through the air."

"We're . . . You're not there anymore, Dell."

"Everywhere I've been, the more experienced a soldier is, the more he will be afraid of a crazy person. Why? Because a crazy person has no—I'm not sure how to say it—boundary lines, maybe? It's not what they're capable of doing; it's that they're capable of doing *anything*. Who wants to guess? It's so much easier to just step to the side when you see them coming."

"Lancer isn't a—"

"I say 'soldier,' I just mean a man whose life is hunting, or being hunted. In the jungle, there is no law. But in a dark alley, there is no law, either. If a policeman thinks there's something dangerous in that alley, he might just charge ahead. That would be very brave or very stupid. But if someone like me is waiting in that darkness, the end result would be the same."

"You're saying, no matter what we showed him, Lancer might still think a crazy man *could* have done it?"

"Yes."

"You wouldn't have said all that for no reason."

"I didn't. Remember when I asked you if Mack was a man of honor?"

"I remember. And I haven't changed my answer. But you spent all day with him—are you saying you don't feel the same way?"

"No. He must be an honorable man to take the risks he takes for so little money. And to make it his life's work. But I think maybe I did not explain what I meant by—"

"Dell, I know what you meant. You were asking, if he faced going to prison for a long time, maybe the rest of his life, would he talk, yes?"

"Yes."

"I . . . I don't know. I think he would not. If the cause was just, yes, I *do* think that. But whatever you don't want him to tell, why tell it to him at all?"

"Because it is not what he would *know,* it is what he would have to *do.*"

"*Tu parles français. Peut-être pas avec mon . . . allegeance,*" my woman said, a tiny smile starting to coax its way loose. "But I don't speak . . . 'criminal,' maybe? So why all these riddles? Especially from you?"

"Like we talked about before, Dolly, there's one sure way to convince Lancer that Homer couldn't have killed that Nazi. One sure way to convince this whole town. If that happened, the DA couldn't justify holding Homer, yes?"

"Go against the town? Against public opinion? A man who campaigned like a fiend even when he was the only candidate running? Never. But what could be a sure way?"

"Find another Nazi. Take him to the same spot where we know it must have happened. Kill him, throw him in the ocean, and wait for his body to wash up."

"Wash up in that same exact spot?"

"Dolly, you know it wouldn't have to be that precise. Are you really saying, if another man whose body was covered with Nazi tattoos died from the same single-strike blow and washed up thirty miles from here, they'd *still* hold on to Homer?"

She sat down. Twirled one of her auburn curls, the way she does when she's thinking.

Time passed. I don't know how much. Dolly looked up at me. "I know you hate them, Dell."

"I always will hate them. That is my inheritance."

"But you don't even—"

"Only one man ever called me 'son,' Dolly. Not 'son' like I might say to a younger man, especially a less experienced one. 'Son' as if he was my father. He saved me, then he showed me how I could continue that work. To save myself. I never saw him again. But his hate for them is inside me as surely as if I had been born with it."

"And you've never—since it's been us, together, I mean— killed one of them because you hated them all. I shouldn't have even *thought* that, Dell."

I deliberately slid around the question my wife had buried inside her sweet words. "It would take two men. We couldn't lure anyone up to that spot, especially after dark. We'd have to kill him someplace else, wrap him good, and carry the body up to the same spot before we dumped it into the ocean."

"Dell, truly—there's no other way?"

"I'll look for one," I promised. I was heading for the basement as I spoke, so Dolly knew I wouldn't be doing that looking outside the house. Not for a while, anyway.

I opened the line.

If anything was waiting for me, I knew it would be short enough for me to memorize. Not that I'd have a choice—it would self-destruct ten seconds after it showed on the screen.

```
|<Infiltrated. Transmissions to GV regular. Unclear
from content if sender is agent-in-place, or paid
informant.>|
```

"GV" was generic "government." FBI, CIA, Homeland Security, Justice Department . . . a long list of agencies. The odds against them sharing info with each other were too extreme to express.

The shadow-breeze could probably do a trace-back—in America, no agency ever death-wipes data. That's why one moron leaving his laptop in his car could compromise a hundred lives. But if it was a paid informant, there might be a quicker way. I used the coding I knew by heart, typed as quickly as I could:

```
|>Transmitter connected to open cases?<|
```

As always, each word I typed vanished as soon as I hit the space bar after it. So now all I could do was go back to waiting, and hope Mack could keep Homer from falling apart while I did.

I didn't like myself much for doing it, but it had to be done.

If there was one man around here that any White Power recruiter would consider a prize, it was a behemoth everyone called "Bluto." Not to his face—he might get confused enough to break your back.

His real name was Franklin Wayne, and he loved MaryLou McCoy. He was nowhere near the dimwit other high-school kids thought he was, but he was good enough ·at smashing through offensive lines for some "boosters" to get, his father a no-show job and a house to live in, just to get Franklin to transfer to school here.

The thing was, in Franklin's mind, I'd saved MaryLou from a life sentence. Worse, MaryLou loved Franklin, too—even though she told everyone she was gay. Maybe Mack could unravel that last part. What counted was that MaryLou trusted Franklin. I don't know what she might have told him about our Plan B in case her trial hadn't come out the way it had, but I suspected she'd never said a word, protecting him from himself.

Franklin had been a plow mule all his life. Used by everyone for whatever field they needed tilled. Everyone but MaryLou.

And, up to now, me.

He'd done some things to help MaryLou. A lot of things. Things I'd told him to do. But I wasn't giving him orders—once I told him that those things would help MaryLou, he *wanted* to do them. And I hadn't tricked him—without Franklin's help, everything might have come out differently.

I knew I could get Franklin to do some things again. But they wouldn't be for MaryLou. So he'd have to trust me. Which he would, but I couldn't exactly sit down with MaryLou and talk it over first. She wasn't coming "home" on summer vacation. Why would she? Her parents were parasitic filth, her father maybe something even worse. And the baby sister she'd given up her entire future to protect had run off . . . but not before she shoved her contempt for MaryLou in the sobbing girl's face, in front of the whole town. In a place this size, anything a jury saw, the whole town would see.

I knew where Danielle would have run to. I could probably find her if I tried. But I didn't care if she lived or died, and those feelings weren't split fifty-fifty.

There was just no way to talk to Franklin unless MaryLou was in on it. It would have to be in person—Franklin could blurt out something on a cell phone that could cause problems. But that wasn't why I'd asked Dolly to find MaryLou for me. If the woman I loved thought I was even considering using a damaged young man like Franklin in something that could get him killed without getting the approval of the girl he loved first, she might start to reconsider her own feelings for me.

There's some risks I'd never take.

"All Dolly said was that you wanted to talk to me about something," the tall, rawboned young woman with wide-set pale-blue eyes said.

She'd showered quickly after practice, pulled her long dark hair into a ponytail while it was still wet, and walked over to where I'd been waiting.

"And you knew it had to be something too important to talk about over a telephone line."

She nodded. "Franklin."

"Yeah," I answered what had never been a question. I wasn't worried about trusting a woman who knew I'd kept a promise I'd made to her once—a promise to kill a man. It had been the only way I could get her to defend herself.

I am always truthful with myself. I knew that I would have promised MaryLou anything to get her back on mission. Not because I cared about her, but because my Dolly did. Fiercely. And I would happily die a thousand times over before I'd let Dolly's faith that I could "do something" turn out to have been unjustified.

"I tried to get him to come down here himself," she said, wistfully. Then her tone turned cold. "I know I could get him a total ride here, even without him ever going back on the field. All I'd have to do is do a little thinking out loud about transferring back to some school closer to where I came from . . . You know, so Franklin and I could be together. They'd have his scholarship papers waiting before I got back to the dorm.

"I've already set the school record for strikeouts in one season, and I'm going to have the best ERA in the league this year . . . again."

I didn't miss the difference between "where I came from" and "home." Or the bitter flavor of her words. Any athlete of her caliber could write her own ticket—what would an extra scholarship cost the school, compared with what it would be getting—actually, *keeping*—for its money?

So I just told her what I was thinking about. I didn't gloss it, but I underestimated how she'd react.

"And you're telling me because—what?—you think Franklin would have to ask my permission? No, that wouldn't be it—every time he comes down here, sometimes for a whole weekend, it's always 'Mr. Dell' this, and 'Mr. Dell' that. He still thinks you're some kind of magician, the way you saved my life.

"So . . . Ah, okay! The only way you can be sure Franklin wouldn't let something slip if the cops came around asking questions is if he thinks he'd be protecting me. How'm I doing so far, 'Mr. Dell'?" she asked. The bitterness of her tone made it no question at all.

"Bad."

"Really?" she said, her voice now just short of downright hostile.

"Yeah, really. If all I wanted was to make sure Franklin never talked, I'd just make sure he couldn't."

Her blue eyes met mine. Not for the first time. But now she was searching for something else—trying to find my soul.

"You're a real piece of . . . dry ice, aren't you?"

"This isn't about me. Or what I am. I was good enough for some things, wasn't I? I trust you with what could put me away forever, and you get all insane because I trust you with something *else*?"

"When you said you could make sure—"

"Don't be such a little princess, okay? You're not stupid. I could have made sure *you* wouldn't let something slip, too, right? Did I do that? No. But could I have? Sure."

"I'm sorry," she said, holding my eyes, meaning it. That's when it hit me.

"You really do love him, huh?"

"I . . . I guess I do."

"There's no 'guess' on Franklin's part. That's why I wanted you to be there when I break it down for him. What he'd have to do, I mean."

"What would he have to do?"

"Just let some people find him. Find him, and pitch him on joining, the same way the school pitched him on playing football."

"And?"

"And get them to come to meet with him. Or even just one of them."

"That's when you'd—?"

"Yeah."

"No good."

"Just like that?"

"Just like that. They'd never see you coming, I know that. But they'd know Franklin. Know where to find him. Find him *again*, I mean. You're going to be his bodyguard?"

"No. It'd be quick. It has to be quick. Whoever comes to

Franklin with a recruiting pitch the first time—one man or even a few of them—they wouldn't be leaving."

"But what if they, I don't know, had already put his name on a list? You know, like a scout would write 'worth a look,' or something like that?"

"They wouldn't. If they did, and they *couldn't* persuade Franklin to join up, they'd be screwing themselves. At the minimum, they'd lose status. At the worst . . ."

She went quiet.

I waited.

"I've got a better idea," the young woman said.

"**Y**ou're not being straight with me," I told her after I listened to her better idea. "You just want to put yourself into this. Into it deep enough so that Franklin would know that anything he might tell anybody, ever, could be enough to wreck your life."

"Uh-uh. That's not it, not even a little bit of it."

"I know," I said and watched a stunned expression cross her face. "The real reason you want to make sure Franklin never says a word is because you still think I might think I have to . . . protect myself from that possibility."

She shook that off like a fighter who'd been hit hard, but nowhere near hard enough to put him down. "Let me ask you something. If you thought Franklin letting something slip would get Dolly in trouble, what would you do then, *Mr. Dell*?"

I nodded. She was right. And she knew it.

"You really want to be in it, MaryLou? In it that deep?"

"Franklin's been shortchanged enough in his life. I'm going to stand up against that, stand up *with* him—even if it means standing on the tracks with a train coming."

Before I filled Dolly in on what had come of my visit to MaryLou, I made a "wait a minute" signal with my hand, and stepped down into my basement.

I read what was waiting for me, then replayed it in my mind over and over, but I still wasn't sure I understood what the cyber-ghost had told me:

```
|<Not fully infiltrated, but strong data-flow.
Informant not on GV payroll. Run by single opera-
tive, unsanctioned.>|
```

Someone inside the same organization that had killed the man Homer took the watch from had his own personal government handler? And this handler wasn't telling his bosses about the arrangement?

If that was right, maybe this "Welter" guy wasn't the first one the off-the-books informant had murdered? A man like that being run by a government agent gone rogue, it wouldn't be the first time. An agent who could pull that off, he could probably name his own salary, too.

Too many questions. And asking them would tell whoever it was on the other end how confused I was by his message. Not a good idea—it could give the cyber-ghost one of his own . . . like it might be time to disappear.

If that happened, the channel would close, forever. So I tried to show him that I could see the lines clearly, and that I'd always color within them:

```
|>Current exchange rate?<|
```

"**C**razy, stupid little—"

"You were the one who got it started, *ma jeune fille.*"

That seemed to calm her down. A little bit, anyway.

"This is all a chain of protection," Dolly said, grimly. "And that's on me," the woman I loved more than my life said, before I could even ask her what she was talking about. "Mack wants to protect Homer. I want to protect Mack—he protects this whole town—so I get you to sign up. You decide the best way to do that is to . . . kill one of them, so now I have to protect *you.*

"And if that isn't enough of a mess, *your* plan is to lure them out by getting them to recruit Franklin. But you can't do that without signing MaryLou up, too. You don't know anything about women. If you did, you'd have known that what *she* wants is to take Franklin's place! That chain, it's turned into a noose around all your necks. And I did that. Me. I did all that."

"All I did was run it past MaryLou, honey. I haven't put anything in motion."

"Not yet."

"Not yet," I agreed. "But that doesn't mean we're only going to have the one chance."

"Yes? And what is that supposed to mean?" Dolly asked. But at least she was sitting down now, taking a sip from her cup of that bitter tea she likes so much.

"It means you missed one thing—whatever happens from here cuts out the weakest link from our chain."

"What?"

"Your pal. This Detective Lancer. He's not inside our circle. Our circle of trust. So there's not going to be any 'reenactment' scene. Sure, it might prove Homer couldn't have done it, but it would only prove it to *him.* And I can't see him going that far out on a limb. He doesn't like the cowardly little DA we have here—what cop would?—but he's not going public with any Sherlock Holmes stuff. It's not his job to dismantle murder cases . . . especially ones like this, ones where there's no way for the DA to lose."

"Oh."

"Dolly, tell me: you trust Lancer like you do Mack?"

"Don't be silly."

"You see now?"

"See what? That we're back to where I started when I said your plan is to kill *another* one of them just to prove Homer didn't kill the first one?"

"Pretty much," I said, shrugging my shoulders. I can't do that like the French do, can't make it say a dozen things at the same time. But I only needed it to say one.

"**H**ow come you always want Mack to come over after dark?"

"Dell, are you just pretending to be dense?"

"Do I have to?"

"No, *mon brave soldat,*" she whispered, kissing the side of my mouth on her way to dropping into my lap. "When it comes to certain things, you are as thick as concrete."

"You, too," I said. And slapped her bottom.

"Stop that! He'll be here any—"

"So?"

"So I don't want to be all silly when he shows up."

"So just sit quietly. And tell me where I'm so thick."

"Ah, Dell. If you could have seen how some of my girls get whenever Mack comes over, you'd understand."

"He's not all that—"

"Oh, yes, he is!" my wife said, snuggling into me to take any jealousy-sting out of her words. "And I'm not letting any of my girls anywhere near him, not if I can help it."

"He may not be a fossil like me, but he's way too old for them, is that it?"

"Will you *stop*? It's not that. Some of my girls, they've been coming over since middle school. I know some are certainly . . . adults now. By law, anyway. It's not the age difference—how could it be, with me being so much younger than you?" she teased. "But Mack just gets uncomfortable when girls go all goo-goo eyes around him. Maybe if—"

"I thought you used up your supply of unmarried girlfriends when you got Debbie and Dr. Joel together."

"Dell! I did not! I can't help it if—"

"*Tu crois qu'en étalant le beurre tu vas cacher le pain?*"

"Hmmph!"

Before I could translate whatever Dolly's sound meant—she uses it for all kinds of things—Rascal let us know that Mack was pulling in behind the house.

"**W**e have to start from here: we *know* Homer didn't kill that guy."

"That's not where we start," I told Mack. "The DA doesn't have to prove Homer killed anyone. All he needs is for some judge to say he's crazy. As far as the whole town's concerned, that's the same as saying he's guilty. Another major victory for the DA. Another load on that 'cooperation between agencies' pile of crap he's always pitching."

"Yeah, I get it. What you said before, right? The only way to get Homer released—*really* released, so he's back to where he was when they picked him up—is to prove someone else did it."

"How many on your caseload?" Dolly asked. Trying to divert him from walking the same road she knew I was going to?

"I don't know, exactly. The Medicaid disability reimburse-ment is the official head count. But that just covers the permanent homeless, the shelter visitors, and the people who live in the residence or with their families."

"Just?" Dolly said, smiling at him like he was being too modest.

"You mean the jail? That's a variable. When they get a guy who's so off-the-wall that they pick up on it right away, they'll stick him in a camera cell, put him on suicide watch, and give me a call. I could get three the same night, or none for a month."

"And the freelance stuff?" she said, still smiling.

"That's only—"

"Every day. Or night. Nobody's paying you to hang out with some of these kids. How else would you have known the nearest place to find skinheads?"

"I don't spend that much time . . ."

"Yes, you do," Dolly said, her tone saying it wouldn't be a good idea to argue with her.

Mack just nodded. Probably knew more about women than I did at his age. *Probably? Who am I kidding?*

"Maybe it's time to think about triage," I said, knowing Dolly would get what I was saying.

She did. "You mean just—"

I cut her off, turned to Mack: "If you get yourself in trouble trying to protect Homer, you risk everything you're involved in. It's taken you years to get so much traction in this place. I don't mean with the homeless, or . . . the mentally ill, or anyone like them. I mean with the people who run the show. You wouldn't just be cutting your connection to the people you work with, you'd probably be cutting all the programs, too. Not just cutting them down, cutting their throats."

Mack's face set itself in hard, sharp lines. "I'm not just walking away. It's not that there's anything special about Homer. It's just me. Walking away, I can't do that."

My wife turned to me. Said, *"Tu n'abandonnes jamais ni tes morts, ni tes blessés, ni tes armes,"* her voice heavy with sadness.

Never abandon your dead, your wounded, or your weapons. The code of La Légion. And she'd gotten it right—Mack was hell-bound to save Homer, and he lived under the same code I once did, except that he wasn't following any orders but his own.

She twisted on the seat of her chair to face Mack. "But you see what Dell's saying?"

"Sure."

"So isn't there a line somewhere?"

"I'm not sure what you're—"

"We take it as far as we can without putting everything else you're doing in danger."

"How would I know where that line would be?"

"You'll know," I assured him, now back on familiar ground— Mack probably knew more than me about a lot of things, but he'd be lost in the jungles I'd worked for so many years. "You'll see it for yourself, as clear as neon at night."

"**W**hat I said to him, that goes double for you," my wife told me, the second Mack closed the back door on his way out.

"Pick a square and stand on it, honey."

"What's that supposed to mean?"

"You think I'd give a damn about some Nazi being killed? Or some crazy man who might have to go to the state hospital? No. So why am I in this at all? You know why, and you know I've already done some things—"

"What things?"

"Things that had some risk to them. But only *while* I was doing them. Now I'm done. In the clear.

"But MaryLou knows something's up. I'm not saying she'd talk—it'd take a lot more than threats to scare *that* girl—but if she thinks Franklin might get dragged into . . ."

"I never meant—"

"You meant to protect Mack, baby. And the work he does. You put your faith in me. What was I supposed to do, use my influence down at City Hall? Hell, I wouldn't even know who to bribe."

"Stop it!"

"Stop what? Stop trying to help Mack get Homer out, or stop reminding you that I only got into the whole thing because you wanted me to?"

I wouldn't have been surprised if Dolly had thrown a punch at me—she'd done it before. But I wasn't ready for tears.

"I shouldn't have ever said a word, Dell. I'm sorry. I never meant for you to be in any . . ."

"I know," I said, speaking the truth to set up the forthcoming lie. "But now that I see how important Mack's work is, I want to help him." Then I covered the lie with a blanket of total truth: "I'll be careful, little girl. Very, very careful. You know I'm good at that."

|<Exchange rate dependent on routing.>|

There's more than one level of cryptographer. The reason this leave-no-trace safecracker had gone undetected was not only his masterful touch on the dial, but his knowledge. He knew—and had warned me—that, no matter how well shielded, *any* traffic could be intercepted, even his own.

Now that everything is stored in some data bank, somewhere, getting in wasn't a problem for him. That "cloud" created for data backup just made his work easier. But all traffic is monitored for "chatter." So, even if someone was listening, his own communications were always designed to be read as if they weren't coded.

"Dependent on routing" could only mean one thing—if someone inside the Nazi organization was informing, he was also being *kept* informed. So the payoffs depended on who was getting them. But what kind of agency man would hand over info to any of the same people he was supposed to be keeping under surveillance?

I had to be very careful, just as I'd promised Dolly. So all I sent back was:

```
|>Employee discharged prior to retirement?<|
```

The young man was a few inches taller than me, and at least a hundred pounds heavier, none of it fat. He was holding a huge tree's bole in both hands, gently lowering it into the earth. I treated the operation with the respect it deserved, standing quietly a few feet away.

Franklin patted earth into place. Then stepped back to make sure he'd handled it perfectly. That's when he spotted me. "Mr. Dell! MaryLou said you'd be—"

"I know," I said, speaking extra softly so he'd lower his voice. Any sound coming from Franklin's double-barreled chest would carry a long way, and any excitement amped it way more than usual. "Don't get fussed, Franklin. I know she told you not to talk with me about anything important unless she was there, too."

"Yes, sir. But I told her she didn't need to worry. I'm a big boy now"—not a trace of irony in his words—"and I know I can always trust you, Mr. Dell."

"That's okay, Franklin. You can't blame MaryLou. She knows you can look after yourself. It's just how women are."

"Really?"

"Sure. Didn't your mother—?" Immediately cursing myself for opening that can of dirt. Franklin's mother had no love for her "retard" of a son, but sure found a *use* for him when his football skills earned his worm of a father a no-show job . . . the only one he was qualified for.

"My mother?" The giant looked at me as if I'd lost my mind. "She knows I can look after myself."

Easy enough to translate: *What other choice did I have?*

"Sure. What I meant was, there's no reason to worry Mary-Lou. I only stopped by to see how you were doing."

"He's doing just damn fine," a voice snarled behind me. "And he'd be doing even better if guys like you didn't stop by for a chat while he's working."

Spyros, the horticultural wizard who didn't much care for humans but loved plants, especially trees.

"What other guys?" I asked, not smiling, so he'd know it was a question, not some banter.

"You, you're enough, all by yourself," he said, changing his tone from snarl to sour. And telling me nobody else had been around lately, too.

"Mr. Dell's my friend," Franklin said. His voice still quiet, but now it was as muted as a heavy crowbar.

I could see Spyros deciding how to play this: he didn't like seeing me come around, but he knew Franklin would jump to my defense as quickly as he'd defend Franklin himself if anyone got stupid and called the giant by anything other than his name.

"Yeah, well, Franklin's working, so . . . ?"

"Couldn't I take my lunch break a little early today, Mr. Spyros?"

"Sure," the old man said, grateful that the giant had shown him a way out of the closing vise—his ego on one side, and my presence on the other.

"I don't think MaryLou understands," the giant said.

His lunch box sat next to him on the downed limb of a dead tree, unopened.

"What doesn't she understand?"

"That she doesn't have to . . . protect me, I guess. I mean, that should be my job, shouldn't it, Mr. Dell? To protect her?"

"Franklin, listen close, now: MaryLou absolutely, positively knows you'd protect her. Anytime, anyplace, any*how*, okay?"

"But, then, why would she have to be here just for me to talk to you? About anything important, I mean."

"Because she thought what I wanted to see you about was something that involved her, too."

"Is MaryLou—?"

"MaryLou's fine," I said, trying to keep Franklin from going off the rails. If he thought MaryLou was having trouble with someone at her school, he'd be in his truck and rolling before I could finish another sentence.

"Then why *did* you come over, Mr. Dell?"

"Dolly wants to put some kind of tree—a Japanese something?—out back, but she's not sure if it'd survive in heavy rain. So I told her I'd ask you."

"Me? Not Mr. Spyros?"

"Sure. But if you aren't . . . comfortable with that, I could—"

"I think she means a Japanese maple," the giant said, back on familiar ground. And secretly thrilled to be consulted. "The kind with red leaves. If that's the one, it'll do great, Mr. Dell. That's a very strong tree."

"I knew you'd know," I told him. "Thanks, Franklin."

As I walked away, I could feel the glow of his pleasure at knowing something of value to me more strongly than the sun on my back.

Damn me and my stupid ideas.

The thought stayed with me all the way back to our cottage.

"Dolly, you think a Japanese maple tree would look nice out back?"

"What? Dell, since when do you care about stuff like that? Besides, you know I'd ask Johnny and Martin"—she never said one partner's name without the other's—"if I wanted anything like that."

"I went over to see Franklin. But once I started talking with him, I realized that it wouldn't be a good idea to get him involved. I had to come up with *some* reason for dropping by, so I told him you were interested in having that tree."

"In case he asks me? Or because now we have to get one?"

"Both."

Dolly gave me a look I couldn't translate. I could feel it on my back as I went toward my basement, too. But it didn't feel like sunlight.

When I checked, there was a message.

I copied it as fast as I could, knowing I'd have to study it for a while.

```
|<Employee not discharged. Working solo.
Trade-off = permit issued circa 2011, No.
095-J-4110-L-671-R. To date, high return on
investment.>|
```

A government spook running an operation solo? Nothing special about that. No cop on any level ever gives up his "Confidential Informant" list. There's no central data bank. Maybe it's all about breaking some spectacular case, getting interviewed on TV; maybe they just don't trust each other. But that "Trade-off = permit" had to be connected to the coding system I'd memorized years before.

So: first number before first hyphen, fourth number after second hyphen, second number after fourth hyphen . . . The code always went on in that sequence for as long as the message ran, but the "R" meant "over."

"Over" was another double-edge: could mean "over to you," or "no more info." Only one way to find out, but, first, I'd have to puzzle this one through so I didn't come off as . . . someone you have to explain things to in detail. The more detail needed, the longer the line has to be open. I didn't know the shadow's limit, but I knew I didn't want to test it.

I stared at the three-digit number I'd pulled out of the message to make sure I had it. Then I went back upstairs.

Dolly was at that huge slab of butcher block she uses for everything from making sandwiches to studying medical charts. It was long enough to ensure that any of that mob of teenagers who always seem to be around in the afternoon during school weeks had a place to sit. A place of their own.

"Does this mean anything to you?" I asked, as I put the piece of paper in front of her, my nose full of the fragrance of her fresh-washed hair—she hadn't yet pulled it back and banded it for working outside, or put it up in a chignon the way she does when she wants to look professional.

"Oh-oh-seven? Are you serious, Dell?"

"Dolly . . ."

"I know," she sighed. "Come on, baby. Double-oh-seven, that's from the James Bond movies."

"Uh . . ."

"Ah, if you'd— Never mind," she interrupted herself. "The spy movies, the fun ones, I mean. There's a whole series. Bond, he works for some British spy agency. And that double-oh-seven—they even call him by that name—it means he's licensed to kill."

"How old is this movie? I mean, when did the series start?"

"I don't know. A long time ago. I can get you the exact—"

"No, that's okay."

"What difference would that make?"

"If that's some kind of serial number, like on a car or a gun, it would *have* to be real old. The seventh Brit spy licensed to kill? That'd be—what?—at least a hundred years ago?"

"It's a *movie* series, honey, not a documentary."

"But this oh-oh-seven thing, most anyone would know what it meant?"

"Everyone but you, I think."

I didn't say anything. Not out loud. I was too busy doing the math in my head: a government-agency man, operating on his own, running a CI? Sure. But giving him a license to kill . . . ?

I went into my den, closed the door, set my oxblood leather chair to near-recline, closed my eyes, and tried again.

When Dolly tapped on the door, I said, "Come in, girl. I was just about to go and get you."

Dolly was ahead of me.

I could tell, because she had one of those small notepads with her, and a gel pen in her hand.

"If you'll just move that chair up straight . . ."

She dropped into my lap while I was still sitting up, legs crossed at the knee, pen poised over pad like a secretary in a bad movie.

"Has there ever been a . . . case, I don't know what else to call it . . . of a government-agency man running a separate operation? I mean, running the whole operation on his own, and—" I dictated.

"A covert agency?"

"At least whatever part of an agency he was in, yeah. But it's probably got to be the FBI or the CIA."

"There's a lot more—"

"Sure. But this would have to be info that was public record. After it was exposed, I mean."

"Ah."

"I don't mean a rogue, Dolly. He'd have to still be in whatever agency *while* he was doing this."

" 'This' being . . . ?"

"Let's say he's got an informant inside some major gang. Drugs, my best guess, but that's only a guess. This is the only part I need: the agency man gives the informant a license to kill."

"How could—?"

"Not a written license. Or even a recorded one. If what you want is maximum infiltration, you'd have to pass certain tests. That's why no agency—not even Interpol—has ever placed a man inside one of the kiddie-rape filmmakers' rings—he'd have to do one of those rapes himself. But no informant would ever be made as a rat if he was killing people the gang *wanted* killed. Even better, if the killings were his *job,* see?"

"I . . . think so. If it was ever a news story, I can find it—I've got full Nexis access now that Gabi is in law school, and I can make it look like a much wider search easy enough."

I didn't know what that last part meant, but I wasn't stupid enough to ask.

In the life I have now, there's never a "nothing to do" mode.

Maintenance is critical to machinery of any kind, whether it's metal or flesh.

Before I stopped working, I'd learned something really valuable from a legendary street beast. He wasn't just another man-for-hire; he'd survived doing his work for such a long time that men doing that same work saw him as a kind of guru. What he told me, I never forgot: "When you can't increase speed, you have to decrease distance."

He wasn't talking about building a better cartridge—there's been stuff good enough to do any firearms job around for a long time; it's only the hobbyists and collectors who want the ultra-exotic stuff. What he was saying is that you're not going to move as fast at fifty as you could at half that age . . . but you can be a lot less visible. In a fight—any fight—the closer you get to your enemy before he knows you're coming, the better your chances.

So I do my exercises, but I don't fool myself. I know things I didn't know when I was younger, sure. But the older I get, the more I rely on weapons other than my hands and feet. Or teeth, if it came to that.

Firearms have to be maintained. Knives, too. Cars. Motorcycles. Scopes. Transmitters. The list is so long that by the time I've run through it completely, it's time to start over again.

I've seen too much to believe in God. I do believe there's such a thing as a random chance that some people call "luck." But I know only a fool believes he can summon it.

So I work very hard to keep random chance out of the picture. The best way to do that is not just to always be ready, but to always be ready to go past any boundaries the targets think *must* be there. Or maybe that's just what they hope, like the guerrilla who surrenders, holding his hands high, desperately trying to convince himself that mercenaries actually take prisoners.

"It only took a few minutes," Dolly said, the second I looked up from the thick pile of paper she had handed to me.

"You mean to—?"

"Going back at least as far as the fifties." She rolled through whatever I was going to say as if I'd never started to talk.

"Dolly . . ."

"The FBI has had informants that they *knew* were involved in killings. Not undercover agents, criminals who got a free pass to kill people, Dell. Or at least be around when that happened."

"You mean, *after* the FBI found out—?"

"No!" she interrupted, sharply. "*Before.* I mean the FBI knew these people were in the business of killing. That they'd killed before, and they were sure to kill again. I guess they thought the information they were getting was so valuable that . . . Well, I don't know how to measure such things, but if an informant's a member of an organization that kills all the time, I suppose whatever that informant turned over would be like having a camera and a microphone planted inside. Planted so deep inside that it could never be detected."

"But sooner or later, they'd have to testify, right? The informant, I mean."

"It doesn't seem so. The FBI had informants inside the Klu Klux Klan back when it seemed like they were lynching black people every week. But the only way that ever got out was when the informant himself came forward. Not out of conscience or anything. Because they were writing a book about it, maybe."

"That was a long time ago, honey."

"What are you saying?"

"I read through some of the stuff you printed out. Informants came out a *long* time later. But those three kids—Schwerner, Chaney, and Goodman, right?—they were murdered by cops. In Mississippi. The FBI says it broke the case—the locals weren't going to even *pretend* to be looking for the killers, so the feds had to step in."

"So? Doesn't that—?"

"In the stuff you pulled up, the FBI itself only drops veiled hints. You know, that they 'reached out to all sources'? And there's other stuff that says a Mafia man came all the way from New York to Mississippi, and tortured the truth out of one of the Klansmen. Scarpa, I think his name was."

"Only you don't believe that?"

"That last part? It's a stretch. There weren't any crime-syndicate guys working closer to Mississippi then? They had to go all the way to New York to find one?"

"Well, maybe they had a reason to use—"

"Damn!"

"Dell? What?"

"I . . . I don't know. Let me see that part again," I said, reaching across the butcher block to extract some of the red-tabbed pages of Dolly's huge printout.

"What are you . . . ?"

"Ssssh," I told my wife. Not a word she liked, but I had to grab that thin thread before it vanished.

It was quiet in the kitchen. Even Rascal flopped down on a mat and closed his eyes.

Then I saw it.

"Dolly, those kids—Schwerner, Chaney, and Goodman—they were arrested for speeding. Cut free a few hours later. After dark. The Klan was waiting for them. Their car was found, burned out. But the bodies weren't inside. Now, look here, it's right on the FBI's own site," I said, my finger on a single paragraph: "Acting on an informant tip, we exhumed all three bodies 14 feet below an earthen dam on a local farm."

"Now, *that* could have happened. Some gangster *could* have tortured the location of the bodies out of someone who knew it. But right on this same page it says eighteen people went on trial but only seven of them were convicted, and *none* of them for murder. A man named Edgar Ray Killen, a Baptist preacher, the FBI says was a major conspirator—he walked free."

"Well—"

"Wait, honey. On that same page, it says he was convicted. Of manslaughter. But not until 2005."

"Mississippi Burning," Dolly blurted out. "That was a movie. I think Gene Hackman was the star. He's a great—"

Catching my look, Dolly interrupted her cinema critique and went back to the facts. "The FBI came back down to Mississippi and reopened the case. And it was a *federal* prosecution."

"When did Hoover die?"

"Give me a second . . ." she said, pounding some keys. "Nineteen seventy-two."

"So—way *before* this happened. I mean, before the movie stuff happened."

"What does that mean? Hoover *was* in charge when they broke the case."

"Before that, what was the FBI doing about . . . that kind of thing?"

"I don't know, Dell."

"Me, either. But what it smells like is that Hoover was kind of forced into whatever he did. All that negative press—not just here, overseas, too. And see, right here? One of those kids, he was *from* New York. A white kid. A white *Jewish* kid."

"What's *that* supposed to mean?"

"It had to be the first time a white man was ever lynched in Mississippi, never mind a white Jewish kid from New York. But it couldn't have been the first time a *black* kid was lynched down there. What I can't see is, why would Hoover subcontract that job to some gangster?"

"The job of—?"

"Torturing someone for information. It's not like the FBI couldn't do that themselves. So why . . . ? Dolly, listen, this Scarpa guy, he had to be someone the FBI trusted. Which means that they had him on a *powerful* leash."

"What possible leash could they ever have? I mean, if he was caught, wouldn't he just tell the truth, even to save his own skin?"

"You just said it," I told her, seeing it myself. "The only way they could trust some Mafia guy is if he was *already* in their pocket. Already feeding info to them. A permanent informant.

"So—first they put together enough to drop him for life. Or even execute him. That's when they tell him, 'You know what, pal? Now you're working for *us*.' If he ever balks, they don't even have to get their own hands dirty. Just let it leak that he's been feeding info. Maybe even point to some boss that's doing time because of this guy's 'cooperation.' That way they score twice—the informant they were running disappears . . . and the mob owes them one, too."

That sent Dolly back to the keyboard, her fingers flying like they were having an epileptic fit.

I just waited.

When she finally looked up at me, there were tiny fire-glints in her gray eyes. "Not so long ago, there were a couple of FBI agents convicted of murder, because they let known killers go right *on* killing, in exchange for feeding them information. Here! Take this new stuff—I'm printing it out now—and read it for yourself."

It took a while, especially with all the flipping back and forth, but I finally put the jigsaw puzzle together.

When I looked up, Dolly was still sitting right next to me. Rascal was chewing on something he'd recently scored.

"So you think they—the FBI, I mean, the whole agency, from the top down—you think they were okay with this . . . policy or whatever, while the Klan was running wild, but not anymore?" I asked her.

"I don't know. And I don't see how it matters. The Internet has more conspiracy theories about the FBI than it does about alien abductions. What I found were cases. Not theories, not speculations, actual cases."

"The informants testified?"

"No. That's not what I mean. I mean *other* agents figured things out. Like if a trap was set—maybe a raid that was about to happen—and everyone *except* a certain person walked into it. A pattern, like you're always talking about, Dell. *That's* when they put in their own wiretaps, started their own surveillance.

"And they heard these gangsters bragging about how they had an agent in their pocket—how they knew they wouldn't be questioned about *any* killing they were going to do, even when they told the agent in advance!"

"Damn."

"Yes. And it's even worse. Police detectives have been convicted of actually committing contract murders themselves. This 'Witness Protection Program' you always hear about? Well, some of the people they put in there, after they testified against their own gangs, they just went right on doing what they'd been doing before."

"Killing?"

"Killing, raping, drug dealing . . . everything."

"That's insane. They had to know if they got caught all bets were off."

"Didn't stop them," Dolly said. "At least, it didn't stop all of them."

"That fits with what I . . . found out myself. Only, I don't know which end it was coming from."

"You lost me," Dolly said, walking over to the refrigerator.

"We know three Nazis were chasing another Nazi, right?"

"Yes," she said, pulling out a blue bottle of that "jungle juice" she drinks whenever she finishes working out.

"They found him, and they killed him."

"Yes," she said again. "Which proves it wasn't Homer."

"That's not enough. It's not even close to enough."

"But if we can *prove*—"

"What can we prove, girl? The dead man's not talking, and the three who took him out are in the wind."

"We have to find them, then."

"Not until we know who we're looking for."

"But you said yourself—"

"I said what I said. Nothing more."

"It sounds like enough to me. More than enough."

"Dolly . . . sweetheart, just listen, okay? If the dead guy was an informant for the FBI—or whatever agency—they'd *already* know who killed him. Even if they wanted to keep out of it themselves, they could have tipped off the locals easy enough. Maybe through the attorney general or something, I don't know. But nothing like that's happened."

"You think they're still—?"

"I'm not saying that. Those Boston gang cases you found, they started out as Rhode Island cases. Rhode Island Italians; Boston Irishmen. The agents who were looking the other way, they were getting value for doing that. At least, that's what they claimed when they were named. It says right here"—I pointed at the printouts—"when one of the Irish guys got caught later, he rolled over, but not on his gang; he blew the whistle on the agents, and they gave him a death-penalty pass for doing that.

"And when *another* gangster who was tight with him disappeared—he was gone for years; they just caught him a little while ago—it sure looked as if *he'd* been tipped."

"So what does that mean? Why does it even matter?"

"It matters because it was the feds themselves who prosecuted those FBI agents. The same way they prosecuted a CIA man who sold info to the other side, not so long ago. It matters because it means the agency itself *didn't* know. So, if that's what this is—the whole business with the guy who got killed, or who killed him—they wouldn't know *now*, either.

"See, this can't be a rogue agent, Dolly. Not a retired guy, or someone who quit. Not in business for himself. Not selling information. And not buying it, either. Just looking the other way when this Nazi—the one he gave that 'license' to—*used* that license. So long as that same guy was feeding him intel on *his* own people, he was free to kill anyone he felt like killing.

"For that kind of deal to hold, he'd have to be handing over *really* good stuff. The kind of info that the FBI would take as *prize* intel . . . like on 'domestic terrorism' plots. Remember what I said about Oklahoma City? The FBI's probably had a whole different take on the 'White Power' groups ever since."

"I still don't—"

"What if the guy who got killed *was* an informant? Not some 'licensed to kill' guy, just the usual kind of rat who sells out his own crew to get a deal? And what if the killer found that out from the same fed who'd given him that license?"

"Then that agent, he'd *want* the killers to get away with it."

"Yeah. But it *was* a homicide, so it's better if it gets solved. And Homer, he's the perfect solution."

"So we could never find them? The real killers, I mean. They might have come from thousands of miles away. Sent over here just to—"

"That's right. They might. But until we know . . ."

"How could we know?"

"Let me see what it would cost first."

```
|>Traffic continuing?<|
```

I looked at what I'd typed before hitting that irretrievable "send." Cryptography is only useful if the recipient can decode it. I read it over a couple of times before I was confident that the cracker would know I was asking if the informant was still in place. Undisturbed. And still working.

Working jungle, you're always doing death math. Hunting those who are hunting you. In La Légion, the mission is always defined. Not by you, *for* you. There is no discussion, no debate. You are not permitted even to wonder if the man walking behind you is . . . reliable.

But mercenaries walking those same trails would always wonder. The mission may be "sacred" to a *légionnaire,* but the only thing sacred to a merc is his own survival. And I had gone from a *"soldat pour l'honneur"* to a soldier for money a very long time ago.

I hadn't worked for money since Dolly had said she'd come and be with me. But that didn't mean I'd let my skills go rusty. Not because I couldn't shake lifelong habits—because I could never know when I might need to do the one thing I was good at doing.

If the informant was still passing info to a government agent, his free pass was still in effect. If he wasn't, it wouldn't be that his license had been canceled, it would be that he had.

Part of death math is patience. Always patience.

But I didn't have to be patient about everything.

Now that I knew that getting Franklin involved was not an option, I had one less card in my hand. I knew Dolly wanted me to do . . . something. But I had to find out how much she was willing to risk before I could move on, no matter what direction the compass needle pointed in.

"Seriously, Dell? I was the one who asked you in the first place."

"I didn't know you were such a dancer," I said, quickly adding, "although you're certainly built for it," to take any sting out of my suggestion that she was sliding around the subject instead of facing it square.

But this didn't even get a smile out of her. And I knew what it meant when she stood up, faced me with her hands on her hips, and pinned me with her eyes.

"If you think I'm not answering you straight, try straightening out your questions."

"All right," I said. "You want Homer out of jail; this I already know. And you also know that the man who was killed was killed by his . . . I don't know what to call them. Friends? Comrades? It doesn't matter. You know that if I start working, some of them may end up dead. And that could happen before I have even a *chance* of getting Homer out."

"They would be no loss. To anyone."

"No," I agreed. "They would not. And you have confidence that I could do . . . something that needed doing without being caught, yes?"

"Oh God, Dell!"

I could handle Dolly's temper—she never meant it, anyway. But her remorse was another thing entirely; it tore at my heart like a barbed-wire garrote. All I could do was hold her. And be patient.

"Il n'y a pas eu d'épouse pire que moi depuis Ève."

"C'est la première fois que tu me mens."

"I'm *not* lying, Dell. I *am* the worst wife since Eve. I didn't even . . . think. Listen to me, now. I'm sorry if this makes me sound cold. Or even crazy. But I want you to stop. Stop right now. If Homer ends up in some hospital, I'll be sad about it, but—"

"But you want me to be careful, I know."

"Now you're finishing my sentences for me?" my ready-for-battle wife challenged.

"I just thought—"

"You can do all the thinking you want, but unless you can read my mind, maybe you could just shut up for a minute!"

I made a gesture, a sorry imitation of how the French can say *"Mais oui!"* with their hands. It didn't make her giggle, like I'd hoped, but at least she didn't look so angry anymore.

"What I was going to say was this, Dell: Yes, I have confidence that you could do . . . whatever you felt was necessary, and no one would ever know. But there's always *some* risk. And even the *tiniest* risk to you isn't worth what getting Homer out would mean to me. Understand?"

"Yes."

She stepped back a pace or two. Looked me over like I was a used car she was considering buying. Then she nodded. "I get it. I get it now. You were going to go on and on, weren't you?"

"I don't—"

"You understand just fine, Dell. If I hadn't just realized what I did when I . . . set you loose, if I hadn't stopped you from saying more, you were going to ask me if I was willing to risk something happening to Mack. Tell me I'm wrong," she challenged.

"Well, he's not trained, and what he does is really important, and—"

"Shut up!" Dolly snapped, punching me in the chest. I've been hit softer by men trying to hurt me. But I'd take another few of the same if only my precious girl wouldn't start crying again.

Dolly turned her back on me. "You really hurt my feelings, Dell. I . . . I can be stupid, I know. But for you to think that I'd be more worried about . . . about anyone more than you, that's just . . ."

I put my hands on her shoulders, trying to think of what words might work. All I could think of was "I never thought such a thing, sweetheart. I couldn't. It wouldn't be you, to think that. All I thought was that you might believe that maybe I'm . . . better at some things than I probably am. To disappoint you would be more than I could bear."

It seemed like forever until she turned around and let me hold her.

"**H**ow bad do you want Homer out?"

"You're not looking for adjectives," Mack said.

I just nodded. I guess that wasn't enough for him.

"Spell it out," he said.

"Some people will do anything if they believe their cause is just. But there's a difference between writing an essay and having a quarter-second to make a decision. You might be against capital punishment, but you wouldn't hesitate to shoot a man climbing in your bedroom window at night."

"You're asking, would I kill someone to spring Homer? Like, do a copycat murder, so the cops would think the real culprit's still out there?"

"The real culprit *is* out there."

"Sure. But that doesn't mean—"

"The guy the ocean washed up, he must have trusted whoever killed him to have let them get so close—and behind him, too. Or at least get close enough to show him a gun, walk him up there. If they did it like that, they'd want him to die quiet."

"What if—?"

"There's no 'if' in this. No way they killed him someplace else—they'd have to haul a dead body all the way to the top of those rocks. That's not just a lot of work; it'd take a lot of time, maybe leave an evidence trail, too. The longer you take to do anything, the better the chance somebody will see you doing it.

"Okay, look. None of that's really important. But this is: the killers weren't hired hands—they had to be some kind of Nazis themselves."

"So you're asking, would I kill one of *them,* then?"

"One or more."

"On my own, or with you?"

"What difference?"

"Morally? None, I guess. But I know you've . . . I know I'd have a better chance of not being caught if you were in on it with me."

"You'd have a much better chance of getting them killed, too."

His silence was my answer.

|<Flow continues. Source>>squad responsible for most recent event>|

Only one way for me to respond:

|>Squad. So why only one target?<|

The answer came so quick that the round must have been chambered in anticipation.

|<Target informing. *Not* to agent, to agency.>|

So the Nazis had made "Welter" for a rat. But instead of some general KOS nonsense, they'd put a specialized squad to work. This Welter Jordan must have known a lot more than a few hand signs and a leadership chart.

And he *had* been running. That made him valueless as an informant, so he couldn't look for any help from whatever agency had gotten his sentence shortened. Which told me he didn't have a sleeve ace—hadn't held back anything. Certainly nothing that would get him any more than some paper ID. That wouldn't be near enough—he'd need plastic surgery for a new face, and even more for a complete tattoo-removal.

I almost laughed out loud when I thought it through—the fool had made a deal to betray his White Power comrades, but all it got him was some time cut off his sentence. And before whatever agency he'd made the deal with turned him loose, they'd already bled him white.

Death math, again. Agencies don't share info. Even when they say they're on the same side, with the same objectives, they're adversaries when it comes to funding. So this "Welter" guy had been turned pretty recently—probably reached out himself, while he was still in prison.

But the steady-flow informant had been in place for a good long while. That explained the difference between "agency" and "agent" in the cyber-ghost's last transmission. Whoever was running the still-working informant must have had access to more than just his own files. So he outranked whoever had turned "Welter." Or he'd accessed files he shouldn't have.

I felt safe ruling out that last one. The shadow who went everywhere without leaving a trail was as high-skill as it gets, so he even tracked changes within internal-control systems. Years ago, he'd warned me that any unauthorized intra-agency access would be picked up instantly, and followed in real time. That's why the cops in L.A. finally lost out on the money they used to make by scouring their data banks for info on movie stars: unlisted telephone numbers, traffic violations, stuff like that.

So the agent was a boss, then. Not a field man.

"You think this Detective Lancer would talk to me?"

"No," Dolly said, emphatically. "Didn't I tell you to—?"

"I'm not going to take any risks, honey. Any at all. I was just trying to figure out, if I walked him through the killing—showed him how it *must* have happened—whether that would be enough for him to look past Homer. But . . ."

"But something else might?"

"I don't know yet. But I keep thinking about a newspaper reporter."

"Around *here*?"

"Maybe not physically. One of those—what did you call them—those Internet people? Didn't you say that they were the only real journalists out here?"

"I . . . guess," she said, dubiously.

If nothing else, planting that idea was good enough to buy me some time.

I don't have any of that "tradecraft" stuff you see in movies.

I'd never been trained to be anything but a soldier. Not even an elevated one. A fighter in the field, not some high-rank boss sitting in a command post.

I sat in my cellar and thought about that. Until I realized I was doing this all wrong.

Feeling sorry for myself, that I already knew was wrong. But it wasn't even close to the edge of how I'd been feeling. When I got close enough to see that edge looming, I realized I was being disrespectful to Luc. And that was unforgivable.

So I burned the self-pity out of my mind the only way I could—by going over the tradecraft I *did* know. The survival skills Luc had taught me. When I first entered La Légion, I'd lied when they asked if I could speak French. The same lie I'd told Dolly when I woke up in that field hospital: *Un peu.*

That was Luc's training, and it encouraged some of the *légionnaires* to say stupid things right in front of me, the way some people make disgusting hand signals in front of a blind man, or twirl their forefingers next to their heads when a retarded person is speaking.

That wasn't all. Luc had taught me to read body language. To watch a man's hands—*"Dans cette ville, tout le monde parle avec ses mains. Ce qui est typique des Français. C'est leur façon d'insister sur ce qu'ils disent. Si les mains d'un homme ne collent pas à ses paroles, on ne doit pas lui faire confiance."* Watch their hands. Not for weapons, but because most people talk with their hands, no matter what the language.

And to know a liar's eyes.

From the moment my military training began, the word I heard most often was *"survie."* Survival. The only god in the jungle. Not a god you prayed to, a god you obeyed.

But I already knew more about survival than soldiers three times my age. Even in a city famous for cheese, a gutter rat will starve unless it can forage. And even the most successful foraging will not feed you if you can't defend what you stole.

"Tu ne dois avoir confiance en personne."

"I trusted *you*," I said to Luc, in the language I knew much better than French. I didn't know why that was—whatever years had been stolen from my mind before I'd fled that "clinic" in Belgium must have been in America, or with Americans. "Doesn't that mean I had knowledge? *Some* knowledge?"

"You had nothing," Luc told me, very calmly. "Including choice. I was an old man. You had been told about old men by other little boys who live in the alleys. It was *them* you did not trust. And you were confident that you could defend yourself, if I turned out to be one of those old men they had warned you about, yes?"

I nodded.

"So! You had no *real* knowledge. Why? Because you had no choices, so anything you might have known was of no value. Even your belief that you could defend yourself against an old man was wrong, was it not?"

By then, I had seen what amazing things that old man could fabricate from scraps others tossed into those same alleys I once foraged in. He knew a hundred ways to kill me. Or cripple me, if that had been his pleasure. So all I could do was nod again.

"You were fortunate, *mon fils*. Nothing more. Lucky. You may never be so again in your life. You know what a man who trusts in luck is called?"

"A gambler?"

"Yes. And *all* gamblers lose. Know that. You would think, the more a man does something, the better he becomes at doing it. That is true. But 'better' is not 'perfect.' Life is not equally *rouge ou noir,* as gamblers believe. That may be true of *all* lives, but you are concerned with only one—your own. And no 'law of averages' will ever help an individual. You must never trust in luck. If you spin that wheel too many times, it will betray you. *That* is the only certainty. And you will never know which spin will be your last.

"So, then, what *can* you trust?" By now, I knew such questions were not for me. They were just introductions to his answers. And this was no different. "Your skills," Luc said.

"What you learn so well that your action comes even before thought. When you have choice—not the gambler's *illusion* of choice; not which color of the wheel to wager on—then you must know *which* choice to make. That knowledge must live within you, and spring forth as naturally as a child's instinct to retreat from cold and move toward warmth."

"How do I learn this?"

"Every mistake you survive must become a mistake you never repeat. Never in your life. You trusted me. As I said, you were not 'right,' you were fortunate. Lucky. So—listen now: never trust another person as you did me, not ever again.

"You can never learn how to trust—to trust another person—unless you first face the world with total distrust. *Tu comprends? Distrust *first.* Then you wait. Use that time of waiting to watch carefully, listen closely, and *then* decide. But know this, my son: no matter how careful you are, *all* trust is some form of gambling. The best you can do is push the odds more in your favor."

Even back then, I knew the old man was speaking the truth.

But there was one truth I'd known long before Luc took me to be his son. A truth known to all orphans, and *only* to us: despite the blather of the café sages, you *can* miss what you never had.

When I decided to go with Luc, that had been more than blind luck. It had been the one true blessing in my life, that I trusted him. Some form of compensation that I deserved, though I would never know how it had been granted.

Until Dolly.

|>Locate?<|

The response was so quick that I was still watching my message disappear when it flashed:

```
|<Seattle. Gomes, Lewis _ Brigham, Alan, now SAC.
Promoted via 3 majors: 13base, cpR, 1388R-latter
aborted.>|
```

I closed my eyes, keeping that message on a screen in my mind as I wrote it down on the pad of flash paper I keep next to the transmitter. Then I began the decoding, writing on that same paper. I had to make sure I got it right before the crack of a wooden match would make all of it disappear.

The informant was Lewis Gomes. Conclusion: he was one of the three men on that hunter-killer squad. He had to be—it was the only way it made sense for him to have access to the kind of info he'd been passing along. Whoever was sending that team out knew they were all killers-for-the-cause. And those killings would make them the last ones ever to be suspected of informing.

And they'd also be the last ones suspected by the government—not with an FBI boss running interference for them.

All FBI men are "special agents," but "Alan Brigham, SAC" meant "Special Agent in Charge Alan Brigham." So Brigham had been running the same "007" informant for a long time, and the "3 majors" that he'd been tipped to had propelled him to that higher position.

The repeated "13" and "R" symbols would baffle decoders, because even a random-number generator required a match at some point. When only a single recipient knew the key, it wasn't a code at all—it was a shared language.

So I knew that numbers always *meant* letters, but that letters themselves took their meaning only from connected numbers, and changed again if before, after, or in the middle of numbers. If letters were not touching numbers in some way, the meaning of the letters themselves depended on whether they were capitalized.

"13" was always "M."

"B" in the upper case signals that it is the first letter of a word that logically follows the word connected with all its preceding numbers, but only if placed at the *end* of a string.

"R" following only lower-case letters means "ring," but an "R" following *numbers* means "race."

I put it together, working slowly and carefully, moving from easiest to decode to most complicated. What I knew was that this "SAC" had received information from Gomes about three operations. No indication whether the operations were planned, in progress, or completed, but one had certainly been "aborted."

If the group Gomes had infiltrated—no, *belonged* to— was neo-Nazi in some way, the "1388R" could refer only to the "Master Race" scenario that ran like a buried power line through all those groups, no matter if they had three members or three thousand. RAHOWA. Racial Holy War. Ice People exterminating Mud People. Restoring the planet to its natural state, the one that god—in some versions, Christ; in others, Odin—intended.

And the "cpR" was also straightforward enough, especially if fitted into an ongoing operation leaked to a government agency. A child-pornography ring wouldn't require the participation of the Nazi group to have its existence known to some of the group's members. And I vaguely recalled that several different "leaders" of such organizations had been convicted of crimes that would fit. Best theory, then: Gomes was the source of information that some *individual* was hooked into a child-pornography ring, and the government took it from there.

"13" was "M." So a word that began with an "M" followed by a word beginning with a "B." Morphine base? When I was still the property of La Légion, it was common knowledge that the opium poppy was easiest to grow in hot, dry places. The paste the growers extracted from the poppies had to be turned into morphine base before it was moved as major weight. Morphine base was like moldable clay . . . and it didn't give off an odor. So it first went to Marseilles for the transformation, that route handled by Corsicans.

What I call "common knowledge" was nothing more than information considered to be of such low value that it was passed along like any other cliché. Everyone said the Sicilians must have some kind of working arrangements to move heroin from France to America—they were already established there, and the Unione Corse preferred the safety of its own territory. Compared with the Corsicans, the clannish Sicilians were warmly accepting of strangers.

At first, the product was sold only to blacks in America, but it spread like any other virus. As the market widened, the blacks were able to wrest control of their own neighborhoods. The Italians were better organized, but they didn't have the endless supply of young men willing to die for a chance to change their fate.

I heard that many died in those wars. I didn't know this for a fact—barroom gossip is just what it sounds like it is—but I knew this for certain: Those who died would have been soldiers, not bosses. Or soldiers who wanted to *be* bosses and let their plans be known too soon.

Just before I quit, the mercenary job board had begun to list work in countries like Colombia and Peru. Those aren't dry climates—better for cocaine, really. But heroin was making a strong comeback. Without the old ten-to-one rule—ten tons of opium makes one ton of heroin—a much purer form could be produced. Naturally, that final product would cost the end buyer a lot more, so the profit margins were probably still worth the risk.

That, too, added up. Among certain people, the perception of "class" is what gives any product its value. Cocaine was once the high-class drug for the trendy "recreational" users, like a party favor. Now it's for crackheads, about as low-class as there is.

But heroin isn't for street junkies anymore; it's for the wealthy. The new, high-purity product can be smoked, using designer-glass pipes. No needles means no risk of infection, and no track marks. A nicer, sweeter high, they claim. I don't know about that, but I do know that the extreme prices high-purity heroin fetches would only make it even *more* desirable to those who make the claims.

But how would a neo-Nazi have information on major shipments of this product? What criminal organization would trust such a collection of . . . ? Whatever the people who joined such groups were, they would share the one characteristic no professional would tolerate—unreliability.

The only possibility that I could see would be that some down-the-line bulk purchaser had enlisted a White Power group as a distributor to end users. But that was off—I could feel it—just not right, somehow.

I closed my eyes to help my mind see better. Huh! Hadn't heroin wholesalers once used motorcycle gangs as distributors? Those gangs wouldn't necessarily be Nazis themselves, but some of their members might say too much if they were in places where they felt safe. Among friends, if not brothers-in-arms.

Pretty much the same for child pornography. Whatever RAHOWA group Gomes belonged to wouldn't have to be participating in some ongoing enterprise for him to *know* about it.

What an informant knows, an informant tells. And sells.

This "SAC" had gotten promoted thanks to information he got from Gomes, but the "Master Race" operation was noted as "aborted." I took that to mean that the informant had passed along enough info for the FBI to stop some massive serial-bombing scheme in its tracks. It surprised me that this hadn't made all the wire services. And *not* taking credit for saving lives, much less stopping "terrorism" in its tracks—that didn't fit, either.

But if the FBI had pulled off a *total* takedown, it made sense that they'd want to keep it quiet. "Aborted" might signal that death was the method the government had used. Now, *that* fit nicely. They wouldn't want publicity for executions, and claiming that a couple of dozen people in different places had all "resisted arrest" simultaneously might be a hard sell.

All guesses on my part, I knew. But I also knew I had no other choice: the cyber-shadow was too valuable to ask for anything I could work out by myself.

And I knew I was expected to do just that.

The blog was called *Undercurrents,* a not very subtle reference to the area it covered . . . and to the fact that there were parts of where we lived that tourists would never hear about.

I didn't know if it was the work of one person with a lot of sources, or a collective of people digging on their own and posting whatever they found. But I knew it was way more popular than any of the local newspapers. Maybe people didn't want to spend their money on "news" when all the coverage they got was of local sports and "the arts."

For myself, I thought it really had nothing to do with not wasting money—there was some online rag you could get for free, but nobody paid much attention to it, either. Since it wasn't a real newspaper, the only way it could get access to anything—especially crime news—was to have that "good working relationship" with the DA's Office.

The print papers could at least sell space—anything from

ads for local businesses to extra-fancy obits to houses for sale. And they had to have subscribers—writing "letters to the editor" was a hobby for a lot of folks, and they probably "scrapbooked" all their insights. For all I know, the papers might even turn a profit.

It came down to this: if you wanted anything even pretending to be an "independent investigation," you were stuck with restaurant reviews. And if those restaurants were also advertisers . . .

"Look," Dolly said, pointing at the screen of the tablet she took everywhere with her. When I asked her about that, she'd told me, "It's not as fast as a cable connection, but if all you want is what's already online, it's a lot lighter to lug around than a laptop. And you can type on it just like on a regular keyboard, if you have to."

I didn't say anything about how we had a multi-boosted connection right in the house—I figured she must have been carrying the tablet around while she was out, got a call on her phone, and pulled up the page she was showing me before she'd gotten back.

IS THE WRONG MAN IN JAIL?

The headline was the opposite of the flabbed-up bias that coated every word of "crime news" in the local papers. The story itself was a fact-dense rundown of all the information they had gathered.

Homer Larkin has been held in the County Jail for almost two months, supposedly awaiting trial on the murder of a man whose body washed up on a local beach. *Undercurrents* has learned that local law enforcement does not believe Larkin is in any way involved with this crime. In fact, he is being detained simply to convince the public that the crime has been "solved."

The KNOWN FACTS are as follows:

1. Larkin is a diagnosed schizophrenic, who, prior to his arrest, had been a resident of "Respite," a facility which houses the mentally ill who are NOT believed to be violent.

2. The "body on the beach" has been identified. Fingerprints show him to be one Welter Thom Jordan, an ex-convict recently released from the State Penitentiary after serving a sentence for his participation in a "hate crime" assault that left the victim permanently brain-damaged.

3. Jordan is a known neo-Nazi, as the numerous tattoos found on his body clearly proclaim.

4. The photographer who took the shot of Jordan washed up on the beach—the photo which launched the police "investigation" after it appeared on the front page of three local newspapers—has not been questioned. This is because the mystery photographer's identity remains unknown, despite the safe assumption that every newspaper in question would have cooperated fully. Not only because they act as the Public Relations Department of the District Attorney's Office, but because no journalistic privilege would attach to an anonymous e-mailer of a photograph.

5. Larkin VOLUNTARILY showed police a watch he "found." That watch apparently belonged to Jordan. This is the ONLY shred of evidence "linking" Larkin to the murder.

6. A social worker who knows Larkin well told *Undercurrents* that not only is Larkin nonviolent, he is physically incapable of committing the crime. "Homer's an old man, with advanced osteoporosis and the muscle

tone of a banana slug. He couldn't break a plate glass window with a crowbar."

7. X-rays of the victim's skull show he was killed by a powerful blow with some sort of spiked instrument. The victim's height was approximately five foot ten— roughly eight inches taller than Larkin. As the blow was struck from behind, it would have been physically impossible for Larkin to be the killer.

8. A gang of SHARPs (Skinheads Against Racial Prejudice) had been spotted less than ten miles from where the body washed up the week prior to the murder.

9. An FBI source confirmed that violence between these two extremes of the skinhead spectrum is common, and has been "escalating steadily over the past couple of years."

The "sources" weren't much of a mystery: Dolly's pals for the X-rays, Mack for the social worker's quote, and my vague hints to Dolly for any FBI agent talking to their reporters.

I also knew none of it would be much of a convincer. But the X-ray of the dead man's skull was in the *Undercurrents* story, right on the screen. And neither Jordan's nor Homer's age, height, or physical condition would be in dispute.

So . . . maybe . . . ?

But I should have known better. That sack of bleached dough we have for a district attorney immediately returned fire, using the "legitimate press" for a weapon. His definition of "legitimate" had nothing to do with paper versus cyber—it was his term for any news outlet that quoted him verbatim anytime he spoke but never asked him any questions.

I'll say this for him: the guy was a sensei of empty language. Who could possibly find fault with: "The individual referred to was arrested, and is being held because no bail application has been filed, much less ruled on. He has not been indicted, and the investigation is ongoing."

Hell, who could find *anything* in it?

"**W**hat if we got a lawyer to file a bail application for him?" I asked Dolly.

"A waste of time," she told me. "Homer's innocent, but a bail application isn't about that; it's about money."

"And a million dollars wouldn't do it," Mack added. "They say bail is to make sure the guy shows up for his trial. And there's already a ton of proof that Homer's crazy. So the only way to make sure he shows up is to *keep* him locked up."

"He trusts you, Mack. Couldn't you—?"

"What? Handcuff myself to him? Remember, he'll always be terrified of daylight, and he lost all his trust in those kids he hung out with because he was with them when he was arrested. He's absolutely convinced they sent out a secret signal to summon the police."

"But—"

"He's getting his meds," Mack assured Dolly. "I check on that. And he's in an iso cell, all by himself. It's got glass—on the outside of the bars—but I've got it worked out so he doesn't see sunlight, ever. For most people, that would be torture, but for Homer, it's the only way to keep him from . . ."

He didn't have to finish that sentence.

"So their plan is . . . what?" Dolly bulldogged on. "They're just going to *leave* him there?"

"I saw the lawyer," I told them, and watched the look of surprise spread across Dolly's face.

"Swift?" she asked, meaning the man who'd gone from shlub to star when he won the "Mighty Mary" case a while back.

"Yeah."

"Well, he's good," she said, patting Mack's forearm. "He was the one who got MaryLou off, remember?"

Mack nodded.

"Don't get your hopes up," I told them. "The only way there's *ever* going to be a trial is if Homer's lawyer pushes for one. He's not going to do that. Why should he? This way, he can keep right on billing for his time, and not have to do much of anything. And, sure, we could get Swift to step in and take his best shot. But that wouldn't get it done. The judge—*any* judge, Swift said—would rule that Homer's too crazy to even stand trial. Which means he stays locked up, only in a different place."

When I asked Swift how much I owed him, he gave me a disappointed look. "I had to ask," I told him by way of apology, offering my hand. He shook it, and checked my eyes, and the whole thing was over.

"This way, I can see him every day," Mack added. "If they shipped him to someplace on the other side of the state, he'd lose it. Which means death inside stone walls, one way or the other."

"We have to get him out," Dolly said, crossing her arms over her chest, the way she does when she isn't going to budge. Somehow, when it's just her and me alone and she tries to do that, her chest is too big to pull it off; but when anyone else is around, she manages it. And everyone gets the message.

But everyone doesn't get the *same* message. Dolly had crossed over the line, to that place where she knew I was going no matter what she said. We both knew what that could cost.

The question was: Did Mack?

"**R**emember when I asked you before? About how far you were willing to go?"

Mack just nodded.

"This would be harder. Doesn't matter how flexible your job description is, it wouldn't cover what needs to be done."

He just nodded again.

"You get caught, you're going to prison."

"You, too, right?"

"No," I told him, watching his face close. I had to know, and there was only one way to know for sure.

"I'll be doing this alone?"

"No. But I'm not going to prison. I'm either going free or going in the ground. Understand?"

"If I get caught, I'm going to prison for life—that's what you're saying?"

"Things go haywire, I'm not drawing any lines—not around myself, I'm not. If you stand around and watch, you'll be the only one going on trial. If you want to stand *with* me, you'll have to do what I'm prepared to do."

"How am I supposed to know—?"

"Try it this way. I'm not going to prison, period. I don't care for how little or how long. For me, six months would be the same as life. For you, maybe not such a big deal."

"You're saying—"

"That I'll kill anyone who tries to take me in? Yes."

"So, even if I don't . . . do that, I'll be locked up?"

"If I get away, that depends on what I'd have to do. If I leave bodies behind, probably. And if I don't get away at all, yes."

"It's that black-and-white for you?"

"Everything is."

"Dolly wouldn't want you to—"

"Die? No. Go to prison? No. But now she's got her feet planted, ready to swing. Dolly wants Homer cut loose. And she knows what I might have to do," I said, thinking, *La mission est sacrée.* Not the *légionnaire* mantra, not this time. Mine.

I let Mack light a cigarette. Waited until he was done with the smoke. Waited until he said, "I'm in."

"Pack enough to last you a few days," I told him. "I'll be around to pick you up after dark. Then it's a good ten, twelve-hour drive."

"I can do it," I whispered to my wife.

"Dell, listen. I want Homer out. And, like a fool, I told you I did. But what if—?"

"You know."

"I won't lose you."

"You won't. But—"

"Don't even say it," she said, very calmly. "Blood washes off. Wounds can be healed. Just make sure you—"

"That's something you don't need to say, baby."

"You *better* come back," Dolly said, reaching for me. Her gesture was a loving one, and followed by more.

I'd heard men curse God—all kinds of gods—but that was the first time I'd ever heard anyone threaten one.

"I'd bring you in myself," Mack told the redheaded leader of the teenage crew we'd visited before.

"Yeah? You gonna bring me *out*, too?"

"There's no paper out on you, Timmy. No wants, anywhere."

"I know," the kid said. Something in the way those words came out told me nobody had wanted him for a long time. If ever.

"Homer thinks you gave him up," Mack said, holding up an

opened palm to stop the redhead from interrupting. "I know you didn't. But this isn't something we can fix with logic. Homer's got to see that *I* trust you, okay? Your crew, it was one of his safe places. I wouldn't want him to lose that."

"He's getting out?"

"That's being worked on. I'm going on a little trip now. When I get back, that's when I'd like you to go in with me. It can be after dark," he said, looking around at the inky night as if it was endorsing the statement.

"You want Homer to know you trust *me,* I get that. Unless what you really want to know is if *I* trust you."

"I already know you do," Mack told the redhead.

"Yeah? How?"

Mack nodded in my direction.

The redhead fist-bumped him.

"This isn't my idea of camouflage," Mack said, referring to our "farm-use only" Jeep.

"Mine, either" is all I said.

"When are you going to tell me—?"

"Before we go in."

He went back to being quiet. I went back to driving.

I used a burner cell to dial a number. I let it ring once. Then the gates to what looked like a place to dispose of junked cars swung open. If Mack noticed the "B³" sign on the gate, he kept it to himself.

I'd only found out about this place by accident. Dolly's landscaper friends had let me borrow their new Lexus SUV while I was doing something to help MaryLou. I'd needed paper credentials for that. A letter on Swift's law-office stationery that said I was working for him as a private investigator was a good start, but I wanted to add some more to the package. Johnny and Martin's permission to drive one of their cars had been perfect for that.

But permission to use means returning in the same condition you borrowed, and I hadn't been able to do that. Maybe the Lexus really was an off-road vehicle—it sure didn't drive like it was—but I'd still been forced to hide it deep enough in the brush to put scratches all over it. The car I returned needed a total repaint, and I'd made them take the money to have it done.

Martin was really the car guy—he had an old Facel Vega that he was going to restore "someday," and when I'd talked about a new kind of paint that changes colors depending on the viewing angle, he couldn't pass it up. And when he showed it to us later—showed it *off,* really—he told us where he'd gotten the work done.

"They're the best," he'd told us. "But you have to drive through the worst part of Portland to get there. Whoever heard of a custom-fabrication operation built out of cinder block with a barbed-wire fence, and a whole horde of pit bulls running around loose?"

I wouldn't have had any trouble answering that question, but all I said was, "Apparently, you."

Johnny thought that was pretty funny.

I filed the info away. Later, I checked out my suspicion. Then I did a favor for the boss of that place. When I came into the garage to tell him his problem had been solved, he looked at me strange—how did I even know he'd *had* a problem?

When I just shook my head after he said, "How much?" he looked a little anxious. But he settled down when I told him, "If you'd *asked* me to do it, I would have told you a price. If we'd had a deal, I would have gotten paid. We didn't, so I don't. All I want is for you to know I can be trusted. And that I always pay my way."

He nodded. Among men of our breed, that's the secret handshake.

So, when I drove the Jeep into a big gray garage built out of what they call "penitentiary brick," I told Mack to grab his gear and we walked over to an off-white Ford Taurus. The keys were in the ignition. I opened the trunk, we tossed in our stuff, and I backed out of the garage, to head north.

"Check the glove box," I said to Mack.

"Registered to the B³ garage, whatever that is. Insured. And some keys on a ring."

"The plates will match. And it won't be reported stolen."

"At least it's a lot more comfortable," he said, tilting his seat back and closing his eyes.

I'd rented a lot more than just the car from those B³ guys.

One of the keys on the ring I took from the glove box opened the back door to a "town house"—one of a trio of two-story shacks slammed together on top of a matching set of one-car garages. The whole ramshackle mess squatted at the end of an unpaved road.

The directions had been perfect, and the odometer in the Taurus was dead-accurate. Facing the middle unit, I hit the remote for the garage. That worked perfect, too.

If the units on either side of us were occupied, there wasn't any sign of it. The entire structure didn't look any too stable, and the electricity had been cut off. There were contractors' signs plastered all around the place, and an especially big one standing between twin stakes out front. Apparently, the whole dump was sitting on the future site of one seriously major mansion.

It took us a couple of days to buy enough burner cells so we'd never have to use any of them more than once—incoming or outgoing. Even if the numbers got fingered somehow, all the phones would show up as local purchases.

Since we were only going out after dark to make the buys, I had plenty of time to talk with Mack.

"Ever use a firearm?"

"No. I mean, I've shot guns. On the range—I've got a good friend back in Chicago, a cop. He took me a couple of times. But I don't think that's what you're asking."

"I'm not. Knife?"

"Not like you're talking about, no."

"But you've been in a lot of fights."

"Because of my hands?"

"Because of the way you stand, how you shift your weight . . ."

"Okay."

"You understand why I asked, right?"

"Yeah."

"We can't do this like it was a movie. You could pass for one of them on your face, but that wouldn't hold for longer than it would take for them to check you for ink. Worse, any story you told would come up wrong when they asked for references— you don't have any."

"Then . . . what?"

"All that leaves is for me to try something I'm not good at, so there's a real chance it could go wrong. If it does, there's going to be some kind of killing. Gun, knife, whatever—I already told you, I'm not going to prison."

"You're going to do something you're not good at. If that goes wrong, you're going to do things you *are* good at."

"Yeah. So, if you're going to change your mind, now would be a good time."

"I'm not."

"Okay," I said, opening up what Dolly calls a "notebook." Mine was a portable encryption device, with enough battery to last seventy-two hours if I left it on all the time. If I just used it when I had to, probably good for over a month.

```
|>Pvt # for contacting SAC?<|
```

"What's next?" Mack asked, after I closed the notebook.

"Waiting," I told him.

Later, when I opened the notebook, a ten-digit number was waiting.

I realized it could have been a sat-phone, and if it was, I'd be expected to know what country code to use. But making a sat-call from a burner cell would be like trying to put out a forest fire with a tissue-paper blanket, and the cyber-shadow would know that.

I wrote down the number, watched the screen clear of its own accord, and shut off the notebook.

"You recognize this area code?" I asked Mack.

"Miami," he said, so quickly that he must have known someone down there.

Made much more sense to me—if the informant was strictly one-on-one, the FBI man running him wouldn't want calls from him going through the agency's system. Or even risk being picked up on a random home-and-cell sweep, the kind his bosses probably triggered every once in a while.

I didn't know if the FBI routinely polygraphed every agent like the CIA does, but the prospect didn't worry me. Two reasons: they'd only be polygraphing field agents, and this guy was way above that level now; and that CIA spy, who'd been selling to the other side for years, he'd passed a bunch of polygraphs. By now, every agency would know that certain people would pass any kind of "guilty knowledge" detector.

Maybe all this "profiling" stuff was as silly as it looked on TV, but even the FBI would know there's people who don't *feel* guilty. About anything. It just wasn't in them.

You couldn't bluff such people, either. Tell them they'd just failed a polygraph and they might do any number of things—laugh in your face, tell you the machine was fucked up and demand a retest, get angry—just about anything *except* break down and confess.

If I'd been alone, I would have tried to clear my mind so I could see the field mapped out before I went in. I wasn't trained as a strategist. But Mack was there with me. And whatever we were going to do, it'd have to wait for nightfall anyway. So . . .

"We've got to turn him," I said.

"The FBI man?"

"Yeah. But the only handle we've got to turn him with is that he gave a hunting license to at least one of those three who took out that Jordan guy. We don't know which one. Far as we know, he could have issued the license to that whole team.

"All I've been able to find out is *how* they reach him. They'd have to do it over a line if it was a tip he'd have to act on fast. But data banks aren't any more useful than the data they hold. He'd know that, so there isn't a chance in hell that he'd have *any* of their names or contact info written down on a piece of paper, never mind put into his agency's computer system."

"You're thinking we could—what?—make him talk?"

"No. That's a myth, torture. It makes people talk, all right, but it doesn't make them tell the truth."

Mack just nodded, as if everybody knew that. But I didn't miss the relief on his face—his eyes didn't change, but his facial muscles relaxed just enough for the tell.

"And even if we did get him to give up the killer, so what?" I said. "We'd still be right here."

"Right here?"

"In the same place. Even if he drew us a map, we'd still be working through a maze. Say we knew the name of the guy who killed the Nazi. So what? First, we'd have to find him. That could take way more time than we have. But let's say we got lucky. Say we *do* find him, now what? He's going to confess?"

"I get it."

Those three words from Mack triggered a memory: I'd emptied my weapon in a jungle-dark firefight. I was groping around in the dark, desperation and the need to be careful at war with each other in my head, when my fingers suddenly touched that extra magazine I knew I'd put somewhere close to hand.

That memory: "Killing all the guards won't move *that* boulder," this guy who looked like a university professor was telling me.

A long time ago, when I was still working.

We were in his office. At least, that's what he called it—I figured the only thing that was actually his was the little brass nameplate on the outside door, and he'd be taking that with him when he left. "The boulder's not only too big, it's planted too deeply. There's only one way to move something like that. You know what that would be?"

"A lever. A fulcrum and a lever."

"Very good," he said, drawing on his meerschaum pipe. The scent of the tobacco was a kind of cherry. Bitter cherry. "Do you know where we could get such a combination?"

I just shook my head. People giving lectures don't like to be interrupted, and I was getting paid to listen, anyway.

"The only leverage—the only *true* leverage—always comes

down to the same thing. Information. That's why the people who know always get paid much more than the people who pull on that lever."

Or pull the trigger, I thought. But all I said was "The difference between you and me, you're saying?"

"It doesn't have to be."

I just looked at him. Waiting.

"He has a daughter."

I knew what the man wanted then, but I just sat there. If anyone was going to say it out loud, it would have to be him.

"Three years old. Her mother's nineteen. He's at least seventy years old. Maybe he got injections, maybe he's still . . . capable. Maybe he used his own sperm, frozen years ago. It doesn't matter.

"Here's what *does* matter. *Information* matters. We know that child is his ultimate trophy. The child's existence proves he can cheat Time itself."

I just kept waiting.

"He keeps her in a separate house inside his compound. She is only brought out—taken down from the trophy case, if you will—when he wants to exhibit his . . . prowess, perhaps one might say."

There was still nothing for *me* to say.

"The mother stays with the child. But when her . . . services are required, the child is tended by an amah. You know what that is?"

"Nursemaid."

"Yes," he said, approvingly. "However, for the purposes of this endeavor, it doesn't matter who is tending to the child— the house is guarded individually, you see?"

"That house has its own guards. Not the ones who guard the compound itself, guards *inside* the compound."

"Correct."

"They wouldn't be the only ones."

"Of course not. He has his own personal bodyguards that go wherever he goes. And those are always very close. His personal dwelling—that, too, is guarded."

"And you have the diagrams," I said. If there was any question about that, there was no point in asking it.

He took several rolls of paper from a drawer in the desk he was sitting behind and spread them out, anchoring each end with a heavy brass ruler. The rulers were triangle-shaped, so you could measure in inches or centimeters, or whatever else you needed.

I studied the diagrams, taking my time. Not once did he interrupt my examination. For the moment, our roles were reversed. But those *were* roles, and I wasn't fool enough to think otherwise. He wasn't just the star or the director, he was the author of this play. And its producer, too.

"It would have to be silent," I finally said. "Or else a full-on, all-sides assault."

"And the difference between those alternatives?"

"One takes a much smaller group, but they would have to be *very* highly skilled. The other, it would be a war—and wars take troops."

"One is preferable to the other?"

"A war means you don't pick your targets. The safety of neither this man nor the child could be assured. And you need them *both* alive, one to make certain the other will turn over whatever it is you want."

He nodded, telling me he already knew this—he was just satisfying himself that *I* did, too. And confirming that what he wanted was some kind of *information,* the commodity he prized above all else.

"But no matter which method is used, the task is impossible," I said, very calm in the truth of what I was going to say. "There is a key element missing. Without it, any invaders would be going in blind. Electronic sensors? No-bark attack dogs? Who knows? And if there is *any* alert sounded, the invaders become targets. If one of those targets had the job of extracting the child, then this would all be for nothing. A dead child will not serve your purposes."

"What is this 'key element' you believe is missing?"

"A traitor," I told him.

That's when I understood why that memory had surfaced, unbidden.

Almost 2:00 a.m.

We were at the highest point we could find for what we needed—privacy, and where a cheap cell phone would have the best chance of working.

"Seven nineteen," a voice said.

"I don't know the code you gave your boy," I said. "But that worm has turned. He's still at large, but he's been located. You know how it works once they have him: if he gives you up, he walks; if he doesn't, he never sees the sky at night again. Which choice you think he's gonna make?"

"Who is—?"

"Don't be stupid. He doesn't know your people have got him targeted for takedown. Want proof? *You* didn't. Where do you think I got *your* number? I'm in the worm-removal business. Pick a spot you can get to in an hour. I'll meet you, we'll agree on a price, and I'll take it from there."

"I don't know who you—"

"You get this one chance," I cut him short. "This one chance *only*. Now name a spot and be there in an hour. Or you're on your own."

"Think he'll come alone?"

"Who's he going to get to work backup? He doesn't have time to reach out to a hired gun. The only men he could round up would be agents who work under him. He can't tell *them* to go in shooting. And he can't risk any of them finding out what he already knows *I* do."

"I'm just supposed to sit here, on the fender of the car?"

"Yes."

"And you'll be . . . somewhere close?"

"Right."

"You're the one who has to talk to him, so why—?"

"I can cover you," I told him, moving the night-scoped jungle rifle a little to make it clear. "You can't cover me."

"Okay."

"You understand, the minute he shows, we switch places?" I said, repeating myself. When he nodded, I handed him a Sig P226. "There's no safety on this—just pull steady and firm the first time, then keep pulling; the trigger lightens after the first round."

"I get it."

"Let's be sure, okay? He walks toward you; I start walking when he does. You see him, you move *away* from the direction I'll be coming from. You move to *your* left. As you move, I'll be moving, too. By the time he's close enough, I'll be where you *were.* And you'll be over to your left . . . where it's dark."

"How many times do you want to tell me?"

"Until I'm sure you'll pull that trigger if you have to."

He was cute, I'll give him that.

A red Corvette is as close to generic as you can get in Seattle, and the spot he'd picked was probably a lot closer to his house than an hour's drive.

He'd been playing the same game, the same way, for a long time. Probably thought he still had it under control. He wasn't driving an agency car, and he wouldn't be wired . . . but he'd want to be sure whoever called him wasn't, either.

He pulled in right next to Mack, and came out of his car *fast*. I was close enough to grab a single eyeball with the scope, but I'd lensed it full-wide, knowing I'd only have a few seconds to gather data.

Mid-forties, with a spiky haircut that would have looked right on a guy half his age. Gym muscles, biceps on display in a short-sleeved black shirt. No gun in sight, but that shirt was long-tailed enough to belt-conceal.

"Move over, kid," I said as I slid up on Mack's right. "It's time for the grown-ups to talk."

SAC Alan Brigham turned his head just far enough to realize he couldn't keep Mack and me in his field of vision at the same time. I shifted the rifle to one hand, pointed it at the ground, held it loosely. Telling him I *could* have taken him, if that's what I'd been there to do.

He just watched me, waiting.

"Your man is facing a hard choice. So are you," I said.

"My man?"

"You want to hear 'Gomes,' that make you feel better?" I said, gambling that he'd only licensed one man—one man's name was all I had.

"I don't know what—"

"*That's* your best? Can't be. So maybe you're thinking Gomes *already* turned, and it's my job to get you to spill."

"You know who I am?" he said, making the question a threat.

"You want your name on a tape, is that it? Or maybe you need to hear that if you act stupid my partner will shred you where you stand? Act your age, okay?"

He stood frozen for a ten-count. Then he said, "Lay it out."

"You made a devil's bargain. Gomes gets a license to kill. Every kill ups his status. That gives him access to more and more info. He turns the cream of that over to you, and you keep renewing that license.

"Your agency didn't go public with that last takedown, but you got credited, right? And nobody ever asks you how you're always getting such heavy intel on the White Power guys, do they? At least, not anymore, they don't. Domestic terrorism, that's their key to the treasure chest."

"Is that it?"

"It's more than enough. A devil's bargain—that means only the devil *gets* the bargain. You issued a license you can't cancel. Not now, you can't—it's been used too much. All you can do is cancel the guy who's holding it."

"Spell it out."

"I'll tell you this much, no more: the people who have Gomes on their radar, they have him *good*. Not for anything to do with you. Gomes, he's what they call a 'boy-lover,' and they've got enough to put him all the way down. One of the little boys he was playing with ended up dead, and the whole thing's on video. How do I know that? Because it got sold. For a lot of money.

"The people who want Gomes work for the same outfit you do. But they're not your friends—they've got ambitions of their own. Too bad for you the wrong guy won the last election.

"So forget Gomes, he's getting wrapped up. And soon. But there's one string still dangling, and the other side can't pull it. You know why? Because they don't know it's there."

"Come on!" He wasn't shouting, just the opposite. But his voice was vibrating with tension.

"Your guy doesn't work alone. He's the boss of a three-man team. I take him out, you let the other two in on the deal. You understand what I'm saying? They—*your* people, I'm talking about—they only know about Gomes. And they only lucked into that. Maybe Gomes didn't plan on the kid dying, just wanted the tape for his collection. But he's like all of those sickos—he couldn't bring himself to dump the tapes, not even that one.

"You get it? Get it *now*? Gomes disappears, you not only slip out from under that rockslide that's coming your way, you get to stay in business, too. You expose Gomes to the other two guys he works with because you're on *their* side, understand what I'm saying? So, after that, it'd only be natural for you to warn them when you could . . . and for them to tip you when *they* could. Brother race warriors, they'd do that.

"Now, you're not interested in stuff that gets counted in kilos, and the kiddie-porn stuff is really for Interpol. But when you passed that one on, you cooked Gomes, too. No way you could have known that—Gomes had to be a moron to inform on the same ring that ended up with a copy of that snuff film he made.

"So what are you really losing? You wouldn't want to blow your cover—to your Aryan brothers, I mean—by asking about stuff like that, anyway. But that 'domestic terrorism' bullshit they keep planning, *that's* your ticket to the top—why should you care who's driving the bus?"

He blinked once. So hard I could hear his eyeballs click. Then he just said: "How much?"

"I don't have time to play used-car salesman. Seven figures. The *lowest* seven figure."

"You think I—?"

"Yeah, I do. Or, anyway, that you can get it."

"I don't . . ."

"This is Tuesday. They're set to grab Gomes this coming Monday night—they already know where he's supposed to be. They do that, Gomes, he'll have a decision to make. You know what *that's* going to be—you knew he was a piece of filth all along. Maybe telling you about that kiddie-porn ring made you wonder even more about him.

"You got *any* doubt what he's gonna do? You can't believe he's going to take a Double-Forever in some super-max rather than give you up. And that's not even the worst he's looking at—that tape he made could put him in line for the needle."

"There's no federal death penalty for—"

"The kid he killed? It was on a rez. Not far from a casino. How much more do you want?"

He went silent again.

"You know what I think? I think they're going to milk him dry. And after they get *your* name, they're probably just going to make him disappear. Why embarrass the agency? Of course, the rest of that job is to make sure you never get near a witness stand. You'll probably get a hero's funeral. Killed in a gunfight with a terrorist—now, *that's* something they could get mileage out of, right?"

He was done arguing. About anything. "How can I—?"

"You?" I half sneered. "You can't. I'll tap you—Thursday, midnight. You say 'yes,' it means you're going to get all three of them in one place—a place where I can do what I have to—anytime this weekend. You say 'no'—and not answering your phone *is* 'no'—you're on your own."

"You want me to get a million in cash by this weekend? There's no way I could ever—"

"Ten percent down, three more in ninety days, three the next ninety, the final payment ninety days from that one. One year, and you're paid in full."

"How do you know I wouldn't just . . . ?"

I didn't say anything, letting my silence answer his question.

"**E**asy," I cautioned Mack. "We're pressed for time, sure. But if a cop stops us and looks in the trunk, we're both going to be *doing* time."

Mack didn't answer, but he slowed the Taurus down to ten-over. "How about if I draft?"

"Okay."

He accelerated until we were behind a yellow Camaro, one of those new ones with windows that look like the slits in an armored car. The Camaro was flying, but he'd be the one break-ing the radar gun's beam, not us.

I wished it was raining—the cops don't ever seem to be out in force on the speedways unless it's nice and dry.

"One more time," I said.

"Damn, you *really* go over a plan, don't you?"

"The way I was trained."

"You were trained to do what you're saying we're gonna do next?"

"Yes."

"Were you—? Ah, never mind," he interrupted himself.

It was full-on daylight by the time the Taurus pulled around behind our cottage.

"Go home and get some sleep," I told Mack. "We can only work nights, and we haven't got many of those left."

Dolly and Rascal were both at the door. Dolly took one look at me and said, "Now!" I kept moving until I got to our bedroom.

"**B**ecause I can't teach you to be quiet enough in the time we've got," I answered Mack's question the next night. "When—uh, *if*, I guess—I find him, I'll tap your number. These throw-aways don't even have a vibrate setting, so you keep a decent distance away to keep him from hearing it ring."

"I follow him to his house, then I call you and you meet me there?"

"If it's a house, yeah. If it's one of those little condo things, make sure you get the exact unit. Wherever it is, it's close by. And it's got to have room enough for all the equipment he'll have."

"And then we go in?"

"There's no 'we' in this. *You* go in, right behind him. Then you just keep him there until I show up. . . . Won't be long."

"He'll see our faces."

"Yeah, he will. What's he going to do, call the cops? All you have to do is make sure he understands you're waiting for your boss—that's me—to show up.

"Make sure he hears you when you tell him that he *already* knows me. That we've worked together in the past. He won't know my face, but he'll recognize my voice. And he thinks I *already* know where he lives."

"I'm no good with guns. You already know that."

"You're not going to *shoot* the damn thing. But it's what a guy like him would expect you to have. A prop, like. I've got a shoulder holster for you, too."

"You have a suit?" Dolly asked him.

"For court, yeah."

"Good enough," I said. Quickly, before Dolly could start questioning him about his whole wardrobe. "You know the script. We're not there to terrorize him; we're there to sign him up for a mission."

"You really think a guy who . . . does what he does, you think he's gonna buy all this?"

"Remember, I've known about him for a long time . . . but nothing ever happened. He may not know what I am, but he knows I can be trusted. Otherwise, he wouldn't have gone back to his video stalking.

"He's low-hanging fruit," I said to Mack. "And he's been waiting a long time for the right people to recognize how ripe he is."

The tiny red light blinked on.

He was at work, his usual spot. Easy enough to take him right there, but that wouldn't get us inside his house.

A big sedan threw up gravel as it spun into the Lovers' Lane spot. One *whoop!* from its siren set all the other cars in motion, moving even more frantically as a huge man rolled out from the passenger seat and charged up the hillside, a bright spotlight in one hand. He was heading away from the exiting cars, straight toward where the video ninja had been lurking. You could hear branches snap under his boots, just behind the spotlight's beam, like if Bigfoot was wearing a miner's hat.

The little red light went off. I could hear the video ninja's panicked breathing as he packed up to run. He knew lugging the weight of his equipment would slow him down, but he wasn't about to leave it. *"Tu n'abandonnes jamais ni tes morts, ni tes blessés, ni tes armes!"* ran through my mind as he passed within ten yards of me.

This one would never have comrades, so "never abandon your dead or your wounded" wouldn't be on his screen. But abandoning his weapons, that was unthinkable. For this creature, that would be pulling out the IV feed that was keeping him alive.

I popped open my cell, tapped "3 3 3," and thumbed it off.

Following the video ninja wasn't hard—I just stayed behind him until I was sure that the "north-north-north" message I'd sent would stay accurate. Then I turned and went back the way I came, all the way down to the now deserted make-out spot.

Deserted except for Dolly and Franklin.

"Where'd you get the car?" I asked the giant.

"It's Mr. Spyros's. He's got this Town Car that he uses for limo jobs. Not himself, I mean, he has this service that he runs. Anyway, I asked him could I borrow it just for the night, and leave my truck with him, just like you said, Mr. Dell."

"You did perfect!" I told him, clapping him hard on his chest. I don't think he felt the thump, but I knew that he'd felt the approval. And that Dolly would reinforce it all the way back to wherever he'd met her.

Mack's voice on my cell: "In place."

He gave me an address. I heard him tell the video ninja, "ETA fifteen minutes, max," as I cut the connection.

Turned out to be a house. Small one, with a detached garage, door closed. The Taurus was in the driveway—Mack had probably taken the video stalker as he exited the garage.

I rapped on the door: three times, one time, three times. Nobody answered. I hadn't expected anyone to. What I *did* expect was to find the door unlocked, and Mack seated across from a man in a black jumpsuit. The jumpsuit's hood was down, the man's face blanched and twitching.

"This is Conrad, boss," Mack said to me. "Photo-verified."

Meaning Mack had taken a cell-phone snap of the video ninja's driver's license, or some other form of ID.

"I know," I answered. "We've worked together before."

A little color came back into the video ninja's face. He'd never seen the black Tanto, just felt it, so I didn't bother showing it to him again. I just took a seat next to him. His smell was as familiar to me as my voice had been to him. It's not only dogs who can smell fear, if it's heavy enough.

"Conrad, the agency has a special assignment, one that requires your skills."

"My—"

"Skills, Conrad. For some freelance work. We're authorized up to five thousand, depending on one area we don't have confirmed yet."

"I don't under—"

"Audio. We need video, still photography, *and* audio. I know you're a master of the first two, but—"

"I've got *everything*," he burst out, interrupting me in his eagerness. "Shotgun and directional, both. Under the right conditions, I can narrow in on a single conversation at fifty yards."

"Didn't I tell you?" I said to Mack. "Conrad's the man for the job."

Mack nodded soberly.

"You mind?" I said, reaching inside my jacket for a pack of cigarettes, lighting one up without waiting for a response. Two reasons: I—Adelbert Jackson, me—I don't smoke. And the gesture helped give off that sense of no-way-out I needed the video creature to feel. If he thought he had a choice—a choice about *anything*—he might make the wrong one.

"Okay, this is a rough breakdown," I told him. "We don't have all the details, not yet. We're"—nodding at Mack—"meeting with four men. Four members of a terrorist cell. They don't know they've been identified—under surveillance even as we speak—and we have to keep them from learning otherwise. People like them have a need to believe they're in charge, and we have to cater to that need if we want them to reveal as much as possible.

"What we need is one final audio and video. Of that meeting I just told you about. We already know it's going to be an *outdoor* meeting. At *night,* which is why we need a man with your specific skill-set."

I looked around for an ashtray and didn't see one, so I tapped the gray ash of my glowing cigarette into a small rubber pouch I pulled from my jacket.

"They're going to set the time and place, but we'll be there before they are . . . and you'll be with us. *Your* job will be to find a good spot, and record as much as possible."

I let some gravity into my voice. "This could *not* be more important, Conrad. There's no danger to you—they'll never know you were even there—but, believe me, your country will *never* forget your contribution to our counterterrorism work."

He didn't want to look at me, so he just nodded.

"Give it to him," I said.

Mack handed our nameless agency's new night-video expert one of the unused burner cells I'd rejacketed; its new casing was branded with an indecipherable symbol in small gold printing on its underside.

"This is special-issue," I told him. "You *never* use it, not for anything. It's just a way for us to signal you. As soon as you hear it ring, that's your green light. Start putting together all the equipment you'll need—we'll have to travel some distance from here. Within a few minutes of that green-light signal, we'll come by to pick you up, and then we're off. Understood?"

"Yes, sir," he said, still frightened, but already feeling a calmness he'd never before experienced in his entire life. Not the confidence that comes from being part of a team, but that sense of self when you suddenly realize you're not the permanent outsider you'd always believed yourself to be. Doomed to be.

I would never acknowledge it, but I instantly recognized what the video ninja was feeling inside himself—La Légion had put that same calmness inside of me long ago.

The café dwellers could rant on about the possibility of existentialism, but all us *légionnaires* knew the truth of fatalism—no matter how well trained or well equipped you were, once the shooting started, the bullet either found you or did not.

Still, I would choose them again. To be an outsider all your life was worth . . . what?

"Yes or no?" was all I said.

"Saturday night," the FBI man answered. "The Rainbow Coalition Tavern. That's just off I-5, about three miles northwest of Vancouver. We'll all be in the booth farthest to your left as you walk in. I'll give you forty-five minutes on each side of oh one hundred."

"When you see me, that'll be your signal to walk *out*," I told him. "We can't do this inside."

"We could in that place, trust me."

"Why would I do that? Trust *you*? What's out back, a parking lot?"

"No, parking's only out front. Behind is just empty space. There's no lighting, and no paving, either. Nothing but a few old girders still in place from the demolition, but new construction won't start for at least a few months. They're putting up a whole—"

"Okay. Now, listen: I walk in, you see me. I turn around, walk back out the same door I came in . . . like I'd made a mistake. Then I slide around to the back. You give me a minute, then get out there yourself—you and the other three."

"There's a back door."

"That's up to you. But you use the back door, you better make sure nobody else does. Not until *all* our business is finished."

"Done." He signed off. I hadn't missed his "I'm still in charge" tone, but I guessed that wasn't for me; it was for himself.

We picked him up where he wanted—a pool of darkness just behind the high school.

Dusk hadn't even settled in yet, but if we hadn't been watching, we wouldn't have seen him. Must have been a place he'd used before. No sign of a vehicle, but he had to have gotten there somehow. The one thing I was sure of was that a friend hadn't dropped him off.

I got out of the backseat and said, "Put it all in here," pointing to the trunk Mack had popped open from the driver's seat. I could see Conrad didn't want to let go of his lifelines, but he relaxed a little when he noticed we had padded the whole compartment with those foamy acoustical tiles they use in recording studios.

I pointed at the front seat. He climbed in. When Mack pushed the button, it wasn't the sound of all the doors locking that froze Conrad in place—I was sitting behind Mack, so every time our video man turned to his left, he'd see me.

Probably all unnecessary. The video ninja wasn't going to run, not with all his equipment in our possession. And not with us knowing where to find him. But my training was that there's no such thing as taking too many precautions.

The meeting was for 1:00 a.m. I wasn't lying when I assured our video expert that we had plenty of time—we'd be in place well before midnight.

No rain. Around the coast, that'd be counted as a lucky break, but where we were going, none was expected. Weather wouldn't have changed anything, but at least I could keep my window down—my character smoked, and I wanted to keep reinforcing that in the video man's mind.

He'd seen my face only when he was terrified, before. Now he was more relaxed—not *much* more, but enough to do the work we needed doing. He never spoke, just looked straight ahead or out his window. Probably couldn't have picked me out of a lineup. Even if he wanted to.

And there was no "probably" about this: he'd never want to.

Something was nagging at me, but I couldn't isolate it.

I closed my eyes, blocked out even the sensation of the car moving.

Why did I see the man seated next to Mack as "Conrad"? His name, I mean, the spelling. Why "Conrad," not "Konrad"? How had I known this before I'd ever seen the ID Mack had copied?

Was that because the only "Konrad" I'd ever known was in the same unit I was—I should say, had the same paymaster? He was older than me, but way too young to have fought in World War II. Yet there had been something about him that triggered an embedded memory—Luc's memory, now mine.

We were in the midst of a firefight. At the first crack of a rifle shot, our unit immediately split—taking cover as separated as possible, every man for himself. For reasons I'd never examined, that triggered memory had caused a trigger pull.

When we reassembled, the enemy had disappeared. Some dead, some just gone. No need to count our dead: if you didn't make it back to the preset coordinates by pull-out time, you were *counted* as dead. This wasn't La Légion—we weren't expected to return carrying dead comrades. Or waste time burying them.

Nobody would ever know my bullet had taken Konrad's life.

It had come to me as naturally as breathing. Not something you think about. So why was I thinking about it now?

"This is *perfect*," the video ninja whispered.

I could see why he was so excited: the skeleton of the demolished building still had some girders standing, with a few crossbeams lying haphazardly across. I could smell the exposed iron, already rusting.

His comfort level rose when he saw it was extra-dark back there—even shadows had blacker centers.

"I can use the tripods," he said, like that was an enhancement he hadn't expected.

"You know where we left the car. When we"—pointing at Mack, to make sure he got it—"leave, you won't see anything until I come back. I'll be joined by four men. Things will happen. You won't see Jenkins"—I whispered, then clamped down on the last word like I'd said too much, quickly covering with it with "Mr. Boston"—"until it's over, but you *keep* recording until he tells you to stop. Okay?"

"Yes, sir."

I checked my no-frills Luminox. Not just another prop to enhance the "special agent" routine for the video man—it worked so good that I'd had to rubber-cap it to make sure nobody but me picked up its electro-glow hands. Still shy of midnight. I had no way of knowing if the targets were already inside. I hadn't seen the red Corvette in the parking lot out front on our first pass-by, but that didn't mean anything.

"One more time, Conrad. Run it down for me. By the numbers."

"You're not ever to be in the frame. . . ."

I nodded, making vague sounds of approval so he'd relax a little more.

"I get a wide shot of all four of them. Then I come in close, face by face, and snap stills. Once I've got each one face-captured, I dial back a little so I can cover everything that happens."

"Perfect. Now, listen. *One* of them is going to end up standing next to me, so be very precise. Shoot it like you're my eyes, Conrad. We need the coverage only of what I *see,* not of me myself. Understand?"

"I'm your eyes," he echoed. Not just repeating words, saying it as if he wanted to *be* me, seeing with *my* eyes.

"And my ears," I reminded him.

But he was ahead of me, already fitting equipment in place—becoming more a part of this with every move. Going from voyeur to government agent had done wonders for his . . . I don't know what, exactly. Not confidence, more like maybe he wasn't *just* some sick little man, not anymore. Our certification of him as a team member, an expert with special qualifications, that was the key to a door he hadn't even known was there. Unlocking that door had given him a true *raison d'être,* probably for the first time in his life.

I could feel that in him, even stronger now than the first time it had come.

I threw a complicated series of hand gestures in the direction where Conrad thought Mack was standing. But Mack was actually on the opposite side, holding the full-blued Benelli 12-gauge in one hand. "Remember," I'd reminded him, "start from one side and *sweep.* It holds five, but don't try to count—the blasting will block your ears. Keep pulling until it's empty. Then just drop it on the ground—you've never touched it without gloves—and run for the car.

"If I can, I'll be at the car before you. If I'm not, you get out of here. Don't worry about Conrad. Just *drive!* Don't stop. Don't make calls. Get the car back to where we took it from, put it inside the gates, leave the keys in the ignition . . . and walk away.

"Get a couple of miles under you *before* you call Dolly. . . . Just tell her where to pick you up; she'll know what to do."

I could see he didn't like it. But he'd been out of choices the moment we grabbed Conrad. If he knew I was going to make sure Conrad didn't talk—not to anybody, not ever again—he also knew there was nothing he could do about it.

I left Mack, and walked all the way back to where our video man had set up. "I know you're good at waiting, Conrad. Less than an hour to game time. Roger?"

"Roger!" he answered. A little steel in his voice, fear fading as he again became one with the only element that had ever opened its arms to embrace him.

The red Corvette rolled up at midnight plus twenty and slid into the space farthest to the right.

He strutted in like he owned the place. Maybe he did—the name would be his idea of a joke, and he'd said we could do anything we wanted inside, too.

I waited. Other cars pulled in, other men got out. No way to tell if *his* tools had already been inside, waiting for him.

It didn't matter. When the time came, I slipped on the transparent latex gloves, pulled them tight, rolled my shoulders to make sure my thigh-length field jacket was correctly adjusted, and stepped into the bar.

He was where he'd said he'd be, sitting all the way to the right on one side of a booth, a glossy white nylon jacket unzipped to show a bright-red pullover underneath.

I couldn't see who was across from him, or next to him. Or even if anyone else was there at all. I made a "Damn!" gesture with my right hand, like I'd walked into the wrong place. Then I turned around and walked back the way I'd come in.

I will say this for La Légion: if you survived all their tests, they stopped the lying and treated you like the soldier you had become.

So, before you went into the field for the first time, they made it all clear. No matter how expertly you had been trained, no matter how correctly you might be armed, no matter how perfectly strategic the position you held, there would always be the waiting. And, within that waiting, what you did with your mind could change what was to come.

You were never to think about your preparations. Once in place, you were done with the past. *All* your past, right up to that very second. *"Aucun homme n'a le pouvoir de changer son passé. Mais un homme bien entraîné peut changer son futur."* Your full range of reactions is loaded in your mind, each as carefully as you had loaded your weapons.

There were options, always. But they always lived inside the inescapable dungeon of commitment. To the death. The enemy's, if you performed correctly. If not, your own.

And, then, the final truth. *"Peu importe qui distribue les cartes, la dernière carte à jouer sera toujours celle du Destin."*

I'd done everything I could.

The FBI man knew exactly what he had to do: execute the maneuver so smoothly that he would be standing with me before the others realized what was happening.

I could not be more prepared than I was.

But I knew this, too: I couldn't be sure of him—there was no way for me to know what Conrad would be seeing with *my* eyes.

I was in position.

Committed, but with options inside that commitment. Whoever came out the door would be backlit, so the matte black pistol dangling in my right hand would be invisible to them. If the FBI man was planning to cross me, that glossy white jacket would be my first target.

The back door opened and four men walked toward me. The man in the white jacket was wider than any of the others, but the one standing just slightly behind him to his left was taller.

They came toward me, not in a hurry. Moving slowly enough to show they had no fear . . . but all I saw in their movement was that they didn't want me to think they were going to rush me.

When they got close enough to see my face, I could see theirs. Not kids, but younger than Mack—I guessed somewhere between late twenties and early thirties.

I was going to say something soothing to freeze them for the split second I'd need, but the FBI man was already in motion. He spun around to my right side so the config became the two of us facing the hit squad, just as we'd rehearsed. The man in the middle of those three responded by stepping slightly forward. Had to be Gomes, I thought.

"He's with me," the FBI man said to them. Whether they thought I was another agent or just hired backup, his flat statement was enough to settle them down. "I've got something you all need to hear," he said. "A new target. Hard to believe, but easy to take. Very easy."

All three of them simultaneously clasped their hands together at the waist, in a listening stance.

"You already know Jordan was a rat," the FBI man said. "And it shouldn't have taken *me* to clue you—he was cut loose way short of his full sentence, and there's always a reason for that."

"We didn't even know he was out until—"

"Then the organization is still too weak for the Final Move," the FBI man said, cutting off the speaker, a slender man with a hawkish face standing to the left of Gomes. "Nobody is *ever* locked down where you can't get some girl to write him like she was going to wait for him no matter how long it took. At the worst, they can't stop a lawyer from getting inside. Who cares if they'd be listening in? All we'd need to do is verify he was still there."

"That's not right," Gomes said, his voice pulsating with resentment, playing along with what he must have thought *was* a play. "We were on him quick enough; that wasn't the problem. The problem was, he *knew* we were coming. And even with that, he never got far, considering."

"Considering what? He'd already been out months before you *started* to close in. You know what a rat does when you let him run around loose? You have any idea how much he spilled before—?"

The guy with the hawkish profile wasn't going to lose face, not in front of the other two: "He didn't have anything *to* spill. Anything more, I mean. You think we didn't know he was sprung? We had to lay back, like we didn't know nothing. Thought he'd come right to us."

"Guess he didn't, huh? So who finally sent you after him?"

"The Leader. Same as always."

"Jordan must have known by then. So how'd you get him to trust you?"

"*Trust us?* That's a joke, right?"

"He got done with a rock hammer to the back of his head—"

"Yeah. *This* one," the tallest man said, as he pulled a heavy, spike-ended tool from behind his back. "So?"

"So if he didn't trust you"—pointing at Gomes—"how could *you*"—pointing at the tall man on Gomes's right—"get behind him?"

Gomes barked a not-quite-scared laugh. "What he trusted was that Val"—nodding his head toward the man on his left—"was going to blow his face off if he didn't climb that cliff."

"He didn't argue," the man who must be Val said, grinning as he slowly drew a chromed wheel-gun with a ventilated rib from a back-belt holster. "Show a man a .357 mag, he usually doesn't."

"We told him we had heard some things, and we wanted to give him a chance to put us straight," Gomes said. "Gave him the idea that our orders were to question him, not ice him. But we wanted to be *sure* nobody could come up on us sudden, and the top of that rock was perfect."

"He bought that?"

"I'm pretty sure he did," Gomes answered. "Val showed him the gun just in case he balked. We planned it all out. Jordan, he'd think the *last* place we'd fire a gun would be from up there—the sound would carry for miles."

"Pretty slick," the FBI man said, like he was admitting they'd just taught him something. "Only one thing bothers me. Trust, it's a strange thing, you know? I mean, you've got a rep, don't you? People know why you're in charge, yeah?"

"That's right," Gomes said, a little pride in his voice.

"So why would Jordan trust you? You *personally,* I mean."

"What the fuck are you saying?"

"I'm saying what I said inside, only now I'm making it clear enough for even *you* to understand. Jordan's done, but now, all of a sudden, there's a new rat in the cheese factory."

"Really?" the hawk-faced guy said, no softness in his voice.

"Really," the FBI man said as a dark pistol magically appeared in his extended right hand. *That's a Steyr GB,* flashed in my mind—*I haven't seen one of those since Laos.* "You think I don't know who *you've* been talking to, Gomes?" he spat out.

Gomes didn't even blink. "You giving your*self* up now?"

The FBI man blasted his pet informant—a three-shot burst to the central body mass.

No change in ambient sound—probably not the first time people in that bar had heard gunshots out back.

Or maybe the whole thing was an FBI operation. But I quashed that thought as quickly as it came—this "SAC" had to be a lone wolf, or I would have been in a prison or a grave way before this.

"Who the fuck *are* you, man?" the tallest of the Nazis demanded, still holding the rock hammer.

"FBI," Brigham said, putting some brag behind his words. "You're looking at the only man our people have ever placed inside ZOG's own spy nest."

"You're with—?"

"Remember that load of H that was supposed to finance our Robert Mathews Revenge Brigade? It was Gomes who tipped the FBI. And that *major* boom that never went off? That was your boy Gomes, too."

"Look, man, I *personally* watched Lew earn his spiderweb. Three niggers in one night. No way he was a—"

"Yeah? Then *you* tell me how Gomes got away with so much crude shit. Stuff like you just described. You think the FBI didn't know who took out those same three niggers you just bragged about? Gomes, he's been on the payroll for years."

"And you, you're the one who's been paying him?"

"Yep. With ZOG's own money. That was the only way I could get him to where I needed him to be. And now you two are the team. The *whole* team. Your job is to keep me—"

The tall guy whipped the rock hammer into the FBI man's stomach, striking as instinctively as a scorpion's sting.

But the agent must have picked up the pre-strike flex. He was already stepping back, and the spike didn't get all the way in.

"Fuck!" came out of his mouth as he dropped to one knee. Sounded more surprised than angry, but that didn't stop him from gut-shooting the hammer artist. The man he shot dropped to the dirt, still holding on to his kill toy.

The last one, Val, immediately threw down his shiny gun, stepped away from it, and threw his hands in the air. He didn't know who he was surrendering to, but he knew it didn't matter anymore.

I don't know where he'd been trained, but one thing he'd never learned is that you can't surrender to an enemy who doesn't take prisoners. The FBI man fired twice. Val staggered for a half-second, then slumped to the ground.

I couldn't be sure how many rounds the FBI man's pistol had left, but I had to *make* sure the job was done. I waved a white piece of parachute silk back and forth. That was to signal the video man to stop working. And to send Mack circling behind him, to make sure he did.

"You gonna . . . ?"

"Just hold on," I told the FBI man. "We'll get you fixed up." I picked the agent's heavy pistol out of his hand, asked, "Hardballs?"

"Hollow-points," he grunted. "Mercury-tipped."

I walked over to the hammer man and put a slug into the side of his head. Then I planted another one just above the nose of the guy who'd tried to surrender.

I saved Gomes for last. He'd taken the most lead, but no head shots, so I dropped down next to him to check.

He was gone. No pulse, no breath, limp carotid. I stomped his throat with the heel of my boot. It was so quiet I could hear the hyoid bone crack.

I waved again. Mack came on the run. I stepped over to the FBI man, and put his pistol back into its carry-pouch. Then I pulled up his shirt to check him over. Not much blood. I popped open the kit Dolly always puts together for me when she knows I'm going into the field.

Then by the numbers: press on both sides of the wound to push out any pus until I saw a clean blood-flow, pull the backing off the antibiotic-soaked sponge, and smooth it over the opening; body-wrap him using a wide roll of Coban, and cover it all with silicone Rescue Tape to make sure it would hold.

He never said a word, but even his carefully controlled breathing couldn't put the pain noises on mute.

"Keys," I said to him.

"Left outside pocket," he answered. Three separate words, with a nose breath between them.

I found them. Motioned Mack to get close enough to hear what I was going to say.

"Listen good, now," I told the FBI man. "There's no way to get a car back here. There's no light, and the ground's all rutted—can't take the chance. We're going to walk you around to your car and get you in the driver's seat; you're on your own from there."

"I can't—"

"Yeah, you can," I said. "If you want the ER, drive yourself there. But have a *good* story ready. And better get rid of your pistol—it ties you to those bodies."

"Your money—"

"You've got that in the 'Vette, right?"

"Yeah. But . . . Listen! I got a pickup. With a closed bed. At my house. It's real close to here. You could drive me back here, load up the bodies, and dump them someplace."

"Why would I do that?"

"For the money. Almost three hundred large. In my house. You take me there, I'll show you where it is."

Can I trust Conrad to stay put?

"Go back and make sure everything stays in place," I told Mack. "Understand?"

He nodded.

"Do it fast. Soon as you're *sure,* get to the parking lot. You follow us."

Another nod.

I hoisted the FBI man to his feet, and we started moving. He leaned against me like he was dead drunk.

I followed the bent agent's directions to his house.

He wasn't lying—took maybe seven minutes. Mack had no trouble keeping the red Corvette in sight. Or Conrad under control, I guessed.

The FBI man hadn't been lying about the money, either. Probably not confiscated counterfeit bills, not the way he had them hidden—he had to give Mack the instructions twice, they were so damn complicated.

While Mack was retrieving the agent's stash—and making sure Conrad stayed wherever he'd put him—I used my ceramic knife to cut through the Rescue Tape down to the Coban, then pulled it back to inspect the wound. The sponge had done its work—it showed only faint traces of blood. I squeezed a tube of Dermabond tissue glue over the wound, sealing it closed almost as good as stitches would.

"I guess you figured out I was a medic," I told him. "You want a shot to put you out while we go back and dump the bodies?"

"I don't need that much. But something for the pain would be . . ."

"This'll make it all go away," I promised, tapping a vein at his elbow.

Conrad might have been shaking inside, but Mack whispered that his hands had been sure and steady on his equipment as he reloaded the Taurus.

I couldn't guess at what the FBI man might do if we'd let him come around. Probably not much—take a few days off, down with the flu. But whenever he went out to his garage and found the pickup hadn't been used, he'd do *something*. And looking for me probably wouldn't be one of those things.

But I'd been warned off gambling a long time ago—the shot I'd given him made any guesswork unnecessary.

I'd left the spike in his arm, and the length of rubber hose they'd think he'd used to bring up a vein. The tox screen would still be good, even if they didn't find him until days later—and the three extra baby Ziplocs loaded with 90-plus-percent pure would answer any questions they had left.

What else *would* a junkie do when he realized he had three bodies to dispose of, and was too wounded to drive? A nice little shot to relax himself, then he'd come up with an answer.

The answer he'd always come up with before.

But junkies aren't good at forward-thinking, and he'd probably been pretty anxious when he took his last hit. He hadn't had to use a needle. A well-used pipe was in his living room, behind some books he probably never read.

"You're one of us now," I said to Conrad from my position in the backseat.

He turned and looked at me. Not eye to eye, but closer than he'd ever done before. "How could I be—?"

"You're the one who broke this case, Conrad. It was your photo that started it off. And now you know *exactly* how that man ended up where you saw him . . . on the beach that night.

"So you've just closed the case you opened, didn't you? I mean, we've got one of the killers on video, not only confessing to the murder, but showing the weapon he did it with. Once you send *that* to the papers, what's left?"

"But he's . . . I mean, that guy in the white jacket, he shot—"

"Oh, you can show him doing that," I said, as if it would dismiss any doubt a reasonable man might have. "Doesn't change a thing. Remember, you can't blow our cover, so be sure you edit—"

"I . . . I know. I was your eyes, wasn't I? But I don't know how to get the . . . evidence to the papers. I mean, an e-mail with a photo-attach, that's one thing, but—"

"Oh, we'll handle that part," I assured him. "In fact, we'll take all the tape and disks with us, how's that? The cops won't come into this. *They* won't be able to trace it to you, but the papers, they'll make sure everyone knows it came from the same freelance investigator who sent in that original picture. The one that started this whole investigation."

"You can do that?"

"Guaranteed," I promised.

Once the cops saw those portions of the video we needed them to see—they had no choice about that, not with the leak to *Undercurrents*—the DA called another press conference, and proudly announced that no innocent man was going to be tried for a crime he couldn't have committed.

Not in *his* town.

Homer was released into Mack's custody. After dark, when

it was safe. Mack's first job was to take him over to that band of runaway kids, so Homer could see for himself that they *were* his friends, like he'd always believed they were, until the cops had taken him away.

Mack told me and Dolly that the whole experience was actually a good one for Homer. "It's important that he knows he has friends. It's even more important that he learns to distrust things that don't add up, instead of just listening to the voices."

That still left one more job.

"He's got to go," I said to Mack.

"Why? I mean, what could he actually—?"

"I don't know. What difference? He's not right in the head. Sure, we took all the tapes and the camera cards, but . . ."

"I don't want to do it."

"I wasn't asking you to. I was telling you what's going to happen. Tonight."

He looked at me. Hard, like he was expecting to see something new.

"I'm going with you," he finally said.

"This is a lot of money," Conrad said, looking at the stack of bills I'd handed him.

"It's the going rate," I assured him. "You were the agency's eyes and ears on this one, don't forget."

"You said 'freelance' . . . ?"

"Exactly. Who knows when we might need you again? Could be a week, could be five years. But we know where to find you."

"And if *I* find something, how do I—?"

"Do just what you did this time. Go through the papers. Hit them all, *Undercurrents*, too. We'll be watching."

The word must have tripped a switch. Conrad's hands started to shake. Maybe he picked up on what he had to know was coming next—maybe he'd been waiting on something like that his whole life.

Mack made an "I've got this" gesture, and sat down next to the video man. "You don't have to do what you've been doing," Mack told him. "Not now. You don't have to *keep* doing it."

"I don't—"

"Yeah, you do. You understand just fine, Conrad. If you want, we can work together, turn that around."

"I don't understand. What could—?"

"I only work freelance for the agency, just like you," Mack said, turning so he blocked Conrad's view of me. "My *work*, my *real* work . . . I'm a therapist. So I understand why you . . . watch. And I'm saying you don't *have* to. It'll take some work, and—"

"But he said I should keep—"

"Sure. Keep watching. You're an expert at it. But you don't have to be watching for the same reasons."

"How do you know anything about . . . ?"

"Am I wrong?" Mack said, almost too soft for me to catch.

When we drove away that night, Conrad was still breathing.

Maybe not the safest possible move, but I wasn't living that life anymore.

Mack dropped me off. I was pretty sure I knew his next stop.

When I slipped in the back door, my wife was waiting.

"I'll never get you involved in anything like that, Dell. Not ever again."

"You didn't—"

"You know I did," my wife said. Very, very softly.

And then it was just the two of us.

Andrew Vachss is a lawyer who represents children and youths exclusively. His many works include the Burke, Cross, and Aftershock series, numerous stand-alone novels, and three collections of short stories. His works have been translated into twenty languages and have appeared in *Parade, Antaeus, Esquire, Playboy,* and *The New York Times,* among other publications.

The dedicated website for Andrew Vachss and his work is www.vachss.com.

A NOTE ON THE TYPE

The text of this book was composed in Melior, a typeface designed by Hermann Zapf and issued in 1952. Born in Nuremberg, Germany, in 1918, Zapf has been a strong influence in printing since 1939. Melior, like Times Roman (another popular twentieth-century typeface), was created specifically for use in newspaper composition. With this functional end in mind, Zapf nonetheless chose to base the proportions of his letterforms on those of the golden section. The result is a typeface of unusual strength and surpassing subtlety.

Typeset by Scribe, Philadelphia, Pennsylvania

Printed and bound by Berryville Graphics, Berryville, Virginia

Designed by Betty Lew

LMe